Delphi Diversion

Delphi in Space
Book Twelve

Bob Blanton

Cover by Momir Borocki
momir.borocki@gmail.com

D1706996

Delphi Publishing

Copyright © 2020 by Robert D. Blanton

Cover by Momir Borocki

momir.borocki@gmail.com

All rights reserved. This book or any portion thereof may not be reproduced or used in any manner whatsoever without the express written permission of the publisher except for the use of brief quotations in a book review. Printed in the United States of America First Printing, 2021.

This is a work of fiction. Any resemblance to actual persons living or dead, or actual events is purely coincidental.

https://www.facebook.com/StarshipSakira/

Table of Contents

Chapter 1   You've Got to Be Kidding

Catie threw herself on the padded bench in her day cabin. "Why . . . why do I get stuck in a system where a moon explodes? Hey, if you're listening, how about a little romance? Why can't I meet a prince charming? I could use a little fun once in a while. Why can't we find a unicorn or a planet where everyone loves each other?!"

Catie was aboard the Merlin, one of Delphi's frigates which was returning to Earth from the Onisiwo system. It was there that the new Delphi League had stopped the Fazullan Empire from conquering Onisiwo. After their victory, Catie had spent seven months repatriating the freed Paraxean slaves to the various Paraxean colonies. She had also been responsible for moving the freed Aperanjen slaves to their new colony. And finally, before she could head home, she had sent the Fazullans off to a new world under their new leadership. There the Fazullan Empress could settle her people into a healthier society, one not based on slavery and oppression.

Catie just figured that all that effort deserved a reward, not to have the wormhole they were traversing collapse and drop them into a system next to a gas giant and in the center of what was once a moon. They tracked the debris back to its origins and determined that the moon had actually exploded, shattering into thousands of pieces.

"Princess?" Captain McAvoy knocked at Catie's door. Catie had been ignoring her Comm which had announced the captain's presence over a minute ago. With her Comm being ignored, Captain McAvoy had resorted to the age-old custom of knocking.

They'd just spent four hours under emergency deceleration, so Catie was surprised the captain was up and about. Catie was still exhausted by her short foray to the bridge earlier after they'd reduced the deceleration to a barely tolerable 5-G profile.

"Come on in, Tegan."

"Did I hear screaming?" Captain McAvoy asked once the door closed behind her.

"There might have been some screaming."

"Are you okay?"

"Yes, just frustrated at having to deal with more drama."

"I thought I'd let you know that we managed to clear a path for that ship. And as you can probably tell, we're back to a normal deceleration profile."

When the Merlin had dropped out of the wormhole deep in the system, the first priority was to clear a path for their ship, the Merlin. Then a distress call had alerted them to another ship that was in danger of being plowed into by the debris of the exploding moon.

"Good."

"Do you have any suggestions or preferences about what we should do next?"

"Why don't you sit down and we'll talk about it. ADI?" ADI was Delphi's main DI, digital intelligence. DIs were self-aware and could make independent decisions, unlike AIs which were just smart.

"Yes, Cer Catie."

"Do you have any more data?"

"I'm still analyzing the sensor logs, but I don't have any more information."

"Please notify Daddy and Uncle Blake."

"Captain McAvoy notified your father and Admiral Blake right after the incident. I have kept them updated, although there has been little new information. Your father wants you to call when you have time."

"Sure, as soon as I get a *break*. ADI, are you able to translate their language?"

"Not at this time. I haven't been able to access the computer systems on the ship. Their homeworld is in the communication shadow of their sun, so I have not been able to capture any of their electronic communications to gather enough data to analyze their language."

"Oh!" Catie sat back, much more relaxed now that she had a real problem to work on. "How long have their EM signals been blocked?"

"Two months."

"Catie, want to share what you're thinking?" Captain McAvoy asked. She'd grown used to Catie's 'I have the answer' face.

"ADI, was this civilization detected by one of our solar explorer probes?"

"Yes, . . . That is a clever thought. I will analyze the broadcasts that it recorded; I am accessing them now; it should allow me to create a rudimentary translation program."

"Thank you, ADI. Now Captain, I assume we need to deal with the spaceship. You said it was disabled."

"We do and it is," Captain McAvoy said. "It looks like something took out their control systems. Their distress signal was coming from an emergency system, not their regular communication."

"How do you know?"

"Different antenna. I assume their main antenna burned out. They've started sending something with more content other than a basic SOS; we don't understand the language but it's obviously a longer message."

"Can we try to answer it?"

"We're trying; we have been sending requests to them for information, but it doesn't look like they're receiving them and even if they are, it's unlikely they can understand them."

"Will we cross paths?"

"No, our vectors are ninety degrees to each other and we're traveling at a significantly higher velocity than they are."

"What will it take to match their velocity?"

"A very hard deceleration on our part. We have to come to a virtual stop."

"Can we send a Fox to her and use it to transmit our communications?"

"We can; we're still waiting to recover the ones we sent to clear the path for her. We can vector one of them to her and have it match velocities. Several of them have quantum relays."

"Then we should do that; how long?"

"Cers, it will take ten hours for the Fox to reverse course and match velocities with the ship."

"Okay, we'll see what we can learn then."

"Hi, Daddy, hi, Sam. Where's Allie?" Catie had grown so used to being able to chat with anyone via the quantum relays, that she sometimes forgot that they were tens of light-years apart.

"She's sleeping. Now, how are things going? You look tired," Marc said.

"Marc, you don't tell a woman she looks tired!"

"It's okay, Sam, we both know Daddy doesn't think about such things." Catie didn't mention that, like her father, she usually didn't think of such things either. "I am exhausted. We're still trying to figure things out. Right now, we're trying to help one of their spaceships that's been damaged."

"Have you tried to communicate with the planet?"

"No. I thought we'd try to figure out more before we did. We don't have access to their broadcasts because their communications are still being blocked by their sun. We've sent a probe over to the ship; we think it will give ADI enough information to be able to finish developing a translation for their language; she's starting with what the Solar Explorer picked up back when it came across the system."

"That was smart," Samantha said. "ADI says that you think it was an accident."

"Can't see someone blowing up a moon on purpose. We're still trying to figure out what happened."

"Don't overlook the possibility of a natural disaster," Marc said.

"We won't, we'll know more when we contact their ship. That is if they'll tell us anything."

"Whether they're willing to talk will tell you a lot; we need to know if we want them to join the Delphi League or avoid them. I'll let Captain McAvoy know that you're in charge of the mission."

"Thanks, Daddy." Catie rolled her eyes at her father.

"You had to know that was coming," Samantha teased.

"A girl can dream, can't she?"

"Good luck, Sweetie."

"Bye, Daddy, bye Sam."

Ten hours after Captain McAvoy sent the Fox to act as a communication relay, it was coasting alongside the alien spaceship. They were able to use its cameras to gather more detailed images of the ship. There didn't seem to be any obvious damage to the ship, other than the burned-out antenna.

"Now what?" First Officer Vinci asked.

"I think we wait and see what they do," Captain McAvoy said. "They were transmitting a distress call. Either they'll start transmitting on that channel, or they might have another transmitter that has more bandwidth."

"They do," the communication officer announced. "The Fox is picking up a laser communication beam. It's relaying it here but I can't decode it."

"I wouldn't expect it to be encoded, I'm not sure ADI is ready with a translation program yet. ADI, what's your timeline?"

"Captain, Merlin and I are working on it, but it's difficult with the small amount of data we have. I've programmed their communication frequency and standard compression protocol into your communication system. I would suggest you try a video link."

"Communications, open a video channel."

"Yes, ma'am."

"This is Captain McAvoy of the Delphi Star Ship Merlin. May we be of help?"

The image of a woman in what Captain McAvoy assumed was their version of a shipsuit came up on the display. She appeared remarkably human. Her eyes were green, her complexion a light tan, and her hair was dark and wavy. She smiled at the camera, gave a slight bow, then said, "Αυτός είναι ο καπετάνιος marie του διαστημόπλοιου Hyrata Dionysus. Χρειαζόμαστε άμεση βοήθεια."

"Sounds Greek to me," the communications officer quipped. Everyone gave him a weak smile, to laugh would a breach of bridge protocol, not that his quip wasn't a breach already.

Captain McAvoy smiled at the woman; she pointed to her ear and nodded her head, "yes." Then she pointed at her forehead and shook her head "no."

"I hope they don't have their head shakes reversed from us," she whispered to her crew.

The woman smiled and nodded her head. She pointed to her mouth and then her ear, and nodded her head again. Then she pointed to her mouth and then her forehead and shook her head. She said "μπορώ να ακούσω, δεν καταλαβαίνω." Then she nodded and said, "Ναί," then shook her head and said, "όχι."

"Okay I think we have yes, no, I hear, and I don't understand figured out."

"I agree," ADI said.

"Vinci, come over here. Act like you're having trouble standing up."

"Yes, ma'am."

The first officer walked over next to the captain and feigned collapsing. Captain McAvoy had stood up while he approached. When he collapsed, she grabbed him and helped him to stand.

"How can we help?" Captain McAvoy asked, pointing to First Officer Vinci.

The woman took her hand and made like a kid flying a plane moving her hand like it was an airplane. She had it turn directions as she flew it and shook her head no. "No."

Then she flew it straight and ran it into her other hand. "I understand," Captain McAvoy said. Then she flew her hand like the woman had, then took her other hand and grabbed it and brought it to her chest.

The woman shook her head yes and smiled. "Yes, παρακαλώ."

"First Officer, let's put an asteroid mover on that ship. Once we've done that, we'll demonstrate that we can control their ship. Hopefully, ADI will have a rudimentary translation program up by then."

"Yes, ma'am." First Officer Vinci called the crew chief in flight bay three and instructed him to pull an asteroid mover out of cargo and get it into space. The asteroid movers were a small fusion reactor and three gravity drives mounted on a frame. Natalia Ortiz, an engineer and wife of one of Artemis's miners, had designed them for Marc so that they could automatically send ice asteroids to Artemis, Earth's first colony planet, for their terraforming activities. Each drive would anchor to the asteroid at a different location. When the frame was fully extended there were over one hundred meters between drives.

"The gravity drives are in place," First Officer Vinci informed Captain McAvoy.

"Then let's slow her down. In fact, let's turn her around so she's heading back in-system. That should help to reduce their stress level."

"Yes ma'am."

Captain McAvoy turned back to the display. "Open a channel with our friends."

"Channel open."

The woman's face came back up on the display. She was saying words and short phrases. She was startled when she realized that Captain McAvoy was back.

"Hello," she said. The word was heavily accented but it was correct.

"Hello," Captain McAvoy said, the look on her face must have given away her confusion.

"ADI is help."

"Captain, I've been working with Captain Galanos of the Geraki to build up my knowledge of their language."

"Interesting."

"Yes, I've been using the program we use to teach language, showing the captain pictures and videos and having her provide the proper words. That plus the content I got from the solar explorer has helped me create a basic translation program."

"So, I should just talk?"

"Of course."

"Captain Galanos, I'm happy to see we're finally able to communicate. Please forgive us if the translation is not exactly correct, we're just learning your language."

"ADI learns fast."

"Yes she does. I assume she asked if you had a computer database she could access."

Captain Galanos paused as ADI flashed a few images on her display.

"Yes, database. She did ask about it, but she used a different word. No we do not. All of our electronics have been destroyed by a large EM pulse."

"I see. Do you know the source of this pulse?"

"No. We were afraid it was from you. We were very worried when we saw all your fighters coming toward us. Thank you for clearing a path for us. Can you explain how you can be standing on the bridge of such a small ship?"

Captain McAvoy laughed as she realized that Captain Galanos thought they were aboard the Fox. "The ship next to you is one of our fighters. It was the only thing we had that could match velocities with you and act as a communication relay. We are traveling too fast into your system so matching velocities with you would have taken too much time."

"But your fighter could?"

"Yes, it is being remotely piloted, so it could sustain the force necessary."

"Thank you for the explanation. Now, how have you turned my ship around?"

"We have placed a set of external engines on your ship. They will allow us to steer you back to your homeworld."

"And the pulse?"

"We know nothing of it. But we do suspect that one of the moons around that gas giant behind us blew up, or broke apart."

Captain Galanos's face lit up with shock, she was obviously distraught.

"Did you have a base on the moon?"

"We have base on Stási, that moon, but I have difficulty believing a moon blew up."

Captain McAvoy ran the simulation that ADI had constructed of the debris. It showed that it all came from a central location.

"This is what we have determined from the velocity vectors of all major sections of debris that we've been able to track."

Captain Galanos nodded. "That is where the moon should be. You say there is nothing there now."

"That is correct."

"Oh, may the gods help us. That is unbelievable."

"I'm sorry, it is tragic. We'd like to find a way to figure out what happened. But first, we need to deal with your situation. Do you have enough food, water, air?" Captain McAvoy asked.

"Our air will only last two days. We are working to restart air scrubbers, but it is not going well."

"ADI, how long until we can have a better command of their language?" Captain McAvoy messaged.

"I need more data. If you could send them some Comms, then I could interact with more of the crew and build up a database faster."

"Captain Galanos, we need to learn your language better. Can we send you some communication devices so more of your crew can work with ADI?"

"Yes."

"Can you access your airlock?"

"Yes, it is working."

"First Officer."

"I'm on it."

The first officer had a bag of Comms delivered to the Geraki using one of the Foxes. They would use a bot to send them through the airlock.

By the next morning, ADI was confident that she had developed a translation program that would allow the Helikens, as they called themselves, to communicate with the Merlin's crew.

"Captain Galanos, I hope you had a good night."

"It was as good as it could be. We are all still in shock."

"I can understand that. We have been discussing how to deal with your air problem. How many people are in your crew?"

"Crew is six, plus eight scientists as passengers for the base."

Captain McAvoy messaged the chief steward. "Chief, can we set up isolation cabins for fourteen people?"

"If they double up, we have enough space. Otherwise, you'll need to tell some pilots to sleep in their Foxes."

"I'm sure doubling up will not be a problem." The captain turned back to Captain Galanos. "We could accommodate you over here. We need to know your dietary needs and what air mixture you breathe."

"Captain, I have already verified that they breathe an oxygen, nitrogen mix similar to ours. While on their ship, they do the same as we do and breathe an oxygen, helium mixture to protect against sudden decompression."

"I see. I've been told that we breathe similar air. If you can bring your food with you, we can put you in isolation. I'm sure our cooks can handle whatever you're eating."

"I'm sure they can since all of our food is freeze-dried."

"Maybe we can improve upon that once we know more about your diet."

"Providing us with good air will be sufficient."

First Officer Vinci switched to a private channel. "Captain, we could send one of our scrubbers over there."

"I am aware of that. But I'm inclined to get them out of that ship until we know more about what happened."

"Yes, ma'am."

"It will take two days before our shuttle can reach you," Captain McAvoy said. They had switched to an aggressive deceleration profile to allow them to slow down enough that the alien ship could catch up with them. "Have the doctor suit up and meet the shuttle in flight bay three. Tell them they need to prepare for emergency acceleration to reach the alien ship."

"I'm on my way," Dr. Moreau announced. "ADI has sent me all the pertinent details."

"Captain Galanos, we're sending a shuttle to get you and bring you to our ship. You'll need to travel in your spacesuits until you get into your cabins here. We'll isolate the cabins and the passageway, giving you your own environmental bubble. Please bring any personal possessions you would like to have with you. We'll provide additional clothing and sundries. Our doctor will be with you and will take samples of the air from your ship, and then from you once you're in your cabins."

"I understand."

"Catie, how do you want to proceed?" Captain McAvoy asked.

"We need to figure out what happened."

"I agree. What about our new guests?"

"Once they're here, can we do a slow approach to their planet, fast enough to give us a little gravity, but slow enough that we have plenty of time to figure things out? We can always speed up."

"If you slow down until the shuttle reaches you, then proceed at 0.2Gs it will take you about twenty-six days to travel the 14 AUs to their planet," ADI informed them. "Once they're off their ship, you can increase its acceleration so that it catches up with you."

"That sounds about right. Tegan, when will they be on board?"

"As if ADI hasn't already told you. They're in the shuttle now, so they should be on board in ten hours, we're going to accelerate the shuttle at 1.2Gs. Are you going to suit up and meet them?"

"Just try to stop me."

Catie and Captain McAvoy were in the flight bay when the shuttle landed. They were wearing full spacesuits to protect themselves from any pathogens as well as the potential of sudden decompression. But Catie thought it was nice to be able to avoid having to wait to actually depressurize the bay. The shuttle was designed to form a capsule that could slide through an iris. The iris sealed against the shuttle minimizing the loss of air; they lost about ten percent, but that was easily made up.

"How do you feel about being Princess Catie again?" Captain McAvoy asked.

"I'm not happy about it, but what can I do?"

"Maybe if you weren't so good at it." Captain McAvoy laughed; she knew how much Catie would prefer to be the captain instead of the princess.

"Captain!" Dr. Moreau spoke on a channel with Catie and the captain.

"Dr. Moreau?"

"Three crew members, including the captain are blind in their left eye. It appears they have ocular implants that were burned out by the EM pulse. All the scientists seem to be okay. We'll need to ask them about what other implants they might have."

"You haven't asked already?"

"They weren't too happy when I asked about the ocular implants, so I thought I would wait."

"Very well."

The shuttle glided to a stop and settled down on the deck. The flight bay door closed and the shuttle hatch opened. Captain Galanos and Ensign Racine walked down the boarding ramp to Captain McAvoy and Catie. Their gait was awkward due to the low gravity.

"Captain Galanos, I'd like to welcome you and your crew aboard the Merlin. This is Princess Catherine of Delphi. She is the leader of our mission. Princess Catherine, Captain Galanos."

"I'm so pleased to meet you, Princess. And I want to thank you and Captain McAvoy for rescuing us. We hope we can find a way to repay you." Captain Galanos turned and pointed at the shuttle. "That is a very impressive shuttle, such high acceleration capacity. And there is gravity here, can you explain?"

"We're under modest acceleration which gives us the sense of gravity," Catie said. "We can discuss more about technology later. For now, we are happy to help. We had plans to visit your system, this event just accelerated it. We are part of a league of planets that facilitates trade among its members and helps them to defend each other."

"You knew of us before?"

"We have been sending probes out to explore the galaxy. We have initially been focused on finding planets to colonize, but the probes record any discovery of inhabited systems. It was the data from the probe that helped ADI to start translating your language."

Captain Galanos nodded her head. "I see. I'm sure we have many questions for each other."

"We agree. And to help with that, along with the communication devices we have already given you, I'd like to add these additional components. The glasses will pair with the units you already have. The small plugs go into one of your ears so you can hear without disturbing your neighbors. If you wear them, ADI will be able to work with you to learn your language more completely. They have been sterilized and the bag will be sterilized again as you go through the airlock."

"That is kind of you."

Catie handed Captain Galanos the bag with the extra gear. "Ensign Racine will lead you to your quarters. Our doctors are still analyzing the air and saliva samples she took to determine if it is safe for us to interact without these spacesuits. The steward will give you fresh shipsuits. For now, you and your people should get some rest."

"Thank you."

Captain Galanos and her crew followed Ensign Racine to the airlock. Each of them was carrying a small bag with their personal possessions and doing a decent job of maneuvering in the low gravity.

"Ma'ams, we left some probes and surveillance pucks in the ship," Ensign Racine messaged Catie and Captain McAvoy.

"Smart."

"Dr. Moreau, what's our status?" Catie and Captain McAvoy were meeting in Catie's day cabin to discuss their plans after yesterday's big events.

"Our tests of the air on their ship show that there are no active pathogens, which one would expect since they've been in isolation on it for months. Likewise, our air has no pathogens, since we've been in isolation for the week since we left Onisiwo."

"So, can we let them out of isolation?"

"You can, but we'll have to monitor the situation closely. Our DNAs are very similar, so it is likely that we will be affected by the same pathogens. When we reach their planet, we'll have to consider vaccinations before we can move about freely."

"Very well. I'm sure they'll enjoy access to the ship's recreation areas. Based on what you've said, I'm guessing we can eat the same food."

"Yes, I've examined what they brought with them; it is all edible by us. And I'm sure the converse will be true as well. But we should do a few experiments to make sure there are no allergies before we have them eat our food."

"Agreed."

"Once we have access to the systems on their planet, we'll be able to learn about what vaccines we might need to administer."

"What about their eyes?" Catie asked.

"Given the similarity in DNA, I've taken the liberty of printing new eyes for them. I'm still running tests to verify whether they'll be compatible, but I'm confident they will be. The eyes should be ready for transplant tomorrow."

"I appreciate the initiative," Catie said. "We'll discuss it with them when we interview the captain."

"Thank you, Doctor. We'll talk to you later," Captain McAvoy said, dismissing the doctor.

"That's interesting. We look so much alike and our DNAs are similar," Catie said.

"It makes one wonder if we're biologically compatible."

Catie snorted. "Like we need more humans."

"But maybe these guys are a better quality of people," Captain McAvoy teased. "They certainly look good."

"Are you shopping for a husband?"

Captain McAvoy laughed. "Well, having one who lives on another planet would certainly mean he would give me plenty of space."

"I would guess so. Now, why don't we ask the captain to come visit? Tell her she can bring one or two of her crew."

"Merlin, please ask Captain Galanos to join us," Captain McAvoy instructed the ship's AI.

"Yes, Captain, I am calling her now," Merlin replied. ". . . She has indicated that she would like to bring two of her crew."

"Tell her that is fine."

"Yes, Captain."

A few minutes later the sentry announced the Helikens. When they entered the cabin, the three Helikens bowed to Catie, then turned and bowed to Captain McAvoy.

"Princess, thank you for seeing us. This is Commander Petrou, my chief engineer, and this is Ensign Prince Nikitas, my communication officer," Captain Galanos said.

Giving the Helikens Comms and specs had allowed ADI to improve her translation program over the last few days. The Helikens had been enthusiastic about sharing their language with her.

The Helikens were all wearing the Delphi shipsuits the steward had given them. Catie was wearing her Princess uniform, just a stylized version of the standard Delphi Captain's uniform, and Captain McAvoy was wearing her day uniform, slacks and jacket over a shipsuit. Catie couldn't help but notice that Ensign Prince Nikitas filled out his shipsuit very well; he looked about the same size as her Uncle Blake. He also had a winning smile to go with startling blue eyes and wavy blond hair.

"Please be seated," Catie said. They all moved to the large dining/conference table that was in the day cabin. It could seat eight and had very comfortable chairs. Catie gave everyone a welcoming smile; her smile lingered on the prince for a bit longer than the others. "Our doctor has assured us that we can breathe the same air and not be a danger to each other. She also believes we can eat the same food; she only worries about allergies. She needs to do some tests to verify that you can eat our food, but it is likely that by tonight you'll be able to join us for dinner."

"That would be appreciated. We are all very tired of the rations we've been eating for the last six months. But you must also be tired of your rations."

"Oh, that is not a problem for us. We are able to prepare fresh food," Catie said. "We have a small hydroponics facility to grow vegetables and we have a wide assortment of meat. Our chef is quite proud of the meals he serves the crew."

"That will be good news for my crew. Now, you have some questions?"

"Yes, we're still trying to understand what happened. I'm hoping you'll be willing to share some information about the moon and the activities there."

"Princess, we also would like to know what happened. The moon housed an observatory and a lab. However, their research and experiments are classified."

"I understand. Can you at least describe the facility? Was it on the surface or below the surface?"

"The lab was below the surface. It was quite deep to protect it from any asteroid or other stray space debris that might strike the moon."

"How big was the moon?"

"It was 5400 kilometers in diameter and massed about 1.3452 times ten to the 18 tonnes," Ensign Nikitas said, giving Catie a big smile.

Catie liked the smile; his swarthy complexion highlighted his white teeth. Catie noticed all three Helikens had a similar complexion. Captain Galanos had wavy black hair; Ensign Nikitas had wavy hair like the captain except his was blond; while Commander Petrou's black hair was short with tight curls, similar to the tiny afros that Black women on Earth often sported.

"That was a big moon," Captain McAvoy said to break the silence.

"Yes, it was one of the largest moons in our solar system."

"Did they have an escape pod? Anything that they might have used to leave the moon?"

"Not that I'm aware of," Captain Galanos said. "It would not have mattered anyway. The moon is too far from our planet or the asteroid belt for them to be able to reach help, and we were still weeks away. We couldn't afford to leave a spaceship there. We relied on our annual visits to resupply them and rotate the scientists."

"Is it possible that they detonated a bomb or something like that which caused the event?"

Catie caught a slight flicker of recognition pass over Commander Petrou's face. The commander quickly regained her composure.

"I can't imagine something like that happening," Captain Galanos replied. She hadn't flinched one bit, keeping a straight, neutral face the whole time. "Couldn't it have been a natural disaster of some kind?"

"It's hard to imagine one that would have been isolated to the moon, and as you could see, there's no evidence of an asteroid or large interstellar object," Catie replied. "Have you talked to your scientists to see if they have any theories?"

"I have. They reached the same conclusion. A natural disaster that could destroy a moon is extremely unlikely. One would have expected to find some other impact to the system or, as you said, a large asteroid among the debris."

"Were there any recent missions to the moon?"

"No, we would have been the first ship to arrive there for about a year."

"I see. Is there anything else you can share with us?"

"We're happy to share, but we cannot imagine what happened."

"Then while we're here, could you tell us more about your world and its politics?"

"We have a single world government made up of sixteen nation-states. Four of the nation-states are constitutional monarchies, while the other twelve have an elected president. They all have a parliament with two houses, The People's House and the Senate. The prime minister is elected by The People's House and forms the executive branch," Commander Petrou said.

"Commander Petrou is a political junky. She loves to follow the politics of the various nation-states," Captain Galanos explained.

"It's so opposite of engineering. I find it entertaining."

"I'm curious, is there a lot of contention between the various political parties?" Captain McAvoy asked. "There certainly is on Earth."

"We have a few extremist parties in the various nation-states, especially the constitutional monarchies. Typically, they want to break away from the world government and go it alone. They think they're being held back by the other nation-states," Commander Petrou said.

"We see the same thing on Earth. Some people just don't want to share."

"Now, on a personal note, Captain, our doctor indicated you and Commander Petrou, along with another member of your crew, have lost vision in your left eyes. Something about an ocular implant," Catie asked.

"Yes, the EM pulse destroyed the electronics in the implants, and the heat injured our optic nerves," Captain Galanos said.

"We believe our doctor can help you there. Do you have any other implants that were affected?"

"Our navigator also had a processing implant that was destroyed along with his ocular implant. He seems to be okay, but we don't know if there was any damage to his brain."

"It would be hard to tell," Ensign Nikitas whispered to Commander Petrou. Unfortunately, the Comms picked it up and everyone heard his comment. Captain Galanos glared at him.

"The doctor will be waiting for you in sickbay to discuss options. Ensign Nikitas, I notice that you're the only officer that didn't have an ocular implant. Is there a reason for that, possibly something we could help with?"

"No, unless you have a treatment for overprotective fathers. My father refuses to allow me to get any implants for precisely this reason. Possibly, in this case, he was not being overprotective."

"I can relate to overprotective fathers." Catie laughed, thinking of the various argument she'd had with her father about risks. "We'll let you go visit sickbay; Dr. Moreau is waiting."

"So, what did you think of that?" Captain McAvoy asked. "Other than the fact that the prince was exceptionally good looking."

"I didn't notice."

"Yes you did, your blood pressure went up ten percent and your heart rate jumped sixteen beats per minute," ADI messaged.

"I don't want the captain to know that!" Catie messaged back.

"Catie, I can't see how you couldn't notice," Captain McAvoy teased. "But anyway, did you catch the flicker in Commander Petrou's eyes when you asked about an accident?"

"Yes. The captain and the ensign didn't blink, but the commander's eyes flared. I'm sure she thinks that something happened in the lab."

"But with the whole moon destroyed, I don't see how we can find out."

"I've been thinking about that. ADI, please join us."

"Hello, Captain."

"Hello, ADI."

"Whatever event happened, we know when it occurred, correct?" Catie asked.

"By tracing the debris back I have an approximate time for the event," ADI explained.

"Then, why can't we put one of our jump probes out on the fringe and jump it out far enough that it will pick up the light and EM energy from before the event and during it?"

"You mean go back in time and look?" Captain McAvoy asked.

"Essentially. ADI?"

"You would need to add a better telescope to the probe. I might also need to jump it around to get the correct angle on the moon."

"That sounds fine. Wouldn't we do better if we put the probe above the ecliptic? That should help to avoid getting blocked by the planet and the moon."

"Good idea," Captain McAvoy said. "People always forget about going outside the ecliptic. That would be especially helpful if we have to back up even further in time."

"Okay, ADI, do you have the design of the telescope you want?"

"Yes."

"How long to make it?"

"Eight hours, but we have to stop our acceleration during that time."

"Can we use a Fox to deploy the probe?"

"We can. It will need to be mounted above the wings so that the Fox will be able to exit the flight bay."

"That shouldn't be a problem," Captain McAvoy said.

"Tegan, let's do the zero-gravity coast tonight when most of us are asleep."

"Yes, Princess. ADI, if you'll take care of the printing, I'll inform the crew."

Catie frowned at Captain McAvoy for calling her princess but didn't say anything.

"Captain, I've taken the liberty of telling Merlin to announce the zero-G period. I left it for you to issue the orders to the ship's pilot."

"Thanks for leaving me something to do," Captain McAvoy teased.

"I can't do *everything*," ADI teased back.

Chapter 2   Back in Time

"Catie, you remember Tina," Morgan said. Catie and Morgan were entering Flight Bay One, to do their morning run. Cristina was stretching just inside the airlock.

"Sure. Hi Tina, fancy meeting you here."

"Morgan said you wouldn't mind if I joined your workout. I heard some comments from the crew about your sparring match with the first officer back on the Roebuck. When I asked Morgan about it, she told me how good you were at Aikido and Krav Maga."

"She did, did she?"

"Hey, just telling the truth. Tina wanted to get some more hand-to-hand training, so I thought we could use a third partner. It'll let us work on two-on-one scenarios."

"Sounds like fun. But first a ten-K run."

"Morgan told me that would be the price of admission," Cristina said as they all headed out running around the perimeter of the flight bay.

"Whew, you guys set a fast pace," Cristina said as the three women finally finished their run.

"If you can't beat them, you have to outrun them," Catie said. "Besides, if you're a bit tired, we'll have more fun introducing you to Krav Maga."

"Morgan said you were evil."

"*Moi?*"

"We've got the gym booked at 0500, so we'd better head there. It looks bad if you book it and then show up late." Morgan swatted Cristina on the butt then quickly jumped into the airlock and started the cycle.

"Hey, that's not fair!"

"You can get even later," Catie whispered.

When they got to the gym, they showed Cristina some basic Aikido forms while they cooled down from their run. Cristina already had some of the basics down from working with one of the other Marines. Catie watched her closely as they went through the moves. Cristina was close to Catie's height and weight, which would be nice. Morgan had two inches and ten kilos on Catie and it was beginning to show. Catie had trained for more years and was faster, but Morgan was closing the skill gap faster than Catie was closing the muscle gap. Catie was still faster, and at seventeen, she wouldn't be gaining much more weight or getting much taller, so she needed to focus on staying ahead of Morgan in skill.

"Hey, I saw Prince Charming yesterday. He's pretty gorgeous," Morgan said as she and Catie started circling each other on the mat.

"He's an alien."

"Well, doc says we're pretty compatible. I didn't ask her any specifics, but I'm guessing." Morgan's hand flashed out in a strike to Catie's solar plexus. Catie turned sideways and trapped Morgan's hand against her chest as she kept spinning.

"Ow! That was . . ."

"A good move!" Catie finished for her.

"You guys play rough," Cristina said.

"Hey, the doc can fix just about anything, so we don't hold back much. Just no eye gouges," Morgan said.

"Can't the doc fix that?"

"Sure, but it takes a few days. Can't be putting the princess out of action. And a pirate princess doesn't have the same cachet as a princess."

Cristina laughed. "I don't know. I think Catie would look pretty good with an eye patch."

After a couple of rounds of sparring, pairing each of them against the other, they moved to some two-on-one practice. Morgan was looking forward to getting to Catie with Cristina's help.

Morgan and Cristina were circling Catie, make various feints to try to catch her off guard. Then Morgan moved in, throwing a quick combo, and knocking Catie's kick aside. As Catie bounced back, Cristina grabbed her from behind. Morgan came in for the kill. Catie slammed the back of her head into Cristina's nose, then, using Cristina's backward motion to create space between her and Morgan, she raised both legs into the air. Morgan blocked Catie's first kick, the second leg caught her in the knee.

"Down!" Morgan yelled as she grabbed her knee.

Catie used the momentum from her kick to spin around and throw Cristina over her hip.

"I give!" Cristina yelled before Catie could slam the heel of her foot into her solar plexus.

"Damn, Catie. That's the second time this month you've taken out my knee," Morgan whined.

"Sorry!"

"Yeah, right. I can tell you're all broken up about it. Now you have to help me to sickbay."

"I can help you," Cristina said. "I need the doctor to fix my nose; the princess has a hard head."

"People keep saying that, but it doesn't change her behavior."

"Har, har."

"Come on Tina, let's go. Catie probably has a date with Prince Charming."

◆ ◆ ◆

After her shower, Catie went to the wardroom for breakfast. The chef just put out a buffet for breakfast and lunch, reserving dinner for sit-down meals. Catie grabbed some bacon and eggs before joining Captain McAvoy at a corner table.

"Good morning, Princess. Ensign Racine tells me you've broken a couple of her Marines."

Catie blushed. "Oops. I guess the doctor would have to tell her. It wasn't anything permanent." Although Morgan was Catie's head of security, she was on detachment from the Marines, and Morgan pulled in additional Marines to augment Catie's security detail as needed.

Captain McAvoy laughed. "I guess not. But she did point out that Morgan seems to need repairs every few weeks."

"She gives as good as she gets."

"I'm sure. But apparently, the doctors don't report any injuries that occur to the princess."

"Those only go to Daddy. By the way, why is Racine still an ensign? She did an amazing job during the Fazullan battle, and she seems to be on top of everything."

"I don't know, let me look." Captain McAvoy focused on her HUD as Racine's record came up. "She has a good fitness report from Major Prescott. She's not on the current promotion list, but it looks like she's recommended for the next one."

"Oh," Catie said, disappointed.

"You could give her a field promotion if you'd like."

"I'm not sure that would be doing her any favors. A field promotion from Princess Catherine might look like favoritism."

"I could promote her. If you'd put a note in my file that I was agreeing with your recommendation."

"That works for me."

"I'll take care of it tomorrow."

"Good morning, may we join you?" Captain Galanos asked as she and Ensign Nikitas walked up to Catie and Captain McAvoy. Captain Galanos was wearing a patch over her left eye.

"Please, I see you've had your eye replaced," Catie said. "Where is Commander Petrou?"

"The doctor took care of our eyes this morning right after we started accelerating again. Commander Petrou decided to take the rest of the morning to recover. These medical capabilities that you have are amazing, I hope you will share them with us. I'm also curious about the zero-acceleration last night."

"I'm sure Dr. Moreau will be happy to work with your doctors and share some of our medical technology." Catie nodded to Captain McAvoy to indicate she should field the second question.

"About the zero-acceleration, we thought we'd give the engines a rest after the hard day they had. Catching up to you put a big strain on them."

"I'm sure it did. I'm surprised you had enough reaction mass to accelerate so hard and still have enough to hold constant acceleration."

Captain McAvoy looked at Catie, leaving it up to her to decide if she would reveal the existence of gravity drives. Catie winked at her, suggesting that she go ahead and answer. "Oh, we don't use reaction mass. We have what we call gravity drives. They work with the gravimetric waves from your sun to accelerate us."

"Our scientists have speculated about gravity drives. But what do you do when you're outside the gravity well of a sun?" Ensign Nikitas asked.

"Then we use reaction mass. But we try to avoid acceleration when we're outside the gravity well."

"Interesting," Captain Galanos said. "I wonder if you would be willing to share this technology with us."

With the conversation shifting to trade, Catie decided to answer. "We do sell the grav drives, as we call them. They require a fusion reactor to run. Based on what we've seen of your ship, it seems you power your ships with fusion reactors."

"We do, and I'm sure our planet would wish to buy some of these drives. I'm starting to think we were lucky to meet you, that is, besides your saving our lives and all."

Everyone at the table gave Captain Galanos a laugh.

"Ensign Nikitas, where does the prince in your rank come from, are you actually a prince?" Catie asked.

"Ah, as Commander Petrou mentioned, our planet has four constitutional monarchies. I am the son of one of our princes. Of course, we all started off on one continent, but we've spread to the other continents. Even the countries with presidents still have

30

principalities within them. The principalities have an economic presence on each continent. Most of the principalities are relatively small, it's more about wealth and control of key technologies than land. And as she said, four of our nation-states are essentially very large principalities."

"That's interesting. We have a few principalities on Earth, but they are all based on family ownership of land granted to them from some monarch."

"There were no monarchs when Helike was born, so all of our princes were self-proclaimed."

"Self-proclaimed?" Catie asked.

"Their control of certain technologies allowed them to set themselves up as princes and gather followers. They had all been leading citizens before."

"Your history sounds very interesting; when we have time, I'll have to ask you more about it."

Four days after they sent the probe out, they got their first images of the event.

"Oh my god. It's hard to believe that happened," Catie gasped.

They were watching the destruction of the moon. ADI was still working on getting more detailed images, but more detail wasn't necessary to be able to see the moon break apart. Everything about the moon looked normal, then suddenly flames shot out of several fissures across its surface, and seconds later the moon broke into nine large pieces and flew apart. Seconds after the moon flew apart, the Merlin appeared where the center of the moon had been. They could see each piece racing away from the center of the event. The largest piece was thrown into the gas giant, where it set up a huge secondary event as the mass blasted into the atmosphere, throwing up founts of gas and liquid. The rest of the pieces flew out away from the planet and what was the center of the moon. All of the pieces were accompanied by tons of debris, smaller rocks and whatnot, that had been blasted out of the moon.

"What could have caused that?" Captain McAvoy asked.

"I don't know, that must have been like a gigaton of power."

"I calculate eight hundred nonillion joules," ADI said.

"That's ten to the thirty-two," Catie gasped. "It has to have been an antimatter explosion. Even then it would take a few megatons of antimatter. Who would be stupid enough to have that much in one place?"

"Possibly there was a secondary explosion," ADI suggested.

"Oh, so you think the antimatter explosion created enough pressure and heat to start a fusion reaction?"

"Yes, that is my supposition. A fusion reaction would consume all the air and lighter material at the moon's core. Until the moon actually fractured and released the pressure, the fusion would have continued consuming the material around the initial blast."

"Okay, so, not so stupid. But it still would have taken an enormous amount of antimatter to cause that."

"I agree."

"So, what does this mean?" Captain McAvoy asked.

"We don't know yet. We need more information," Catie said.

"I'm working as fast as I can," ADI said with a huff.

Catie laughed. "We know you are, we're just anxious. Call us when you have more data."

"I have a new video prepared for viewing," ADI announced two days later.

"Let's see it," Catie said as she joined Captain McAvoy in the captain's day cabin.

"As you can see, there is a spaceship at the moon just before the event. It leaves the moon here." ADI showed the timestamp as Event – 10:00:00

"Okay, keep playing."

The spaceship moved away from the moon, accelerating hard. "They are accelerating at their max capability based on Captain Galanos's ship."

"Thank you."

ADI fast-forwarded the video as the ship moved away from the moon.

"Hey, I thought you had the timer based on the event," Catie said. "It's at zero, but we don't see anything."

"That is correct," ADI said using a superior tone. "I have determined that the primary event occurred at this time. There were five separate events."

"Clever, but you don't need to be snooty."

"I was going for enlightening."

"Missed by a mile. But five events?"

"Let me explain, here at 00:00 seconds the first event occurs. There was a small EM pulse that indicated that a small amount of antimatter was released, combined with the available matter, and exploded. Base on the radiation, it was not a controlled combination of antimatter and its corresponding matter. Then a few milliseconds later a second event occurs. I would surmise that there was a second storage container of antimatter that was compromised. Then the third event occurred, which would have been the fusion of the helium in the air. I surmise that they breathe an oxygen-helium mix like on their spaceship, so there would have been a lot of helium available. That explosion created enough heat and pressure to start fusion of all the available fuel. So at 4.9 seconds, you can see the first fracture of the moon. This is the event that released the fourth and much larger EMP, which disabled Captain Galanos's ship as well as this unknown ship. At this time, they are no longer accelerating."

"Okay, so what happens to them?"

"At 5.3 seconds, the moon breaks apart. At 8.2 seconds, one of the moon fragments collides with the unknown ship. Here at 8.3 seconds, you can see a secondary explosion that consumes the ship, the fifth event."

"That would indicate that they were carrying antimatter," Catie said.

"I agree with your supposition."

"Do you have anything else to tell us?"

"It was at 8.4 seconds that the Merlin exited the wormhole. Other than that, this is all I have at this time. I will continue to collect data to enhance the images."

"I think we need to know when that ship arrived and where it came from," Captain McAvoy suggested.

"I agree. ADI, what about communication between the moon base and the ship?"

"I see indications of communications, but it appears that they are using a tight laser beam to communicate."

"Should we position a probe to capture that communication?"

"It is unlikely that I would be able to decode the message since it is probable that they would have encrypted it."

"But who knows what we may learn later. We might come across the key," Catie said.

"It would require moving the probe into a position which is disadvantageous for gathering more data on the event."

"We should put the other two probes we have out there. Then you could move them around to intercept the communication and get more viewing angles of the region to help figure out what happened."

"That would be helpful," ADI said.

"I think you're going to want to put one below the ecliptic," Captain McAvoy said. "We don't know where the ship came from, and there is even a possibility that there is something behind the planet, its other moons, or one of the other planets."

"Okay, why don't we send them out. We'll release them along the ecliptic and ADI can move them into place. That will allow us to recover the Fox. I'm sure you don't want to give up another Fox just so it can hang out to pick up the probes," Catie said.

"Agreed. We'll leave the first Fox we sent out to recover the probes or help ADI reposition them. ADI, I assume you'll make the arrangements to print two more telescopes."

"That won't be necessary. I took the opportunity when we printed the first one to print an additional five. That made it a full print job, and I anticipated we would want to change the probe configuration to include such telescopes in the future."

"Nice anticipations. Okay, now what?" Captain McAvoy asked.

"Do we bring in Captain Galanos?"

"Do you trust her?"

"ADI?"

"I have not detected any guile in Captain Galanos's interactions with you. She is upfront about not telling you the purpose of the base. I would be able to be more certain if we did a psych interrogation."

"We can't do that to a potential ally!"

"We did it to the Onisiwoens."

"But only the bad ones, they were criminals. ADI, I'm disappointed that you would even suggest such a thing."

"Sorry, I'm only trying to help. Your rules about what we can do and when keep changing."

"They're situational. But I think you're right about the captain. I trust her. I think we should share this with her and see if we can persuade her to help. But first, we'd better talk to Daddy and Uncle Blake."

Chapter 3   Who Are They?

"Hi, Daddy, Uncle Blake."

"Hi, Princess, and I mean that in both senses of the word," Marc teased.

"Pfft," Catie let her father know what she thought of his princess comment. "Did you guys review the video?"

"Yes, ADI walked us through it. Wait just a few moments, Sam wants to join us."

"Hi, Catie," Samantha said as she joined the call.

"What am I, chopped liver?" Blake said.

"No, just a pain in the ass as usual," Samantha replied. "Are we ready?"

"So, I assume everyone saw the video and had ADI explain our thinking. Any comments?" Catie asked. She was thinking about how her poor father had to put up with these kinds of antics every month at the board meetings; it never bothered her then, in fact, she was a primary contributor, but now that it was her meeting, they annoyed her.

"Yes," Marc said. "We need to know what the story is. Do we want to open relations with this system or quarantine it?"

"Quarantine?" Catie asked.

"Yes, force them to stay in their system until we're confident they're not going to run around blowing everyone up."

"We would like to avoid that. I hope it's just a matter of poor safety protocols," Samantha said.

"I don't believe that. I'm betting on sabotage," Catie said.

"Sabotage that blows you up as well."

"Uncle Blake, I don't think they accounted for the fusion reactions that occurred after the antimatter reaction."

"So instead of being careless, they're stupid."

"Seems like that might be it. But there were also some bad people. There were over eighty people at that moon base."

"Couldn't they have all been in the ship?" Samantha asked.

"ADI says that based on Captain Galanos's ship, the max number they could carry and make it back to their homeworld would have been twenty."

"Then it sounds like Princess Catherine has to do some investigating. Keep us posted."

Catie let out a very loud sigh. "I will."

"Captain Galanos, thank you for joining us," Catie said as Captain Galanos joined Catie and Captain McAvoy in Catie's day cabin.

"Princess, I'm happy to be here. Is there a problem?"

"Not with you or your crew, but I think there is a problem. Please have a seat and we'll explain."

"Now, you have me worried," Captain Galanos said as she took a seat at the conference table across from Catie and Captain McAvoy.

"That may be a good thing. We've been investigating the event that destroyed Stási."

"Interesting, how are you accomplishing that?"

"Let us show you what we've found first, then I'll explain."

ADI ran the video of the destruction of Stási for Captain Galanos. She had added graphic effects to show the EMP events along with the time code.

"That looks very plausible. But how does a recreation of the event help us?"

"It is not a recreation. It is an actual video of the event taken by a telescope on a probe that is several light-days away from here," Catie said.

"How is this possible? Even if you had such a probe, it would still have to transmit the data to you." Captain Galanos gave Catie and Captain McAvoy a doubtful look.

"First, we have what we call quantum relays. Do you understand quantum coupling?"

"Of course, every student of science knows about quantum coupling." Captain Galanos seemed to be offended that they would think she didn't know. "But a quantum relay?"

"We have them, so we can communicate with the probe instantly, even though it is so far away. Now, second, do you know what a tunnel through space-time is?"

"Yes, our scientists speculate that such things exist."

"Good. We call them wormholes and we can create one. That is how we traveled here. The event that destroyed your moon collapsed the wormhole we were traveling in and deposited us at the location of the event."

"No, no, this cannot be true." Captain Galanos was shaking her head.

"It is. Surely you must question how we could have arrived in your solar system so suddenly. Our homeworld is over fifty light-years away."

"But to a tunnel between two points, how can that be possible? They would have to be perfectly balanced and that cannot be."

"Our speculation is that when we travel through the wormhole, our ship moves to another dimension, then it exits that dimension into our dimension at the new location. That means that the two points are never actually connected."

"Okay. Let's suppose I believe this wormhole theory. What does that mean?"

"It means we are able to effectively go back in time and view the event. By using a wormhole to travel out light days from the event, we can capture the electromagnetic radiation and light energy from the event and send it back to us so we can study it."

"I thought you said that was a probe."

"It is. Our larger probes can generate their own wormholes."

"Okay, so this video, what does it prove?"

"Our analysis says that in all probability what happened was that there was a supply of antimatter in your lab. The containment vessel holding the antimatter failed and suddenly released a huge burst of energy."

"But there should not have been enough antimatter that its detonation would have destroyed the moon!"

"We agree with you, but we don't think that anybody accounted for the fact that with a sealed underground bunker, the energy released by the antimatter created enough heat and pressure to start fusion. The fusion consumed the available fuel, releasing energy and creating more pressure, which continued the fusion until the moon cracked and released the pressure. That is why we see multiple EMP events. One when the antimatter is released, another when a second store of antimatter detonates, and one when what was essentially a fusion bomb goes off."

"Oh my. That is horrible! There were eighty-two people on that moon."

"Yes, you told us. But there is more."

"More?"

"Watch."

ADI now played the high-resolution image that showed the ship trying to leave the base. When the video showed the ship being destroyed, Captain Galanos cried, "What is that? This is a trick!"

"I can assure you that this is not a trick. There was a spaceship leaving the base just before the antimatter was released and the first explosion occurred."

"All of our ships are accounted for. There are only three others like the Geraki, and we were in contact with two of them until our communications were burned out. And we passed the third as we were leaving Helike, it could not have made it out here before us."

"I think that means that there is a fifth ship," Catie said. "We are going to back up farther in time to see if we can learn when it arrived and where it came from. And that is why we need your help. We think it is critical that we understand the purpose of that ship being at Stási. We hope you can help us to unravel this mystery."

"Why is this important to you?"

"We have to decide if we will open relations with your world or go home and leave you to your destiny."

"But what if it is not our world government that is at fault? What if it is one of our princes, someone who is trying to grab more power?"

"Then we would like to help."

"I need time to think!"

"We understand. Please do not share this information with anyone yet. We would like to know more before we involve others."

Captain Galanos gave Catie a skeptical look. "I will wait. I need time to absorb this information and look into myself to see what I must do. I will talk with you again before I do anything."

"Thank you."

"Well, what do you think?" Catie asked Captain McAvoy after Captain Galanos left.

"It was quite a shock to her. I'm sure anyone would be shocked to discover that they really had a Bond villain running around their planet."

"You think they have James Bond movies?"

"I'm sure they have something like him. If not, then we could get rich introducing the concept to them."

Catie laughed. "I wonder what they call their 007."

"Who knows, maybe their superspy is a woman."

"Yeah, that'd be the day."

"Hi, Nattie, I'm between disasters, so I thought I'd call."

"Catie, just a second; let me grab Jules."

"Hah, I knew that nickname would stick."

Natalia came back into view of the camera holding her baby. At ten months, he was quite a handful.

"Hi, Jules. Are you driving Mommy crazy? You know that's your job. Yes it is."

"Hey, don't give him any ideas. He's starting to walk and he's become a danger to anything below three feet."

"Ahh, let me see him walk. Damn, I miss all the good stuff."

"Language!"

"Oh, sorry. I'm sure he never hears you or Paul say anything bad."

"We're trying," Natalia said as she set Julian down on the floor, encouraging him to take a few steps.

Catie spied a stuffed teddy bear across the room. "Jules, go get your teddy for Auntie Catie. Come on, that's a boy."

Julian stumbled across the room to his teddy bear. As he reached down for it, he lost his balance and fell. He immediately stuck his thumb in his mouth and lay down on top of the stuffed animal.

"Oh, he hurt himself."

"No, he didn't, he's just embarrassed that he fell. Allie is walking circles around him. He thinks it's making him look bad."

"Oh, but she's two months older than he is."

"You can't tell him that. She was walking before he really started crawling."

"No way!"

"You see that thumb in his mouth. That's what happens every time he gets stressed. It's hard to crawl with your thumb in your mouth. He quickly decided walking was a better deal."

Catie laughed. "I can sympathize. Sometimes I think I need my Binky."

"I'll bet. Now tell me about these crazy Helikens. I hear they like to play around with antimatter."

"Who told you?"

"Hey, I know people."

"We're pretty sure that's what happened. We showed our data to their captain. Now we're waiting for her to process it. We want her to help us figure out who was behind it."

"More like you should be helping her to figure out who was behind it."

41

Catie rocked back in her chair a bit stunned. "You know, you're right. It's her planet. She needs to feel more in charge. We'll try that when she comes back."

"Good. You don't want to come across all paternalistic, like they're some child race that you're going to punish or something."

"I never come across like that!"

"Right, you're always the concerned, helpful type that just wants to understand. You never think you've got all the answers."

"Nattie!"

"Just saying."

"Okay, okay, I'll try to avoid being condescending and superior. We really do want to help them."

"Good."

"Hey, have you taught Jules any moves yet?"

"Catie, he's ten months old. We've just gotten him to sleep through the night. We're being careful to avoid putting any stress on him lest he backslide."

Catie laughed. "Yeah, I remember you could wake up in the middle of the night at the sound of a pin dropping, but you would be grouchy the whole day."

"Paul's noticed the same thing. He really wants to keep Jules sleeping through the night."

"Captain Galanos, please have a seat. Captain McAvoy will be here in a moment. I hope you slept well."

"Princess," Captain Galanos acknowledged Catie. "My sleep was very troubled, but I have reached a decision."

Captain McAvoy entered Catie's day cabin and nodded to Catie and Captain Galanos.

"You have? Can you tell us?"

"I'm willing to help you investigate the incident at Stási."

"Thank you, but it is we who will be helping you investigate." Catie noticed Captain McAvoy's eyes go wide. "It is your system after all. Our interest is simply to determine whether your world is a good candidate for us to trade with. We only have to leave and avoid your system if things are not as we would like. You have to live here."

Captain Galanos sat up straighter and took a deep breath. "Thank you for your offer of help. I would like to include Commander Petrou and Ensign Nikitas. I trust them completely and believe that they will be able to help."

"We trust your decision," Catie said. "Would you like to brief them yourself, or would you like to have us do it?"

"I think it would help if I could brief them. Can I have the material you have shown me?"

"ADI will present the material when you ask her. She will be listening to your Comm for her cue. Let her know if you want her to narrate or would rather do it yourself. You're welcome to practice with her."

"Thank you."

"Our pleasure. Let us know when you want to meet again."

"I will. I assume that you haven't determined where the ship came from."

"We're still trying to determine that. We should know when it arrived at Stási in the next day or so. Then we'll expand our search to determine where it came from. We'll keep you informed."

"Thank you," Captain Galanos said as she stood up to leave.

"We are eager to help. Let us know if you think of anything else we might do."

Once Captain Galanos left, Captain McAvoy turned to Catie. "Good move telling her that we're helping her investigate."

"Yes, a friend suggested that we shouldn't look like we were trying to take over."

"Smart friend."

◆ ◆ ◆

The next day it was a somber trio of Helikens that joined Catie and Captain McAvoy in the captain's day cabin to discuss the situation.

"Welcome, please have a seat. My steward will be bringing refreshments," Captain McAvoy said.

"He should be bringing us something with alcohol," Commander Petrou said.

"Maybe after our meeting."

"That would probably be best."

The steward knocked on the door as he entered the room with a tray. "I have a pot of coffee here and pitchers of water and orange juice. Let me know if you would like anything else."

"This will be fine. Thank you, Allister."

Once the steward left, Captain McAvoy turned to the group, "Well, any ideas?"

"I think it has to be Polemistia or Agriosa," Commander Petrou said. "They are the most aggressive nations and they're the only ones besides Primus with the capability to build a ship without help from another nation."

"I agree," Ensign Nikitas said. "Both of them have large isolationist movements, and I suspect that there are members of their royal families involved in those movements."

"We have five weeks before we reach Helike. We could slow down more if you feel we need more time."

"Aha!" Ensign Nikitas slapped the table with his hand, "I knew it."

"You knew what?" Catie asked.

"That you were traveling slower than usual."

"And how did you arrive at that conclusion?"

"I overheard one of the crew complaining about having to use the shoulder restraint when they were running. They said that 'this quarter-G thing was a pain'. I would conclude from that, that you normally accelerate at one G."

Catie gave Captain McAvoy a look.

"I'll take care of it," Captain McAvoy said with a frown. "We would prefer that you didn't share that information."

"You can count on our discretion," Captain Galanos said, giving the ensign a hard look, suggesting that she would have liked to have been informed of his supposition before the meeting.

"Other thoughts or suppositions?"

"Captain Galanos says that you're trying to discover where the ship came from and when it arrived," Ensign Nikitas said.

"That is correct. We've determined that it arrived between one week to four months before the event. We'll soon have that narrowed down. Then we'll be able to start looking for where it came from."

"Were there any communications from the ship?"

"We believe so. But we expect it to be encoded."

"If they were making normal transmission to the base, I should be able to help decode them. I have my encryption keys with me," Ensign Nikitas said.

"Excellent. We'll let you know when we have captured some of their transmissions. Anything else?"

"The ship had to have come from the asteroid belt. It would be impossible for anyone to build and launch a ship from Helike without being detected. We can show you where Polemistia or Agriosa are mining the belt if you can bring up a chart."

An image of the asteroid belt came up on the display.

"This is an amazing image. Such detail in this area." Ensign Nikitas pointed to the lower half of the image.

"That is on this side of your sun, and our probes have been able to gather quite a bit of data from there. The other regions will be imaged over time."

"I see, but this is good enough for our use. Their bases are along here." Ensign Nikitas pointed to the lower left quadrant. "All the mining activity is concentrated in this region so they may benefit from the space station that is here." He pointed to another area of the belt, closer to the sun.

"Hmm, I wonder, would the EMP have knocked the space station's systems out?" Commander Petrou asked.

"It is possible, but at that distance, the energy would have been dissipated significantly," Catie said.

"Have you intercepted any communications from that area?"

"ADI?"

"That area is currently shadowed by the first gas giant. That would also make it likely that the space station was not affected by the event."

"What about the mining?"

"That area was likely exposed to the event. I would need a more exact location of their mines to be precise, but again, the energy was dissipated significantly before it reached them."

"We don't have the exact coordinates. The mining ships move around a lot," Ensign Nikitas said.

"That's close enough for now. We'll get better data as our other probes get into position."

"Other probes?" Captain Galanos leaned forward and eyed Catie inquisitively.

"Yes, we sent two other probes out. They will be positioned so we can capture the communication beams from the ship as well as allow us to see on the other side of the planet."

"How long will this take?"

"It will take another two days to get them into position. Then we'll have to wait and see whether we need to push them out farther in time."

Ensign Nikitas laughed. "This travel back in time is interesting. It is too bad we cannot go back and change anything."

Captain McAvoy shook her head. "It might sound like a nice idea, but just imagine the damage someone might do if they could actually travel in time. I think it is better that we can only go back and observe."

"I agree," Captain Galanos said. "Now we'll spend some time talking with the other members of our crew, especially the scientists. We may be able to learn some details that will fill in our gaps."

"You could fill in one gap for us," Catie said. "Were they working with antimatter?"

"Yes, you were correct in your assumptions."

"Why are you researching antimatter?"

"Our scientists feel that we would need an antimatter reactor in order to explore other stars."

"Do you know how fast they were able to create the antimatter?"

"I do not know. It was a closely guarded secret. Why do you ask?"

"Well, depending on how fast you could create it, that would determine if you would need to make it in batches. I still don't understand why you would make so much of it. Unless you could only make it in one location, it would be better to make it as you consumed it in the powerplant. It seems to me that the only reason to make large quantities of it would be if you wished to make a bomb."

"Princess, I fear you are correct. Which is why we need to figure out who was responsible," Captain Galanos said.

"I agree. Now, enough doom and gloom. You asked for alcohol when you came in."

Captain McAvoy's steward appeared with a bottle of Glenlivet and five glasses. "Does anyone want ice?" He quickly served everyone a glass.

"To success!"

"To success!"

"This is very good," Ensign Nikitas said.

"The princess's ancestors came from the region where they make this. It seems to be a family favorite. And I can assure you that this is the best, from her personal stock." The captain smiled at Catie, and Catie immediately realized that the steward had raided her cupboard for the whiskey.

"Yes, it is my uncle's favorite beverage. We have to keep it locked up whenever he is around." Catie smiled back at Captain McAvoy,

47

suggesting that she would be added to the list of people for whom the cupboard would need to be locked.

◆ ◆ ◆

"Hi, Uncle Blake."

"Hey, Squirt. What's up?"

"I just thought I'd call and check in." Catie completely ignored the Squirt jibe.

"You must be getting lonely if you're calling me. Hey, how's Prince Charming?"

"ADI, you're a blabbermouth!"

"I am not!" ADI liked to use all the information that was not confidential or specified as private to join in the gossiping and kidding that went on among the board members. So, one might call her a bit of a gossip.

"Yes you are," Blake said. "But it was Morgan who told me."

"Then she's a blabbermouth too. Anyway, he's just the communication officer on the ship we rescued."

"Yeah, right."

"Come on, Uncle Blake!"

"Okay, okay, I couldn't help myself. Morgan said he's pretty cute."

"*And* he's an alien."

"I give up. Now, why did you call?"

"I wondered if you had any thoughts about how we deal with this situation?"

"Have you talked to your father?"

"Sure, but you know how he is."

"Oh, he probably just asked you what you thought. Sometimes I think he thinks he's a psychiatrist."

Catie giggled. "Yeah, 'how does that make you feel, and what would you suggest.' If you didn't know better, you'd think he didn't have any ideas."

"Yeah, I know just how you feel. Anyway, you really need a lot more information. Once you know who's behind it, you'll know if it's a prelude to war, or just somebody trying to get an edge."

"And if it's a prelude to war?"

"We'll have to decide if we stand back and watch or help out."

"That's what I was afraid of."

"Glad I could help."

While they were waiting on the probes to gather more data, Catie used the time to try and decompress. She finally decided she was relaxed enough to call the triplets. They weren't really triplets, just three young girls that they had rescued from a ring of criminals that was prostituting them to pedophiles. The doctors had dulled the memory from that time so that they were pretty much just normal eleven-year-olds now, well, as normal as one could be living on Delphi Station.

"Hey girls!"

"Princesa!" one of the girls screamed, bringing the other two to the display.

"Hello Princesa Catie, we've missed you."

"I'm sorry, but I've been very busy."

"You should have servants take care of things for you. Then you could spend more time with us."

"You can't have servants or employees do everything. It just doesn't work that way. Now, how are you three doing?"

"We're doing good, . . ."

"Well," ANDI cut in to correct their English. ANDI was the DI for Delphi City and was tasked with looking out for the triplets. Even though the danger had passed, he still spent the time to take care of their education and provide them help when needed, much like ADI did for Catie.

"We're doing well."

"That's good. How's school?"

"Good . . .," one of the triplets said, pausing to see if ANDI would correct her. "We have made some new friends. They want to play podball with us."

"That's great. Did you guys decide on the rules?"

"Yes, ANDI helped the twins and us to develop them. They're working well. . . . And ANDI plays games with us now."

Catie was surprised. The last time she'd tried to teach ANDI about humor and games, things hadn't gone too well. "What kind of games?"

"Guessing games. And we play Escape Room with him. He comes up with really difficult scenarios."

"That should make it more fun."

"It does."

"Sounds like you're getting along really well with ANDI."

"We are, but he's still mean. He makes us do extra homework, and he makes us go to bed on time."

"Ahem!" ANDI interrupted.

"Okay, not mean, but strict."

"He's only doing what's best for you. I'm sure Celia sets your bedtime." Celia was the girls' legal guardian. She'd been the one to bring their situation to the attention of the authorities.

"When are you going to be home? You said you'd be here last week."

"I know, but something came up and I have to deal with it. I'll be home as soon as I can. Then I can play podball with you."

"Good. Liz has played with us a couple of times. She's really good."

"Ah, thanks for telling me." Catie marked that down in her memory, she didn't want Liz suckering her into a bet.

Chapter 4   Back, Back in Time

"The ship was at the base for over a month, thirty-seven days and six hours to be more exact. During that time, it covered the base's antenna," Catie announced to the group. "We see it arriving here, and it seemed to be coming from the area of the asteroid belt that Ensign Nikitas suggested."

"Can you be more specific about the location it came from?"

"We're backing up through time slowly. It's a small ship, so we have to be careful or we'll lose it. We'll know exactly where it came from in a few days."

"They would have needed a shipyard to build a ship like that. Where could it be?" Commander Petrou asked.

"I assume it's in the asteroid belt, close to the space station, but not too close," Ensign Nikitas said.

"It is still hard to believe. It would cost at least twenty billion dollars to do that, maybe thirty billion." The Comm translated the Helike currency numbers to U.S. dollars.

"Why?" Catie asked. She couldn't imagine it costing so much. The Merlin was larger and it had only cost six hundred million dollars.

"You have to lift the supplies and you have to come up with the crew. They couldn't have used the space station that much, so that means resupply had to be accomplished some other way, or by paying off the right people. Just lifting all the material and sending it out there would have been very costly."

"And it would have all had to be done in secret," Captain McAvoy added. "You have to realize that they didn't have all the nice technology and infrastructure we had when we built the Merlin."

"What would you like?" the steward asked Morgan. She was having breakfast with Catie in her day cabin, their weekly check-in.

"Can I have a prosciutto and asparagus omelet?"

"Of course. Anything else?"

"Some melon if you have it."

"And to drink?"

"Orange juice and coffee."

"We'll have that right out." The steward Commed the food order to the kitchen. He went to the sideboard and grabbed the coffee pot to fill Morgan's cup.

"I thought you didn't do omelets," Catie said.

"I don't make omelets; that doesn't mean I don't eat them."

Catie laughed. "How's Tracey doing?"

"She's great. Apparently, she's made up with her father. He kind of disowned her when she came out."

"I'm sorry to hear that. But if they made up, that's good."

"Yeah, she's from a small town in Colorado. She went home for her brother's high school graduation. Here let me show you the video." Morgan flicked a video to Catie's HUD so they could watch it together.

"I'll buy you a drink while we wait on your mother and Jackson to get here," the man said. Catie figured that would be Tracey's father.

"You don't have to. It's okay if we just wait in the restaurant," Tracey said.

"Hey, I want to buy my daughter a drink."

"Then lead the way."

They entered the bar and found a corner table. The waitress came up right away to take their order. "Hello Mr. Lawrence, hi, Tracey. Been a while since I've seen you around."

"Hi, Carrie. I've been overseas."

"Right, I remember you joined the Marines. Well, what will you two be having?"

"I'll have a beer, whatever you have on tap," Mr. Lawrence said.

"Glenfiddich, if you have it, neat," Tracey ordered.

"Coming right up."

The waitress left the table to fetch the drinks. There were four men at the table next to them, and you could just make out one of the men saying the word 'Dike'.

Mr. Lawrence got up and grabbed the man by the scruff of his neck and pulled him out of his chair.

"You have something to say?!"

"No, sir, Mr. Lawrence."

"Well, if you do, you say it to my face. Now that's my daughter and I'm proud of her. Yeah, she prefers women. I can't say I can blame her, given the sorry excuse for men we have around here. Now, if that bothers you, you come see me and I'll help you see the error of your ways. Anyone else have something they want to say?!"

There were some rumbles of 'no, sir' but otherwise the bar was quiet. When Mr. Lawrence sat back down, you could tell that Tracey gave him a kiss on the cheek.

"That's great," Catie said. "I can see why nobody had a problem with that. Mr. Lawrence is a big guy. I can also see where Tracey gets her temper."

"Yeah, I think they're a lot alike. Tracey's the oldest and did a lot to help her father around the ranch. She's a regular cowgirl."

"That sounds nice. Have you ever been to her hometown?"

"Not yet."

"Here are your omelets," the steward interrupted them. "Anything else you need?"

"I think we're good for now," Catie said. Once the steward was out of earshot, she asked Morgan, "Does that mean you're planning to visit?"

"Well, . . . we're talking about buying a ranch there."

"Cool. What kind of ranch?"

"Tracey wants to breed Appaloosas."

"Is that a horse or a cow?"

Morgan laughed. "A horse!"

"What's so special about Appaloosas?"

"They're spotted, that's what makes them special. Tracey likes the ones that are similar to quarter horses. She likes to rope and stuff like that."

"What about you?"

"I'm going to learn how to ride. We'll see what else. But it'll be a business, so there'll be plenty for me to do."

"When are you planning to do this?"

"Don't know. Tracey said she'd check out some ranches that are for sale. But we need to save enough money. It'll be tough starting a new business."

"Can her father help?"

"Sure. He might give her some land to start. But he can't really afford to give up that much. He raises shorthorn cattle."

"So, do I need to tell Kal he's got to find me a new bodyguard?"

"I've already given him the hint. But nothing is going to happen right away. That means there's plenty of time."

"Can't you borrow the money?"

"Horses are expensive. We need to save up."

"Hey, not to step on any toes, but what if we formed a company? I could front the money and you guys could run the business."

"You shouldn't do that."

"Why not? I already own the riding stables on Delphi City. We could do something where we brought some of your Appaloosas in. They'd be cool, something a bit special."

"Catie!"

"Come on, Morgan. It's not like I don't have enough money. It'd be fun. And it would give us a reason to say in touch. You've been great for me. I'd like to help."

"I'll talk to Tracey about it."

"Good."

◆ ◆ ◆

Catie's Comm woke her up, "Cer Catie! I need to talk with you and Captain McAvoy now!"

"ADI, what's up?"

"We have an emergency situation. I've discovered survivors from the moon."

Captain McAvoy was already in Catie's day cabin when Catie made it there. She had been on duty, so was already up.

"Captain."

"Princess, what is this about survivors?"

"You know as much as I do. ADI, please explain."

"The probe that we sent below the ecliptic plane detected a shuttle exiting the atmosphere of the gas giant two days before the event. It landed on one of the other moons. It hasn't moved since then."

"Why did it take us so long to detect this?" Captain McAvoy asked.

"*Because* I have been focusing all the probes on the asteroid belt trying to determine where the fake supply ship came from. Once this probe had completed its scans, I refocused it on the timing around the event, trying to learn anything new. We knew that the supply ship left the base for a few hours three days before the event. It is likely that it was chasing the shuttle."

"Why do you think that?"

"It is the only postulate that makes sense given the data. Why would a shuttle be in the gas giant's atmosphere and why would it land on a moon and maintain radio silence for this long unless it was hiding? The timing lines up with when the supply ship temporarily left the base."

"Okay, okay. Captain, we need to send a Lynx to see if there are survivors on that shuttle."

"Of course," Captain McAvoy said. "I'm going to add a Fox to provide cover. We still don't know for sure who the good guys are."

"I agree, let's talk to Captain Galanos first."

◆ ◆ ◆

"Captain Galanos, we have discovered that a shuttle left the base before it exploded."

"Princess, that is amazing. Will you be able to send someone to rescue them?"

"We're preparing a mission now; we don't know if they're still alive but we're hopeful."

"I suggest that we add Ensign Nikitas to the mission, his name is well known. It would help if they were able to be contacted by a well-known Heliken. And it would make their trip back to the Merlin less stressful."

"Merlin, inform Ensign Nikitas to meet the team in flight bay two."

"Yes, Captain."

Chapter 5   Party

The Aperanjens had been restless during the Dutchman's journey to their new colony world. It had been a long and arduous process to wake them all from stasis. After the disaster of waking the first Aperanjen slave, the process was modified. It took longer, but it was definitely safer than having an Aperanjen wake up disoriented and angry. Most of the Aperanjens had been in stasis when the Fazullans captured their ship, and fortunately, most had remained in stasis so had never experienced the horrors of slavery, but those that had been slaves took a lot of convincing before they were willing to accept that the Paraxeans and Humans were their friends.

During the five months since the Sakira had transported the Aperanjen colonists from Earth, the colonists had worked hard to get the colony ready for their fellow colonists from the Fazullan ships. Those ships had held the majority of their original colony mission.

The week before they were scheduled to arrive, the Aperanjens had sent out a large hunting party. They had informed the Delphineans that there would be a big feast when the colonists arrived. Even after being told that it would take days to bring all the colonist pods down, they still insisted that the festival would begin as soon as the Dutchman arrived and the first of the new colonists set foot on the planet.

Captain Payne met with the head of the security detail for the Aperanjen colony before he started the operation to move the colonists. He had over twenty-eight thousand Aperanjens aboard the Dutchman and wanted to make sure everything was squared away before they started unloading.

"Lieutenant Carter, thanks for joining me."

"Not a problem Captain. We're happy to see you. I see you're not unloading the colonist pods yet."

"I wanted to get an appraisal of the situation before we start adding more Aperanjens down there."

"Smart, and very brave of you. I'm sure you've heard from the Aperanjen leader about the delay."

"Yes, he broke my guest chair. I had to borrow one from the owner's cabin while they make me another. Now tell me what we should expect."

"When we arrived on the Sakira with the four thousand Aperanjens from Earth, it was quite an event. The Aperanjens who had stayed behind when the Roebuck left had accomplished a lot, but what could thirty of them really do? The Marines we left with them were not much help, 1.5Gs is pretty tough on us Humans."

"I can imagine. The 1.25-G profile on the Dutchman is hard enough, I can't imagine dealing with a constant 1.5G."

"It's not nice. Even now, my guys are so relieved when they get to come back up to the Sakira for a day. Anyway, when the Sakira arrived, it was a bit of a madhouse. They had a huge festival that screwed everything up. We lost days before things calmed down and we could really get the place organized. I've talked to them about it, and they assure me they're better prepared this time."

"So, do you have any recommendations?"

"They accomplished a lot in the sixteen weeks since we got here. They've got the condo shells up and ready to slide the cabins in. I'd recommend you spread out the timing between bringing the various colonist pods down as much as you can."

"Fifteen of my thirty pods are full of colonists. I can drop a cargo pod every other colonist pod, but that's the best I can do."

"That'll help. Do you have any colonists in the Dutchman's guest cabins?"

"Yes, they're completely full. We wanted to maximize the cargo space so we filled up the cabins instead of adding colonist pods."

"Well, you should get them down to the planet first before they start wandering around the ship wondering what's up."

"Got it."

◆ ◆ ◆

"Joe, I know you've flown a SkyLifter quite a few times, but that's not a cargo pod out there, it's a colonist cabin pod," Amalia said. She was there to certify Joe for handling colonist pods.

"Sure, I know that," Joe said.

"That means that it has a specific orientation as far as gravity goes."

"Yep, got that."

"Then you might want to pay attention to the cargo master out there who's telling you to hook onto the side of it."

"Oh, right," Joe said as he realized that he was heading toward the pod's crown. When you grabbed cargo pods, you usually did it by their crown so you could slide them into place on the cargo ship. But with certain cargo pods or a colonist cabin pod, you had to grab them on the side so that the cargo would be aligned with the thrust it was under when the StarMerchant accelerated or in this case, gravity, when they set it down on the planet.

"The other side," Amalia said, rolling her eyes.

"Sorry! I guess setting it down so that Aperanjens were head down wouldn't be too funny." The colonist pods were full of colonists. And even though they were strapped into their bunks, they would undoubtedly prefer to be pressed into the bunk by gravity instead of into their straps.

"Oh, they'd be laughing all the way down; thinking about what they'd do with the various body parts they tore off of you. They'd probably think your head would make a nice bowling ball."

"They're not that tough."

"Right. One of their fifteen-year-old girls could rip your arms off."

"I could handle a fifteen-year-old."

"You really think so?"

"Well . . . a twelve-year-old at least," Joe said as the SkyLifter finally latched onto the pod.

"Now, I usually let the autopilot do everything it can do. Like now, rotating that pod so that it's correctly oriented toward the planet. It might sound easy, but you have to remember that although the colonists were told to put everything away and strap stuff down, some kid might have left a toy under a chair. So while you're rotating that pod, that toy's going to get pressed against the wall or floor, and when you stop rotating, that toy is going to keep moving, you know, Newton's First Law. That means that toy might wind up hitting that kid's mother upside the head. Now, it's fair to say that she'll want to discipline that kid, but she might also think you need some disciplining as well."

"Got it. Autopilot, set our orientation," Joe ordered.

Captain Payne watched as the first colonist pod was set down. He held his breath as he watched to see if there would be any bumps or if it would be tilted when it first touched down. But he needn't have worried. Joe had let the autopilot handle that and the pod landed perfectly flat with no extra motion. The SkyLifter released the pod and flew over to the cargo pod that it was going to lift back up to the Dutchman. The pilot made quick, precise maneuvers; the moves were a bit too angular in Payne's opinion.

Only minutes after the SkyLifter set the pod down, Aperanjen colonists started to stream out of the pod. This was a light load since there were only about twenty-nine thousand colonists. There were only three or four per cabin, nothing like when they were moving the Paraxeans, then there were four to six per cabin.

Payne continued to watch as the ground crew removed the side of the pod so that they could access the cabins. Each cabin would be pulled out of the pod and moved to one of the skeleton towers in the new city. They'd be slid into place inside the tower, creating a good start to a new condo unit.

As the work crew started moving the cabins, the reception committee started to move the colonists over to the festival area. There they were heartily welcomed by their brethren who'd been working hard to prepare for their arrival.

"Lieutenant Carter said they were going to manage things better this time, so what's up with the party?" Captain Payne asked the Marine sentry.

"They've been working like crazy to get ready for this. They sent out a big hunting party to bring back some deer and they've been cooking them up."

"They do realize it will take two to three days to bring all the colonists down?"

"Yep. I've been told that the party's going to last for a week. If I were you, I'd steer clear of it. You don't want to bump up against a drunk Aperanjen."

"I guess not. You might hurt yourself, and that's before he pushed you away."

"Yep."

Captain Payne started walking back toward his shuttle. His legs were feeling the 1.5-G gravity. He'd thought that spending a few months under 1.25Gs would have prepared him, but without that zero-G pause every second to let his heart pump blood, he wasn't doing so well.

Lieutenant Carter was right, the Aperanjens were prepared. The work crews had been carefully identified. As each colonist pod was landed, the crew immediately started to disassemble the pod. Using one of the lifters, they grabbed each cabin and slid it into place in the frame of the condo building. A second crew immediately welded the unit into place while a third crew connected the wiring and plumbing. By the time they were finished, the next cabin was being slid into place.

The next day the crews from the day before joined the party and new crews took their place. It minimized the contention between the Aperanjens who were partying and the ones who were working. Anyone could stand a day of being excluded from the party, and they did get to join in when night fell.

Kal had been spending a lot of time with Zahan, his Arabian horse. He was trying to get the horse to trust him. He'd finally gotten him to quit laughing at him when he was able to ride over the one-meter hurdles in the jump course without losing his seat. But Zahan steadfastly refused to try the big two-meter jump when Kal was aboard him. He would just go around it, arrogantly snorting to let Kal know that the jump was beyond Kal's skill level. The staff had taken to lowering the jump whenever Kal was scheduled in the ring.

"Come on, boy, you're making me look bad," Kal whispered as he stroked Zahan's neck. He was grooming the horse while he waited for Sandra to show up. Of course, Sandra had been clearing the two-meter jump on Sultan since her first attempt. She had waited for two months while she and the horse got used to each other, but then they'd done the course like the pros they were.

Zahan nuzzled Kal's side, pushing him away.

"What's the matter, you don't trust me? You're not embarrassed by me, are you?"

Kal heard Sandra enter the barn. Her horse, Sultan, was Zahan's twin. Kal had bought the two horses so that Sandra could start competing again. She had been a dedicated equestrian as a teenager and through college. She'd always dreamed of making the Olympics but never made the U.S. team. She claimed it was because they could never afford a good enough horse to compete at that level. Well, Sultan and Zahan were two of the best horses he could buy. Sandra had just won an event in New Zealand and was riding high.

"Kal, are you here?" Sandra called out.

"Over here, I'm just saddling Zahan."

"Oh, good. Armando is just finishing up with Sultan. Are you ready?"

"Yes." Kal led Zahan out of the barn and next to the ring. They didn't have the arena for another twenty minutes, which should give them enough time to warm the horses up. Sandra was already getting a leg up on Sultan.

Sandra settled down on Sultan and smiled at Armando. "Thank you. You are so good with the horses."

"I love them," Armando said.

"And they love you. Kal, do you want to ride down to the lake and back?"

"That should be a good warm-up." It was a bit cool at 0700, but this was the time their schedules allowed. Sandra had an especially busy schedule as the events director for the Four Seasons Resort. Although Kal, as the top general in Delphi Forces, had a full schedule, he could choose whenever he wanted to take a two-hour break to ride or catch a few waves; it was easy to make the time up later.

They trotted the horses down to the lake. Kal was amazed at the quality of Zahan's trot; it was so smooth that he almost didn't need to post, and the posting took almost no effort. He glanced over at Sandra who was chatting with Sultan. Sometimes he thought she talked more to the horse than she did to him.

"A light canter back?" Sandra asked.

"Sounds right." Kal patted Zahan on the shoulder. "No racing, this is just a warmup."

Zahan and Sultan loved to canter and had a smooth rhythmic motion, which was important since that was the dominant gait when jumping.

"Jumps on the right!" Sandra called out, reminding Kal that there were four well-spaced jumps before they got back to the ring. They were easy jumps to help the horse and rider get into sync before they took the ring. Kal and Zahan glided over the jumps easily, then slowed to a trot for the final leg back the ring.

"Kal, do you want to go first?"

"Sure. *Now, don't make me look bad!*" Kal whispered as he gave Zahan a pat on the neck. He nodded to Armando, letting him know to open the gate. "All right, this is it."

Zahan started his canter as Kal mentally reviewed the course. He aimed Zahan for the first jump, an easy one-meter jump. That's when he noticed that the crew hadn't lowered the big jump for him. They usually did, since everyone knew that Zahan refused to jump it with Kal on his back. "*Damn,*" Kal whispered as he realized he would be embarrassed again.

Zahan made the next two jumps smoothly and started the big circle for the two-meter jump. "Come on boy, we can do it." Then Kal realized that Zahan was heading right for the takeoff point. He forced himself to relax as he gave Zahan his head. The horse knew where he wanted to be, Kal only hoped that his plan wasn't to skid to a stop.

As they glided over the jump, Kal heard Sandra cheering them. "Okay, two more easy jumps and you're good."

As Kal guided Zahan out of the ring, Sandra was grinning from ear to ear. "Wow, you did it. I'm so proud of you."

"It was all Zahan, he finally decided to see if I could stay on."

"He's a smart horse. Do you have my ring?"

"What?!"

"Do you have my ring?"

"You mean that's what it takes? I get Zahan to jump the two-meter gate, and you're willing to marry me?"

"Hey, if he's figured out that he can trust you, I'm sure I can."

"I'll bring the ring when we go out to dinner tonight." Kal shook his head in amazement. He'd been asking Sandra to marry him for a couple of months and she'd always said it wasn't the right time yet. Kal dismounted and handed Zahan's reins to Armando, "I'll take care of Sandra and Sultan if you'll cool him down."

"Thank you. I love to ride him."

Of course, there never was any doubt that Sandra and Sultan would ride clean.

Kal gave Sandra a not-too-short kiss as he met her at the Four Seasons' restaurant. She'd had to work until late to deal with a new convention coming to Delphi City.

"How did the planning meeting go?" Kal asked.

"Long and boring. You'd think it was their first convention. They're worried about the most ridiculous things. Now that's the last talk about work. This is supposed to be a romantic dinner."

"Of course." Kal motioned to the Maître d' to indicate they were ready to be seated.

"Are you going to propose now? Should we order a bottle of champagne?"

"I've already ordered the champagne, but you're going to have to wait until dessert for the proposal."

Sandra gave Kal a pout but changed it to a smile when the sommelier showed up with the champagne.

"To our future," they toasted together.

"I heard they're going to send the Roebuck to check out some more planets for Earth colonies," Sandra said.

"I wonder where you heard that." Kal knew full well that Sandra would have heard it from Jackie, Blake's fiancée.

"I will not reveal my source, but what I'd like to know is if you're going to lead the mission."

"Not a chance. Marc, Catie, and Liz are the ones with the wanderlust. I'm happy right here in Delphi City."

"So, never?"

"Maybe after I've raised a family. Might be a good way to get away from the kids."

Sandra laughed. "So, you want kids."

"You know I do. One or two. But once they're in college we could run away to a colony planet. Just send money back for them. We've got a long life ahead of us with the youth treatments. We might even decide to have a second set of kids."

"I'm not sure about that."

"Why don't we talk about your next competition? Is it in New Zealand again?"

"Yes, are you going to come and watch?"

"I plan to. It's a big one, isn't it?"

"Yes. If I win, I might get invited to join the New Zealand Olympic team."

"You know that might not be necessary."

"What?"

"Joining the New Zealand Olympic team."

"*Why* not?"

"I've heard a rumor that Delphi Nation is going to send a team to the Olympics next year."

"What?!"

"I was chatting with Sam and she said it would be a good idea. Especially since we have this hotshot equestrian."

"You're serious, aren't you?"

"Yes. We're putting in an Olympic-sized pool, a new track, a cycling velodrome, and we already have a jumping area and cross-country jump track."

"And what about our top sniper, they'd be sure to win a medal in shooting?"

"Oh, I'm sure Mariana will be there."

"Silly, I meant you!"

"I guess I can see if I can make the team."

"You'd better. What other events are we going to field teams in?"

"Quite a few; I forgot to mention the skate park and the BMX bike park, you know we have to cater to the youth. But we should be able to field a good track and field team. Lots of good Jamaican runners have immigrated here. We also have some strange people who like to fence, don't know what that's about."

"You'd better watch out or one of them will hear you and challenge you to a duel."

"Ohh, scared I am. I think the only team events they're planning are field hockey and water polo."

"What about gymnastics?"

"We don't even have anyone doing gymnastics."

"How did that happen?"

"Don't know. I'd think the twins would be naturals."

"Hey, maybe we can get some kind of microgravity event added. They'd be sure to win gold."

"I'll mention it to Sam. That sounds like something she'd like. So, are you up for captaining the equestrian team?"

"You know I am."

When the waiter removed their last dishes from their entrée, Sandra gave Kal an expectant look. "Well?"

"Well, what?"

"Are you going to make me beg?"

Kal laughed and got out of his chair and bent down on one knee. "Sandra Bishop, would you do me the honor of agreeing to be my wife?"

"Yes, if you're willing to put up with me."

"I'm afraid I'm hooked."

"So am I."

There was applause from the diners around them as Kal placed the engagement ring on Sandra's finger.

"Now for dessert," Kal said.

"I think we should have dessert on the Mea Huli. I took the liberty of reserving it."

"Oh, I like a woman who takes charge."

"That's a good thing because I plan on taking charge of a lot of things tonight."

Chapter 6   A Story to Tell

Once the Lynx was in sight of the small shuttle nestled in the moon's crater, the pilot gave Ensign Nikitas a nod, letting him know he was clear to open communication.

"Shuttle, this is Ensign Nikitas of the HSS Geraki, do you need assistance? Over."

There was no response from the shuttle.

"Shuttle, we can see your power signature, if you cannot communicate, pulse your engines. We're here to help. Over."

On the shuttle, the pilot was sitting in the corner looking at the woman who was occupying the pilot's seat. "Come on, the Geraki is Captain Galanos's ship. I know about her. She's a good person. And everyone knows Prince Nikitas."

"I know them too," the woman said. "How do you work this radio?"

Since the woman was holding a laser pistol, the pilot decided that he would just tell her. "Flip that blue switch up. Then you can just key the mic to talk."

The woman nodded and keyed the mic. "Ensign Nikitas, we could use some help."

"Do you need help repairing your shuttle, or do you need us to exfiltrate you? Over."

The woman gave the pilot a questioning look.

"Do you want them to come get us out of here? I vote for that; I'm not sure this thing will fly, and I'd like to get out of it and into some kind of shower as soon as we can."

"We would like you to exfiltrate us," the woman said.

"Do you have EVA suits? Over."

"Yes."

"We will set our shuttle down next to yours. We'll signal you when our airlock is open. Will you need help? Over."

The woman looked at the pilot; when he shook his head no, she dropped the pistol and replied. "No, we can make it on our own." Her entire body sagged as she dropped the mic and let go of all the tension she'd been holding.

"We will be setting down in two minutes. When you enter the airlock, keep your helmets on until the decontamination cycle is complete."

The pilot walked over to the control console and took the mic. "Will do. Out."

"Our airlock is ready. Over," Ensign Nikitas communicated to the survivors.

The woman and the pilot exited the shuttle. They moved cautiously along the moon's surface; clearly, the woman was not very adept at moving in the low gravity of the moon. The pilot looked at the Lynx and shook his head. *"What the hell is that thing?"* He helped the woman up into the airlock before jumping up himself. He pounded on the airlock's inner door to signal that they were inside.

The outer door closed, and strong UV light filled the airlock. The pilot tapped on the woman's helmet to remind her to close her eyes. After a few minutes, the pilot could tell that the airlock was filling with air. He checked the pressure gauge on his wrist and when it reached 0.8 atmospheres, he started to remove his helmet. The woman immediately followed suit.

Ensign Nikitas and Dr. Moreau were standing beside the airlock when it opened.

Ensign Nikitas gagged as soon as it did. "Sorry," he coughed.

"I know we're a bit ripe." The pilot laughed at the distressed look on Ensign Nikitas's face.

"You can say that again. There's a shower down that way, we put some shipsuits in it for you to change into. We brought a selection of sizes. Why don't you take care of that and then the doctor can examine you?"

"Thank you," The woman said as she headed into the shower room. She motioned toward the shower with her head, telling the pilot to follow her in. They'd just spent over two weeks on the shuttle together, modesty was long forgotten.

Showered and in clean shipsuits, the two survivors looked almost normal. Dr. Moreau had pronounced them healthy, although malnourished. The woman was reluctant to talk, but the pilot was chatty.

"Hey, pretty strange shuttle you have here. It's nice and big, but you do know that those wings don't do anything out here in space."

"I'm told that it is also capable of atmospheric flight," Ensign Nikitas said.

"Boy, I didn't know we had anything like this. And a shower, man that is crazy. Who designed this thing?"

"I don't know. But you should be happy it had a shower; we spaced your suits." Ensign Nikitas gave the pilot a look that said that without the shower they might have spaced him as well.

"Well, I don't blame you for that. I was getting ready to space myself. Those shuttles were not designed to be lived in. Hey, we must be moving pretty fast. I feel a lot of weight here against my seat."

"We're trying to catch up with the Merlin. It's the big ship. We'll land this shuttle in its flight bay. It's heading back to Helike."

"I could fall asleep in these chairs. They're super plush."

"It'll lean back, why don't you go ahead and take a nap, you look tired." Ensign Nikitas was really the one who was tired of chatting.

It took three days for the Lynx to finally rejoin the Merlin. Dr. Moreau had strongly advised that they wait to talk to the survivors until they had a chance to catch up on their sleep.

"How are they?" Catie asked Dr. Moreau.

"They seem to be getting better. Two and a half weeks on just water and a week's worth of rations is tough. But they'll be fine."

"Good."

"Thanks for suggesting we take a few shipsuits with us. We threw the two of them in the shower and left them there with a selection of suits to change into after they showered."

"Pretty ripe, were they?"

"You could say that. Let them settle in for tonight. They should be rested enough to chat with you tomorrow morning. I've given them something to help with the shock."

Catie cut the link with the doctor and went back to chat with Captain McAvoy. They'd had to shuffle a few of the pilots around to make room for two additional guests. The two had asked for separate accommodations even though they'd just spent over two weeks in a shuttle about half as big as a Lynx. One couldn't blame them for being tired of each other.

"Our two survivors are Dr. Rubis and the pilot Lieutenant Vlachos. They should be here momentarily. Captain Galanos has suggested we talk with Lieutenant Vlachos first," Catie informed the group.

"Have they said anything?"

"You mean besides, thank you? Not yet. I was told that the pilot was rather chatty on the way back. But he clammed up when they reached the Merlin."

The Marine knocked on the door before opening it. "Princess, your guest."

"Come on in. I hope you slept well," Catie greeted the first of the survivors. "This is Captain McAvoy, the captain of the Merlin, and you may know Captain Galanos, the captain of the HSS Geraki."

"We've never met, but I've heard of her," Lieutenant Vlachos replied. He seemed to be confused about Captain McAvoy and Catie's presence. Catie decided that she would let him stay confused. He was a virtual giant, almost two meters tall. He had dark wavy hair and dark brown eyes. His complexion was only a bit darker than Captain Galanos's.

Catie nodded to Captain Galanos, indicating she should start asking the questions.

"Lieutenant Vlachos, what can you tell us about what happened?"

"I probably don't know anything you'd be interested in. I just happened to be the pilot on the shuttle when the doctor hijacked it."

"Hijacked it?"

"Yes, she showed up with a laser pistol and told me to start flying. I started to argue, but she said that if I didn't fly her out of there, we would be dead within the week and I'd be dead right away."

"And you believed her?"

"Well, it looked pretty certain she was serious about me being dead, so I did what she said."

"Go ahead and tell us exactly what happened."

"I always do a readiness check on the shuttle every morning. I guess she knew that because she was waiting for me when I showed up. She had this weird looking laser pistol. I wasn't sure it was real, but she fired off a pulse to convince me, then told me to open the shuttle up.

"She followed me in and had me close the door. Then she told me that we had to escape without them seeing us. That if anyone on the supply ship saw us, they'd just blow us up without asking any questions. Like I said, I wasn't sure I should believe her, but I figured if we were caught, I could explain that I'd been hijacked. They'd probably know the doctor was a bit nuts and believe me.

"Anyway, the shuttle was about twenty degrees along the moon's surface, away from where the supply ship usually docked. It was next to a separate exit, kind of an emergency escape if an accident happened and the main tunnel collapsed. Apparently, the people on the supply ship didn't know that, they only started doing that last year.

"I launched the shuttle and started a fast descent toward the planet trying to keep the moon between us and the supply ship as well as the base's sensor array. We were about half a million kilometers from the moon when they must have seen us. I saw that supply ship tear away from the moon like it was on fire. I steepened our descent hoping to get inside the atmosphere before they got in range, but we were too slow.

"They pulled into range when we still had over two hundred thousand kilometers to go, so I started to corkscrew our path. I used to fly fighters. That shuttle was like flying a brick, and without shielding, we could only sustain about one second of a laser pulse, so I had to do something. They shot at us as soon as they could, no warning, no demand to surrender, so then I knew the doctor was telling the truth. I started to juke the shuttle around; it was clumsy, but I just needed to keep their weapons guy guessing. Damn speed of light is a bitch when you're trying to evade enemy fire. You only get the time it takes them to draw a bead on you to get out of the way of their shot.

"I dumped a bunch of fuel and ignited it, hoping to confuse their sensors. It bought us some time, but not much. We took a hit and it punctured the hull. I yelled patch and pointed at the cabinet. The doctor might be an egghead, but she was sharp enough to know we needed air to breathe. She got up and grabbed a patch and had it over the hole in seconds.

"I yelled at her to strap back in and threw the shuttle into a tumble. It was erratic enough to confuse their weapons operator, and he probably figured he'd nailed us, so he didn't try too hard after that. I used thrusters to keep us in a controlled tumble and got the nose angled right just before we hit the atmosphere.

"Once we were inside the atmosphere, I put us back on our main vector to make sure we maintained escape velocity and pushed the engines. We came out of the atmosphere about a million kilometers from where we entered it. I kept us close to the atmosphere, in the very upper part to hide our signature. We were coasting, but if they picked us up on sensors, they'd have been able to separate us from the atmospheric noise. They must have decided we were done for because they went back to the base.

"After all that, I landed us on that moon and we waited."

"Did you observe anything else?"

"Well, a couple of days later, there was a big disturbance in the atmosphere of that gas giant. It looked like someone had set off a bomb or something, the atmosphere just flared with a big storm. That went on for a few days."

"What was the doctor's plan?"

"She said we were to wait for as long as we could hold out, then we were to send a message to Helike about what had happened on Stási base. I told her I wasn't sure we'd be able to raise Helike, but she said we had to try. I thought we might be able to establish communication with the station in the asteroid belt; when I told her that she seemed to relax."

"And what happened next?"

"We just waited. I figured she might not be crazy after all, and she seems like a nice person. We spent over two weeks on that shuttle and I never wanted to strangle her, but of course, she had that laser pistol the whole time."

"Okay, that was quite an adventure. Would you like to stay while we interview her?"

"Yes, ma'am. But first, could you tell me what happened to the base on Stási?"

"It was destroyed. In fact, the moon was destroyed."

Lieutenant Vlachos was shocked at the news. "The whole moon?!"

"Yes. Someone or something released the antimatter."

"Antimatter, that's what they were making. Hell, if I'd have known that I would have refused that assignment, only idiots fool around with antimatter."

"I can sympathize with those sentiments. We're investigating what caused the antimatter to be released," Captain Galanos said. "These people are helping us."

"I didn't know we had such advanced ships. That shuttle you sent to rescue us is one amazing ship. And this Merlin is bigger than anything I thought we had."

"We'll explain that later. For now, we need you to sit quietly and only talk if I ask you a direct question. Can you do that?"

"Yes, ma'am. Just like at the academy."

Captain Galanos nodded to Catie who then messaged the Marine to bring Dr. Rubis in.

When she entered, Dr. Rubis smiled shyly at Lieutenant Vlachos then turned her attention to Captain Galanos. "What happened to our base on Stási?" she asked.

"It was destroyed, but apparently you expected that to happen," Captain Galanos replied.

"I did."

"Can you explain?"

"Would you like me to tell you the whole story?"

"Yes, I think that would be best."

"I first arrived at the base on Stási aboard your ship, almost two years ago. My degree is in magnetic physics. I was responsible for the design of the containment vessels." Dr. Rubis paused and looked at Catie.

"It's alright, they both know the purpose of the base," Captain Galanos reassured her.

Dr. Rubis nodded solemnly. "Good. Then you know we were researching how to manufacture antimatter. Things went well for the first year. We developed a technique for the manufacture and were setting up experiments to determine just how much we could make at one time and how fast we could produce it. It was after the next supply ship arrived that things changed. They brought six more scientists with them, including a new director for the lab. He changed things, forced more regimentation on our schedules, restricted access to the lab except for when we were on duty and were scheduled to run an experiment. It bothered me at first, but after a while, I got used to it. I had more time for my own research and studies since limiting my access to the lab meant that I could not work overtime on the projects there, so I did research in my room. Just mathematical equations and such since I did not have access to any equipment.

"Then I noticed that our supply of tritium was being depleted faster than expected. That had to mean that much more energy was being drawn from the fusion reactor. It didn't make sense. I brought the discrepancy to the attention of the director. He told me that it was a clerical error and he would take care of it. He assured me that the supply of tritium was exactly what it should be, but I didn't believe him. The process for accessing the logs on the tritium was changed and I could no longer check on our stocks. I tried to figure out what could be using up so much power. The answer had to be that we were producing more antimatter than we were supposed to."

"Were you able to confirm that?"

"I think so. I started marking the containment vessel before the end of my shift. It should have taken two days to fill it. But by the next day, there was always a new vessel. Then I overheard two of the other scientists arguing about how fast the production process could be run. One was convinced that it was only able to produce half as much antimatter as the theory said it should. My guess was that they were the ones who were running the accelerated production experiments and the results did not come out as they had expected. I kept tracking the containment vessels. We were using over three times as many as we should have. Someone was modifying the records so it did not show that, but I could tell by the rate we were going through the parts. I guess they didn't think to hide those records."

Dr. Rubis stared at the wall struggling to control her breathing. Tears welled up in her eyes and she sniffed a few times as she struggled to control her emotions.

"What made you think they were going to kill you?" Captain Galanos prompted her.

"When the supply ship arrived early, we were all shocked. I knew someone who worked in the communication shack, and she said that it had made amazing time. She said they started talking to the ship as soon as Stási rounded the planet and we had a direct line of sight. She told me she was confused because her friend was supposed to be on the supply ship as their communication officer."

"Petty Officer Fotopoulos," Captain McAvoy suggested.

"Yes, that was the name. She told me that the communication officer told her that Fotopoulos had come down with the flu and couldn't make the flight. She didn't believe him; she had an email from Fotopoulos and she wasn't sick. And by that time, she was in quarantine, so how could she catch the flu?

"Anyway, that made me suspicious. I started trying to listen in on other conversations. I heard enough to convince me that when the supply ship left, they would make sure there was an accident that would kill all of us."

"What did you hear?"

"I heard the director say that nobody would notice the shortage of rations. That we wouldn't be needing food as soon as they left. I heard other comments as well. And the fact that the director was leaving. Nobody said that. I had been messaging with my colleagues back on Helike and they never mentioned that."

"Do you believe that they would set a bomb so that it looked like there had been an accident?"

"Yes."

Catie couldn't resist asking a question. "What I don't understand is why they would have left so much antimatter behind? If their point was to steal it, why leave more than just enough to destroy the lab? The explosion that destroyed the moon had to have started with several kilos of antimatter."

"That is bothering me also," Captain Galanos said.

"Ahem," Lieutenant Vlachos coughed.

"Yes, Lieutenant Vlachos?"

"Ma'am. I'm no scientist, but based on what she said and a few things I remember, what if there were two groups stealing antimatter? If only one of them left on the cargo ship and took their antimatter with them, then there would have been a lot still on the moon."

"Two groups?"

"That would make sense based on the containment vessels we were consuming. The other two shifts must both have been running the production at max speed," Dr. Rubis said.

Captain Galanos nodded at Dr. Rubis then turned back to the pilot. "Go on."

"Well, Dr. Rubis said she heard the two scientists arguing about how much they were making. And I heard the doctor in charge of the fusion reactor arguing about the fact that he wasn't getting to go home. He said he was supposed to rotate back to Helike. The director told him there must have been a mistake, and he would have to wait for the next supply ship."

"That would have been another year."

"Yes, and the director told him that the time would just fly by. He was being kind of nasty when he said it."

"If that were true, then it would explain the explosion," Catie said. "But it is hard to believe that there were two plots going on at the same time."

"Well, we do have two suspects. Maybe they're both guilty."

"Okay, that's enough for now," Captain Galanos said. "I need both of you to promise not to share any of this with anyone without my express consent."

"Yes, ma'am."

"Can you assure me that you'll find out who did this?" Dr. Rubis asked.

"That's the plan. We'll give you some more information tomorrow. But for now, go back to your cabins and rest."

"Rest, I'm going to that mess to eat. I've lost at least ten kilos," Lieutenant Vlachos said. "You coming doctor?"

"Yes."

Captain Galanos waited until the two survivors were out of the cabin, then she turned to Catie and Captain McAvoy. "Well, what do you think?"

"Her hijacking the shuttle seems a bit far-fetched," Captain McAvoy said.

"Maybe, but she had a laser pistol and maybe he was suspicious anyway. He wasn't risking much. Then, like he said, when the supply ship fired on them, it confirmed for him that Dr. Rubis was telling the truth."

"I agree," Catie said. "I don't see any reason to doubt them. They were taking a huge risk. What else could have been behind it? There was nothing on the shuttle except their meager supplies."

"Alright. I'll brief Ensign Nikitas and Commander Petrou. We should meet again tomorrow and see what we can figure out."

Chapter 7 Prince Charming

Captain McAvoy had invited all the officers from the Merlin and the Geraki to dine with her.

"It's hard to believe they survived," First Officer Vinci said. "Can you imagine spending two weeks on that ship knowing you would never be able to reach safety? Just hanging on so you could warn the government."

"No, and it's not like it was a Lynx. It didn't have any facilities on it. They were pretty ripe when we brought them aboard," Lieutenant Racine said.

"Dr. Rubis is a very brave woman," Ensign Nikitas said.

"She's lucky she kidnapped Lieutenant Vlachos instead of one of the other pilots. He was surprisingly cooperative," Commander Petrou said. "Another pilot might have made a maneuver to slam her into a bulkhead so they could disarm her."

"She was convincing, and he was patient," Captain Galanos said. "Both very good qualities."

As they were finishing up the meal, Ensign Nikitas turned to Catie and asked, "Princess, tell us about some of the worlds you've colonized?"

"When we started the expedition that explored the first two planets we were targeting, I was hoping to see some really exotic creatures. Dinosaurs, huge reptiles from our prehistory. Some of them were over fifteen meters tall. Or a unicorn, which is a horse with a single horn on its head. They're imaginary creatures that were made up by writers on Earth."

"What's a horse?"

Catie threw a picture of a horse up on the display.

"We have animals like this, but this is much more beautiful," Ensign Nikitas said. "We call ours álogos. Our writers describe creatures much like that one. We have been trying to breed our álogos to look more like this."

"I'm interested in seeing how close you've gotten," Catie said.

"I have pictures in my cabin. I'll bring them tomorrow. But go on with your story."

"Anyway, Dr. Teltar told me that it was unlikely we would see any such creatures, especially dinosaurs, since we had selected worlds that were well established. His theory is that dinosaurs are an evolutionary anomaly associated with the first emergence of life on land. So, you can imagine my surprise and delight when a triceratops emerged from the jungle. It wasn't really a dinosaur, but it had three horns.

"My friend, Liz, and I were resting in the sun when it started snorting at a jeep we were sending out. A jeep is like a truck, but smaller. We raced down to the gate to get a better look. They raced the jeep back inside the fence and we all stood there hoping it would just go away. It was huge, and our fence wasn't going to stop it if the monster decided it wanted in.

"Something made it mad and it rushed the fence. It turned at the last minute for some reason. The fence was electrified and as it ran down alongside it, it tore down all our hard work. Finally, it was knocked out. My uncle went out to examine it. He was wearing an armored spacesuit which was a good thing because while we were all staring at the triceratops, a tiger was stalking us. It leapt up and grabbed Uncle Blake and started to drag him away. Liz eventually hit it with enough stun rounds that it dropped Uncle Blake and stalked off."

"That must have been terrifying," Captain Galanos said.

"It was a little. But we knew Uncle Blake's armor would protect him. He kept yelling for us to shoot it. Here, look at the video."

Catie flicked the video of the end of the scene. Everyone oohed when the triceratops tore the fence down. And they all jumped when the tiger grabbed Blake.

"That thing came out of nowhere!" Commander Petrou gasped.

"It did. Uncle Blake was really mad. And everyone started to sing songs about tigers after that."

"That was mean," Captain Galanos said.

"We were just teasing him. I send him the video whenever he makes me really mad, that or one of the songs."

"What else did you see?"

"Nothing else was that spectacular. Although the landscapes were amazing. Imagine thousands of miles of plains or forest without any sign of people. No buildings, roads, or fences. Just more land."

"We have some areas like that on Helike. I should have brought my photos to share," Ensign Nikitas said.

"You have photos, what kind of photos?" Catie asked.

"Umm, like I said, photos of the land around Helike."

"He's got family photos, even some of them show him when he was a little boy," Commander Petrou said. "He was a cute kid."

"Oh, you have to show them to me."

"I'll bring them next time."

"No, come on. Let's go look at them." Catie grabbed a bottle of wine and two glasses before she pushed Nikitas out into the passageway.

When they reached his cabin, she poured them both a glass of wine and they took a seat on the padded bench which sat against the wall. "Show me one of when you were a little boy."

"This is me on my first pony; I was so proud of myself when I finally rode him without my father's help. I remember years later when I was sixteen, I saw the pony in the field. It was so small. I could almost straddle it with my feet on the ground. But when I was five, that thing was huge." Ensign Kozma Nikitas handed Catie the picture.

"Aww, you were so cute."

"Proud and fierce, not cute."

Catie took a drink of her wine. She was feeling warm from the alcohol, but it felt nice. She'd already had two glasses with dinner.

"Come on, show me some others."

"First you should show me some of yours."

Catie flicked a picture onto the display. It showed her sitting at a little desk next to her father's desk. They were both writing.

"How old were you?"

"Five."

"You could read and write when you were five?"

"Yes, I was very studious and wanted to be like my father. He was always working in his office at home. And I liked to be with him, so I practiced my writing all the time."

"Didn't you play?"

"I had dolls and a dollhouse. I had it all organized. Each doll had its job. Just like my mother organized our house. I had chores to do, even when I was five."

"What kind of chores?"

"I had to clean my room, put away my toys, and help set the table for Sunday dinner."

"Wow, those were serious chores. Did you do them?"

"Mostly, or so I'm told. Mommy threatened to take away my books if I didn't do them."

"Come on, show me some more."

Catie flicked another picture to the display. "Here I am graduating the sixth grade."

"You look pretty young."

"I was nine."

"What about your next graduation picture?"

"Here it is." Catie flicked a picture of her graduating from the Academy.

"Hey, that seems like a big gap; sixth grade to a military academy."

"Starting when I was twelve, I did home-schooling, so my studies were all at different grade levels. I was doing college-level work in math while I was still doing high-school-level work in English."

Ensign Nikitas poured them both more wine. "Come on, you have to have some more interesting pictures."

"You first."

"I don't have access to all mine, just the ones I keep with me."

"So, you have to have more than one."

Ensign Nikitas pulled another from the box and handed it to Catie. It showed him in a military uniform. He was tall, standing next to a woman who was wearing a white gown and a tiara. "That's when I graduated from what we call secondary school, it was a military school. Before that, I went to a local primary school. After secondary school, I went to college at our military academy."

"How old were you here?"

"Sixteen. That's my mother next to me."

"She's beautiful. She must be proud of you."

"I hope so. And here I am graduating from the academy."

The second picture looked almost identical to the first, except he was taller and looked just a bit older.

"So how old are you here?"

"Twenty."

"Your mother looks just the same."

"She still does. She's quite beautiful, and her family has a history of maintaining that beauty well into their sixties. Now cough up an embarrassing picture of you."

Catie flicked a photo of her in the mud in Guatemala. Nikitas laughed. "You mean they made the princess crawl in the mud?"

"They didn't know who I was," Catie said. "I went to the Academy using a different name. The doctors changed my appearance so that nobody recognized me."

"That was brave."

Ensign Nikitas and Catie continued to sip their wine as they went through more pictures. Catie's commentary was slowing down with each picture, and eventually, it stopped. When Nikitas looked at her, he realized that she had fallen asleep.

"Princess . . . Princess!" He gave her a little shake.

Catie just shifted her position until she was leaning on his shoulder. She snorted a little and then hummed a bit.

"Damn!" Nikitas whispered. He shook his head and looked at the padded bench they were sitting on. It just wouldn't do. He flicked the bunk down from the wall, then picked Catie up and carried her over to it. He laid her down, pulled off her shipboots, and pulled the blanket over her. He pulled the upper bunk down, and after kicking his boots off, he crawled in and lay down. *"I hope this isn't a capital offense."*

Catie woke up. Her head was a bit fuzzy and something wasn't right. She snuggled down under the covers, adjusting her head on the pillow. *"Wait, what am I doing wearing my jacket?"*

She raised her head and looked around and bumped her head on the upper bunk. *"What am I doing in a bunk?"* Her sleeping cabin had an actual bed, she hadn't slept in a bunk for at least two years. Then the memories started to come back. *"Oh no! ADI!"*

"Yes, Cer Catie."

"Where am I?"

"You are in a bunk."

"ADI!"

"You are in the lower bunk in Ensign Nikitas's quarters. He is sleeping in the upper bunk."

There was a slight groan in the room.

"Correction, he was sleeping in the upper bunk. He is now holding his head and moaning."

Catie crawled out of the bunk. "Kozma, what happened?"

Ensign Nikitas sat up, banging his head on the ceiling. "Ouch. Nothing happened. You fell asleep. I think it was the wine, although I might have been boring you."

"Oh, did we drink that whole bottle?"

"Yeah, we did. I guess that was a mistake."

"Definitely. Did anything else happen?"

"I just put you to bed."

"He was a perfect gentleman," ADI said. "If he hadn't been, I'd have popped a cap in his ass!"

"ADI? How is she listening? And what does pop a cap mean?"

"ADI almost always listens in on my Comm. She can talk on any Comm she wants to, so she's letting you hear her also."

"And this cap?"

"It's slang for shooting you."

"Why would she say such a thing?"

"I guess because she would have shot you if you had misbehaved."

"How would she do that? And how would she know if I misbehaved?"

"Haven't you noticed the cameras in the corners of your cabin?"

"Yes. Don't tell me she can access them."

"Okay I won't, but Merlin can. He uses them to make sure there are no dangers to the ship. And if Merlin can access them, then ADI can."

"I see. And how was she going to pop a cap?"

"The cameras each have a laser in them. So, she could have fired one. I'm sure she would only have singed you; you know, to tell you to behave."

"Maybe it would have been best if she had shot me. I am in so much trouble."

"No you're not. ADI told me that you were a perfect gentleman."

"But Captain Galanos might not agree. Oh, to die so young."

Catie laughed at Ensign Nikitas's antics. "ADI, how can I get out of here without anyone noticing?"

"If you remove your outer uniform, then anyone who sees you in just your shipsuit will assume you're coming back from your run."

"But what do we do about my uniform?"

"Perhaps Ensign Nikitas can package it up and bring it to you later. He could imply it was something of his that you had requested."

"I could do that," Ensign Nikitas said, warming up to the idea that he might escape Captain Galanos's retribution.

"But I need to get out of his cabin."

"I can give you a small window of time. Enough for you to get to the lift. And I can hold the lift for you."

"Okay," Catie said. She got out of the bunk and removed her jacket and skirt. She folded them and laid them on the desk. Then she found her shoes and looked at them.

"You might want to leave them," ADI said. "Heels are not usually considered a running shoe. People will probably not notice your feet."

"What about Morgan?"

"She is currently running with Cristina. I informed her that you had decided to sleep in."

"Thanks. When do I make a break for it?"

"In one minute."

Catie went over to Ensign Nikitas and kissed him on the cheek. "Thanks for being such a gentleman."

"Apparently my life depended on it."

Catie laughed as she went to the door and waited.

"Five seconds."

The door slid open and Catie ran down the passageway. She careened around the corner and into the waiting lift. The lift door closed immediately and the lift started up toward her cabin floor. ADI had locked all the doors to the other cabins while Catie made her escape. Fortunately, only one person had walked into a door, and they were confused enough to think they had actually missed the door instead of it not sliding open as it was supposed to.

"Thanks, ADI."

"You're welcome."

Morgan slid in next to Catie who was having breakfast in her cabin. "So?"

"What do you mean, so?"

"So, what happened?"

"I don't understand." Catie gave Morgan an innocent smile.

"Come on. I know you spent the night in Prince Charming's cabin."

Catie gave Morgan a shocked look.

"Come on, you had to know that I would have a security guard standing outside his cabin all night, right?"

Catie's face fell.

"Don't worry, she was discreet. She didn't stand at the door. She was pretty amused by your dash to the elevator though."

"ADI?"

"Morgan's people don't count. I assumed you would know that Morgan had you under surveillance."

"I thought bodyguards were supposed to respect the protectee's privacy."

"They are. But the head of the security detail has to know everything. So, what happened?"

"Nothing, I just fell asleep. Too much wine."

"But what happened before you fell asleep?"

"We didn't do anything!"

"I can tell that, but you had to have done something before you fell asleep."

"We just looked at pictures. And how can you tell we didn't do anything?"

"I just can. Tell me, was he nice?"

"Yes, he showed me a picture of him on his first pony. He was five and so cute. Too bad he's an alien."

"Hey, they're totally compatible."

"How would you know?"

"I know things."

"You mean someone's *slept* with one of them?"

"I'm not sure how much sleeping was involved, but yes."

"Who?"

"Racine."

"No way! How did that happen?"

"She was in the Marine mess and the Heliken eggheads were there. Racine was telling the story about how Takurō keeps losing his leg. She was describing the boarding action on that Fazullan ship. One of the eggheads was skeptical that she could have knocked a Fazullan out, so Racine took him down to the gym and showed him some moves. Then she took him to her cabin and showed him some more moves."

Catie laughed. "I didn't know she had it in her. She's always so squared away, always playing the tough Marine."

"Hey, tough Marines get laid."

"I guess, otherwise where would little Marines come from? I kind of figured that if anyone would have gotten one of the Helikens into bed, it would have been Kasper."

"I didn't say he didn't, just that Racine was first."

"Oh!" Catie gave Morgan a curious look. "You do know everything."

"Hey, as the head of your security detail, I have to have situational awareness."

"You mean you like to gossip."

"No, I like to hear gossip."

"So did Kasper enjoy himself?"

"Let's just say that for the last week he's been walking around with a big smile on his face and looking like he really needs some sleep."

"What about her?"

"She has a big smile, but she gets to nap during the day."

Catie laughed. "People are amazing."

"Well, sex is a powerful drug. And now that we know all the equipment is compatible, you're free to see how charming your prince really is."

"Morgan!"

◆ ◆ ◆

Catie gave Ensign Nikitas a weak smile when they met at the dinner buffet in the wardroom.

"Hi."

"Hello, Princess, would you like to join me at my table?"

"Okay," Catie said, not wanting to be rude. There weren't many people in the wardroom since it was right at shift change. The new off-duty crew officers would want to shower before moving out among the rest of the officers and crew.

"Princess, how has your day been?"

"Fine, how has yours been? Did you brag to all your friends about my being in your cabin all night?"

"Of course not. That would be making sport of something I consider very personal. I'm far too much of a romantic to do that."

"Good, so am I," Catie said. She was greatly relieved. ADI had told her that there hadn't been any comments, but one never knew for sure. She was terrified that there would be comments, but more terrified that he would have thought of her as a conquest instead of a friend.

"I did enjoy our evening. Sharing photos of our lives was fun. We've followed such different paths to reach this same place."

"Only because you were raised like a real prince. I didn't become a princess until I was much older."

"I suspect that was to your advantage. I got far more advice and guidance while I was growing up than I wanted."

"Oh, not being a princess didn't save me from all that advice. And with these Comms, it's so much easier for your parents to counsel you. My parents are divorced, and when my mother moved to Delphi City I was getting twice as much advice as before; it drove me crazy."

"But did you have a gaggle of advisers trailing after you at all times, making sure you did everything correctly?"

"Not really, but it seemed like it at times. It still does. I have a security detail that is always with me. Sometimes it's nice, but it does make me feel overly restricted at times."

"Security detail?"

"Morgan, she runs it and is my main bodyguard."

"Oh, she's very unobtrusive," Ensign Nikitas said as he looked around the wardroom. He spotted Morgan in the corner. She looked like she was just chatting with the steward.

"You see her over there?"

"Yes, I just noticed her."

"She is good."

Chapter 8   Board meeting — July 3rd

"I call this meeting to order," Marc said. "First order of business is our new board member. Catie mentioned to me that we were failing to recognize one of our most valuable assets here at MacKenzie Discoveries."

Everyone in the call looked shocked. There had been no discussion of adding another person to the board, and this was the inner circle.

"All of you already know her, but I'd like to formally introduce our new vice-president of operations, ADI."

Catie heard kissy sounds in her ear as ADI's avatar appeared in the video call. She was tall, dark-haired, and wearing a dark brown business suit, similar to one that Samantha wore when she first joined the board.

"I was so surprised by the invitation. Of course, I am delighted to join the board. And I hope I continue to perform my job up to your high standards," ADI said.

Blake laughed. "I can't believe it has taken us this long to think about it. ADI's been here from the beginning. Good for you, Catie, and welcome to the board, ADI."

"Thank you, Cer Blake."

Everyone took a moment to welcome ADI to the board. Catie kept hearing kissy noises in her ear until the final welcome to the board was made.

Once the welcomes were completed, Marc brought the meeting back on track. "Fred, anything to report?"

"I've heard a rumor that Kal's getting married."

Kal rolled his eyes. "That didn't take long. I assume Latoya told you."

"Of course. And she heard it from Jackie."

"No secrets in this group."

"Who cares about secrets; when?!" Catie asked.

"We haven't set a date. Sandra's going to be busy with the Olympics for the next year."

"Oh, you already told her about that. Is that why she's marrying you?"

"Thanks for the vote of confidence. And I didn't tell her until after she agreed to marry me."

"But not before Zahan let him ride him over the two-meter hurdle," Blake said.

"Can we move on?" Kal asked.

"Yes, Fred, how about something business-related."

"Facebook has made an offer for Compadres.com"

"What's that?" Catie asked.

"It's the social media service we launched last year."

"And why did we do that?"

"So Facebook would want to buy us out."

"Why do they want to buy us out?"

"Because, we're the cool new guys, and you can share with your intergalactic friends, our interface is way better, and we're able to screen out all the bots that just mess things up with fake posts."

"How do we screen the fake posts out?"

"It's pretty easy. ANDI does a profile on all new accounts, when they're made, where the user is at that time. Then he checks them for an existing media presence for the user. Also, he watches their posting behavior. For those that he deems suspicious, he suspends their account and requires an authentication to reactivate it."

"Cool. So, are we going to sell?"

"Only if Facebook agrees to adopt the new UI and the account screening."

"I see, so that's why we did it?"

"Yes. We don't want to manage a social media company, but we're tired of having to deal with all the problems created by these organized groups that are just spreading misinformation."

"Fred, where are the negotiations?" Marc asked.

"Just starting. We'll know more in a month."

"Alright. As you can see, Admiral Michaels wasn't able to make the meeting, he's in negotiations with the U.N. Security Council. Blake, do you have any updates?"

"Colonel Malenkov, now Commander Malenkov has completed his fast Academy training. He is now the first officer on the Sakira."

"Do you think you can trust him?" Kal asked.

"I believe so, we'll have ADI track him using the Sakira's AI if he does something suspicious . . ."

"I'll put a cap in his ass!"

"ADI!" Catie scolded.

"Sorry, I just like that expression."

"Blake."

"What ADI said is essentially true. But I think he's committed to a united Earth and more freedom for Russia."

"I agree," ADI added.

"What about Commander Bastien?" Catie asked.

"She also completed her training. She's slated to be third officer on the Roebuck when we send her out on the next planet exploration mission."

"Third officer?"

"Hey, as I recall you were the third officer on the Roebuck's first mission. She'll have plenty of opportunities to move up."

"That brings us to our next order of business. Who should be the governor of the next colony?" Marc asked.

"Aren't you going to do it?" Catie asked.

"We're discussing the possibility," Samantha said.

"We need to know what other options we have," Marc said sheepishly.

"What about Admiral Michaels?" Catie asked.

"And who would take over his responsibilities?" Blake asked.

"You." Catie gave her Uncle Blake a big smile. "You're getting good at handling politicians."

"If you weren't a billion miles away, I'd come over there and smack you upside the head," Blake said. "There is no way I'm going to deal with the Security Council every day."

"And I am not moving off-planet!" Admiral Michaels messaged. "And I want a raise."

"I've been keeping him updated," ADI explained.

"Thanks, I think," Marc said. "So, other options. Blake, I assume you're still not interested."

"Correct."

"Kal?"

"Sandra and I already discussed this. We're not leaving the planet in the foreseeable future."

"What about Catie?" Blake asked.

"Uncle Blake!"

"Turnabout is fair play."

"Quit squabbling!" Samantha said. "We need real options."

"Off the top of my head, Captain Clark or Margaret," Liz said.

"Good suggestions, others?"

"What about Captain Desjardins or Captain Clements?" Kal asked.

"I'm not sure if I should be offended that nobody mentioned my name, but I'm not doing it," Liz said. "Don't you have someone on Artemis that might fit the bill?"

"I've thought about having Helena Bachmann take over here if we move on, but I'm not sure she's ready to start one up."

Marc looked around the virtual room. Everyone was arrayed as if they were in the same conference room. Nobody looked like they had other suggestions.

"Okay, well, that gives us some names to consider. Blake, will you feel out the two captains and Captain Clark?"

"Yes," Blake agreed reluctantly. He wasn't happy about one of them moving on and creating another hole for him to fill.

As the meeting was winding down, Marc decided to bring up a different topic.

"I've been talking with Paul. He says it feels kind of stupid for us to be working so hard mining the platinum metals here on Artemis's surface to lift up into orbit and ship out system, when in twenty years or so we'll start to need it and will probably need to start mining the asteroid belt for it."

"Yes, but do you really want to send miners out to the asteroid belt to mine? You're not really set up to do that," Blake said.

"We could bring the asteroids here to Artemis, just like the ice asteroids."

"You could. But you'd still need to send miners up to mine it. They'd be too heavy to bring down to the surface."

"We mine them in orbit at Earth."

"But the miners have a nice space station to rest in. You know how much they hated it when they were having to go out and live on an Oryx for a few weeks."

"I know, but . . ."

Samantha was nudging Marc to get his attention, finally, he noticed. When he looked at her, she immediately pointed at Catie. Catie was deep in thought.

"Okay, Catie, what have you thought up? Catie!"

"Oh, sorry, what did you want?"

"You just thought of something and were designing it in your head, right?"

"Yes."

"Well, spit it out."

"Well, you know, a lot of science fiction books describe mining the asteroids as a huge rock crusher just breaking them up and separating the good stuff out."

"Yes, but that seems a bit unwieldy."

"But what if you scaled it down? Designed one that would just process the little ones."

"Would that be cost-effective?"

"Why not, it just keeps flying around sucking the little guys in. It would clean up the belt for later when you want to go after the bigger ones."

"But wouldn't you just be cluttering it back up with the leftover debris?" Blake asked.

"I don't think so. I think you would crush the asteroid, heat the debris up so that everything besides the metals was gas or liquid. You let the metals settle out and eject the rest. It would freeze back into a nice ball."

"That sounds interesting. What do you think it would take to run it? How big a crew?"

"I think you could automate it. Send a crew out every few months to pick up the metals and do any necessary repairs."

"Okay, why don't you work with Paul and whoever else you need, and come up with a design?"

"Okay. Should I do it under MacKenzies or form a new company?"

"Fred?"

"Form a new company. I can see every system buying one or two of these. Catie, what do you think they'll cost to build?"

"Two hundred million, maybe three. You've got to have gravity drives and a big fusion reactor. I assume we'd just use fusion."

"Right, I don't want any antimatter reactors unattended," Marc said.

"Okay, I'll send out a prospectus and you guys can figure out who's going to buy in."

"One last announcement: we've finished the canal on Artemis. We're holding the opening ceremony tomorrow."

"You finished it? I thought you needed to make it wider," Catie said.

"Nope, we might do that in a few decades if traffic gets too heavy."

"You mean it's going to be a one-way canal?"

"No, traffic will go two ways. We've installed passing lanes in three places. That means that ships will be able to pull to the side to allow another to pass."

"Hmm," Catie mused doubtfully.

"Hey, the Suez Canal was only one lane when it first opened."

"I didn't know that."

"Well, now you do. Anyway, it's a big milestone for the colony."

"Catie and Liz, hang back if you would. I want to review orders for Artemis," Marc said before he closed the meeting.

Catie sat back down at her desk and pulled up the load list and started reviewing it.

Eighteen hundred jeeps: 1 Pod
Five hundred tractors: 1.5 Pods
Two hundred tractor tires, five hundred jeep tires: ¼ pod
Twelve large power generators: ½ pod
Tooling, heavy equipment: 2 pods
Misc. components for bots, appliances, etc.: ½ pod
Assorted livestock: 1 pod

"You're sure ordering a lot of heavy stuff."

"Yes. You know we can't afford to set up the machinery to cast big parts for tractors and such. We're fine assembling things like appliances and such from their parts, but it's not cost-effective to set up a big foundry or to tool up to make things like tires or jeeps. We'll get there eventually."

"Why so many tractors and jeeps?"

"We're coming up on our second anniversary, so we'll be handing out the land grants. The farmers will need tractors, and both they and the ranchers will need jeeps."

"Why not ATVs?"

"Oh, missed that. We'll want four hundred of them, also."

"Ka-Ching!" Liz said with a fist pump.

"You pirates!"

"You taught me," Catie said. "Are you keeping the scaffolding for the jeeps?"

"Yes, I sent you the spec for them. We'll put them in our assembly plant for the appliances."

"Why are you starting up an assembly plant already?"

"Jobs, we want to kick off our manufacturing sector. Appliance assembly is the perfect start. Low tooling, and we need lots of them, and the space savings and cost savings from shipping parts versus assembled appliances are significant. I understand the Paraxean colonies are going to adopt the same process."

"Great," Catie groaned at all the extra work that would be created by having to find all the parts and package them up into a pod. "I also see you're ordering lots of fixtures, but no sinks or toilets."

"We just started up a porcelain factory. It's simple tooling, just right for where we are."

"Okay." Catie liked that, the fixtures were high-value low bulk compared to the sinks and toilets.

"When are you going to start assembling your own jeeps?"

"Maybe next year. By then the second group of colonists will be getting their grants. The demand will ramp up, so we should be able to support an assembly plant."

"Okay, we'll start working on a shipping design for all those parts. Are you going to start making your own tires?"

"No, the tooling is too much. But it's a pain, they wear out too fast."

"Even the tractor tires?" Liz asked.

"Especially them."

"You know you could coat them with the flexible polysteel. They wouldn't have much traction on the road, but it wouldn't matter in the field," Liz said. "In fact, as I recall, some farmers use metal wheels."

"We'll have someone look into that."

"Hey, we make money shipping tires!" Catie messaged.

"Sometimes you have to be a team player," Liz messaged back.

"Now, it looks like you still have four pods to fill."

"I know, but we've got a few unusual orders. Our fishermen are ready to upgrade their fleet. The small cabin cruisers we brought out on the Sakira just aren't cutting it."

"Okay, so what kind of ships do you want? And how many?"

"Twelve otter trawlers."

Catie brought up the specs on the trawlers.

"Oh, you should have let us know about this before. We'll need to buy them. I assume used is okay," Liz said.

"Yes."

"Well, we can get four in each pod, so you're going to use up three of your remaining four. We can put some stuff around them, but it would have been better if we had time to chop off their upper structure, then we could carry at least twice as many."

"We also need a new cargo ship."

"Ugh, one of those won't fit. We'd have to break it apart, and I don't see how we would have the time."

"Couldn't you make a special double pod?"

"You really want that ship?" Liz asked.

"We need to start moving freight around. We could wait for the next shipment, but it would be nice to get at least one."

"We'll see what we can do. I'll work on a design; it'll give me a chance to use my mechanical engineering degree."

"Anything else?"

"That, along with the other stuff you've added, means we don't have enough pods. Do you want to give up a colonist pod?" Catie asked.

"I know; I thought you could use the space for the SkyLifter."

"Then how would we move your cargo down?"

"We could use one of our lifters."

"Sure, if you loan one to us."

"We thought we'd rent it to you," Marc said.

"Daddy, why? You're the one who wants the extra pod."

"But you're going to make more money by shipping an extra one."

Catie sighed and rolled her eyes. "Okay, how much?"

"Ten percent?"

"Of the shipping cost for the one pod?"

"No, of the full load."

"No way! We're not going to make that much money on the extra pod. I'd rather just skip the extra pod."

"Come on, make a counteroffer?"

"Okay, fifty percent of the shipping cost on the cheapest pod."

"What, you pirate! How about fifty percent of the average cost per pod?"

"Excluding the colonist pods?"

"Okay."

"Deal."

◆ ◆ ◆

Gavril sat down and waited for them to bring his lawyer in. He would show these mooks he was smarter than they were. He was just over eight months into his ten-year sentence for running a ring which prostituted minors.

"I'm surprised you asked to see me," his lawyer said as he sat across the table from Gavril.

"Why, you're still my lawyer aren't you?"

"I am as long as your uncle pays my fees. But I don't see how I can help you."

"Well, there more than one thing a lawyer can do. You see I need to have a way to communicate with some friends on the outside. And you're the only one I can talk to without these mooks listening in."

The lawyer chuckled. "I see why the guard told me that he didn't think you paid attention at your orientation meeting."

"What's that got to do with anything?" Gavril asked.

"Let me explain why that's a bad idea. You see, our conversation is being recorded."

"That's illegal, what happened to attorney-client privilege?"

"That still exists; let me explain. As I said, our conversation is recorded and one of their AIs listens to the conversation and notes any times where we don't seem to be talking about your defense, such as right now. If the AI notes that there were suspicious exchanges, then a committee that doesn't know anything about us, listens to those parts of our conversation. If they determine that we are talking about something illegal, then they tell the court and a warrant is issued which allows another committee to listen to our whole conversation. The AI blanks out our names and such to make sure your rights are not violated if it all turns out to be innocent. But that committee marks all parts of our conversation that do not pertain to your defense, and those parts are sent to a judge who decides whether to issue charges."

"That's not fair."

"They say it is. Anyway, if we're talking about something illegal, then the judge sends the information to the police, who would then investigate. If they catch me doing something illegal, then I'm going to be inside with you, and you're going to have a few years added to your sentence after you spend some time in solitary. Now, can you see why this is a waste of our time?"

"Damn. What do I do?"

"You serve your time, stay out of trouble. You might even want to take a few classes, who knows what you'll learn by the time you get out. But you need to be prepared for the fact that when you do get out, nobody is going to know or care who you are. And you're going to be monitored for the rest of your life. I suggest going straight would seem to be the best course."

"That isn't going to happen."

"Then I suspect you'll just find yourself back here. Now, if you don't have anything related to your defense, I'll excuse myself."

Chapter 9 Canal Opening

Marc was standing at the prow of the fishing vessel that would inaugurate the canal. The owner had done an admirable job of cleaning up the boat, and from the pleasant smell one wouldn't know it was a fishing boat.

"Hello, Governor."

Marc looked down to see Katya and Sebrina standing next to him. "I'm surprised to see you here. I assumed you would be making deliveries."

"We got the concession agreement from the captain. Would you like a drink?" Katya asked.

"Of course, I'll have a lemonade," Marc laughed. They had arranged catering for the trip, but only for the lunch that would be served when they reached the city. It wasn't until they boarded the boat at 0800 that he realized that they might have made a mistake.

"And you, Sam, what would you like?" Sebrina asked.

"Orange juice."

"Sam, why didn't we take care of catering drinks and snacks for the whole journey?"

"We did."

"Oh, I see," Marc said, realizing that the girls had made a deal with Samantha to give them the catering.

"They were the only ones to come and ask," Samantha said. "You always say initiative should be rewarded."

"Here you go, Governor. That's one dollar, just press here," Katya said as she held out her Comm to Marc.

◆ ◆ ◆

They sailed into the canal. It was ten kilometers to the first lock that would raise them the first five meters of the twenty-two meters they needed before they reached the height of the city. Marc broke a bottle of Champagne against the lock gate before it was opened to admit the ship.

"What a waste of Champagne," he said. Then he heard a cork pop. Turning he saw Samantha adding Champagne to her orange juice.

"A mimosa," Samantha said, "you should have ordered orange juice."

Marc poured the rest of his lemonade out and signaled to Katya. Once he had his mimosa, he raised his glass for a toast.

"Governor, where do we get the water to fill the lock, from upstream?" Katya asked.

"Yes, but it is immediately replaced by water from the city lake. We pump water up to the lake to keep everything at the right level."

"How does that help?"

"The lake is very large compared to the size of a lock. So it can replace the water we pull out of the upper canal without noticing it. We can then slowly pump the water to replace what is used."

"Why not just pump the water into the lock from the river?"

"Energy and time. To pump water into the lock as fast as we would like would take a lot of energy. And even with very big pumps, we couldn't do it as fast as this. That's why we built the lake."

"I thought it was for fishing and playing."

"That was a nice side benefit."

"Oh. And how come we're only raising up five meters this time. Why not seven meters?"

"Because we cannot have the water level in the canal higher than the land next to it. We have to follow the contour of the land."

"Oh, duh. I should have seen that."

"You've been busy selling."

◆ ◆ ◆

When they sailed into the City Dock, there was a large crowd waiting. They'd all made the two-kilometer trek to the dock since the city hadn't quite grown enough to border the canal yet. There was a big show of Marc commissioning the new dock. After an hour for lunch and partying, the ship was preparing to leave for the final leg upstream where it would rejoin the river.

"Where did everybody go?" Marc asked.

"Hey, the trip between the fishing village and the city is all most people care about. The rest of the trip is just a repeat of the first half." Samantha laughed as Marc looked around and started to count heads. "Let it go. They've had their fun. We can have a nice quiet cruise to the end."

"Quiet is right."

Liz couldn't remember being happier than the day she and Catie promoted First Mate Hayden Watson to Captain of the Resolve. The constant flying between planets had started to wear her out. Now she just needed to coordinate loads, and occasionally give one of the captains a break. Although coordinating today's load wasn't exactly a picnic. The work to buy the ships and get them loaded onto the Resolve wasn't bad, although buying the twelve otter trawlers had been a hassle. They'd paid too much for them due to the time constraint, but that was Marc's problem.

But the livestock was a real pain. One of the farmers had refused to honor the sale when he realized they were shipping his horses to Artemis. He thought it would be cruel to the horses. But they were going to great pains to make sure the livestock didn't experience any problems. They were using an empty quad to gather the livestock, six hundred horses, four thousand cows, all pregnant according to the vet, six thousand sheep, again all pregnant, and five thousand goats and two thousand pigs, and you guessed it, they were all pregnant as well.

"That pod looks like Noah's Ark," the foreman told Liz.

"Well, Noah only had to deal with pairs."

"Yeah, but you only have pregnant females. You don't have to worry about some stallion getting excited halfway to Artemis."

"That's true. And I don't have to clean the thing, so I guess I shouldn't complain," Liz said as she waved the pilot over to the pod. Switching to his channel she instructed him: "Do not get excited, you have to do a smooth acceleration, no sharp turns. The Resolve is sitting in a stationary orbit over the North Pole. You have to let them slide the pod in while you maintain its position. If any of these animals has a miscarriage, it'll come out of your pay!"

"Yes, ma'am. You've only told me that four times. I've got it etched in my brain. Don't worry, I've practiced the move four times already. Resolve will actually do most of the work. She's going to take over the controls once I match orbits." He was referring to the Resolve's AI.

"Okay, you're hooked on and good to go."

When he reached the Resolve, he handed over the controls to its AI. It wasn't like he couldn't do it, but managing the SkyLifter's orientation with the Resolve's and coordinating with the cargo bots were more variables than he wanted to deal with at one time.

"She's loaded," the pilot informed Captain Watson. "Have a good journey, I'm going fishing." The pilot was rubbing in the fact that he was sitting this trip out since they weren't taking the SkyLifter with them.

"You owe me a bottle of Scotch when we get back," Hayden said as he started easing the Resolve away from Earth. He would have to manage the acceleration profile cautiously. He wasn't looking forward to having to reverse the ship after the jump. That would be an intricate maneuver at high velocity.

"Dr. Rubis, has anything else come to mind?" Captain Galanos asked. She had asked Dr. Rubis to join her, Catie, and Captain McAvoy to go over the situation.

"No."

"Do you have any thoughts on why they were collecting so much antimatter?" Catie asked.

"It would have to be for weapons."

"Is it possible that they got some before, that there is already a supply on Helike?"

"I don't think so. We only started to make it eighteen months ago. And before the new director came, it was easy to keep track of everything."

"Were there any clues as to who is behind it?" Captain Galanos asked.

"Other than the fact that the new director was from Polemistia, I can't think of any. Can't you ask your superiors?"

"We're trying to learn as much as possible before we contact Helike."

"Oh, I see. I assume you're worried that there is some deep conspiracy in the government."

"Yes. We think it's more likely that it's one or two groups operating on their own. We suspect that some of the nation-states might be involved, but it's hard to imagine the people sitting still for such dangerous aggression."

"Yes, I agree with you."

"How are you doing, are you recovering?"

"My body is, but my mind is struggling."

"Have you talked to the doctor about it?" Catie asked.

"Yes, but I don't want to do anything to my memory until the situation is resolved. She has given me some medication to help with the PTSD, but it's hard not to be depressed."

"Yes, I know what you mean. Just thinking about the consequences is hard to take," Captain Galanos said. "But we will figure this out. Our friends here have some amazing technology. And it is possible that just announcing the visit of another race from another star system will be enough that these people will give up on their plans."

"One can only hope."

Chapter 10   Lottery

"Please settle down!" Marc shouted as he brought the meeting to order. There were twenty delegates representing the twenty-eight thousand plus adult colonists on Artemis. He'd tried to whittle the delegation size down to ten, but that had been a losing battle. And of course, almost every colonist was tuned in via their Comm and would be sending questions to their delegate.

"Alright, I now call this meeting to order. You have all had a chance to study the plot layout for the land grants. We're here to answer any questions." Marc pointed to Samantha and the other MacKenzie Discoveries managers.

"Yes, Cer Bachmann," Marc pointed to his favorite delegate. She represented most of the city workers, people who would continue to work in the city, opening shops, or working for businesses.

"We would like you to review the land grant rules."

Marc sighed but knew he had no choice. Everyone wanted to hear him recite them, even though they were written down.

"Each colonist who was over sixteen when they joined the colony and has spent two years in a job assignment defined by the city government and MacKenzie Discoveries is entitled to a land grant. That grant can be a city lot with a shop built on it, a city lot with a house built on it, four hundred hectares of farmland, or eight hundred of ranchland. The farmland and ranchland will have no improvements."

"What about married couples versus singles?"

"People are treated equally, if they worked a job, they get a grant. Couples do get the advantage of combining their entries in the lottery so they will be able to pick their grant at the same time if they wish, but they have to give up twenty-five percent of their lottery entry numbers. Each person receives two lottery numbers, plus any bonus numbers for exceptional service to the colony so couples who combine their numbers only start out with three."

"What if someone wants a town lot, but doesn't want anything built on it?"

"That is not an option. You would do better to select a farm grant or a ranch grant and leave it idle or lease it. We are trying to discourage real-estate speculation."

"Except by MacKenzie Discoveries."

Marc ignored the comment and pointed to another delegate.

"What's to stop someone from turning a ranch into a farm?"

"Nothing except for the fact that the ranch land is generally hillier, does not have water rights for irrigation, and cannot be cleared of trees."

"What!"

"It's in the documentation you received. Ranches must leave the trees in place. If there is a critical need, they can apply for a permit to remove a tree, but that will require them to replace that tree in another location on their ranch. The city will aid farmers in removing trees as they expand their fields."

"I thought we got to own the land?!"

"Most land has zoning restrictions. Ranch land's zoning restriction is limited water rights and you have to leave the trees in place. And we will know if you go around killing them to get around the restriction, so don't go there."

"What's this about no above-ground electrical wires?"

"You cannot run a powerline from the road's access point to someplace on your property unless it's underground."

"But what if we need electricity for a barn or something. We can't afford to be digging two-mile ditches."

"You'll need to install solar panels and either a battery bank or a diesel fuel cell for backup."

"If we have a diesel fuel cell, why do we need solar?"

"The fuel cell will run backward and generate fuel for the night. Diesel will be expensive, so you'll need to decide if solar is cheaper. The way I calculate it, it would be."

"But we could start with the fuel cell then add the solar."

"Yes, if you're trying to save startup cost, that might make sense," Marc said.

"Why are parcels 48 through 62 not available for selection?"

Marc laughed; you couldn't get anything by these guys. "Parcels 48 through 62 are adjacent to the city, as I'm sure you noticed. They are designated for future city growth. As the city grows, they will be subdivided and made available for selection by the new colonists or used for city buildings. As I said we're trying to discourage real-estate speculation."

"Why?"

"Because we don't want people working back deals with future politicians to buy their land for future city projects, and we want to minimize the cost of government. The city has been planned out for approximately five hundred thousand inhabitants. The areas for future suburbs, city auditoriums, schools, and such have been designated. As the city grows, the land will be made available to the city at no cost or will be allocated as land grants to new colonists."

"You mean that you're not going to allow real-estate developments?"

"That will be something the city government will have to decide. As they plan the suburbs, the city will have to decide if they want them developed by a single builder, or will just set the CC&Rs for the community and allow the colonists to coordinate with whoever they wish to build their home. The government will provide the support to put a starter home on the property."

"What's to stop someone from using government money to build some big mansion as part of their city lot?"

"The house size the government agrees to fund is preset, if they wish to expand beyond that they will need to fund that themselves."

"What about when people want to move, or when their kids want to buy a house?"

"When people want to move, they have to find a place that's for sale. Children who are grown up and want to start out on their own have the choice to work for the colony for two years and receive a land grant. However, that land grant might not be in this city. It will depend on the timing and whether this city is still managing land grants. The next city we plan will not be too far away, and you all have seen how fast our transportation can be. In fact, they might want to be in a different city from their parents."

"What about parks?" Cer Bachmann asked.

"We have allocated city parks within the city plan."

"But what about national parks, game reserves, and things like that?"

"We have plans to provide for that. As you know, all future land development will follow this model. MacKenzie Discoveries will be allocated twenty percent of the land as compensation for starting the city and bringing in the colonists. The city will be planned out and the land for it allocated. But when we do that, we will also make decisions on national parks and reserves."

"But you need to allocate some of that land now. Some areas along the coast should be designated as reserves. You have to plan your cities around the reserves so as to minimize the impact of human activity. And I don't think that MacKenzies should get twenty percent of the land designated as reserves."

Marc smiled at Cer Bachmann. She really had thought this out. "That is something that I would expect our secretary of national parks to recommend. Would you like the job?"

Cer Bachmann was taken aback. She was just trying to make sure that Marc did the right thing, she wasn't looking for a job. She was a school teacher now, waiting until they had a university before she moved up to teaching land management.

"Well, would you like the job?" Marc asked again.

"Do I still get my land grant?"

"Of course, it is a critical job. We probably should have designated it sooner."

"Then I'll take it."

Another delegate stood up. "I think MacKenzies is getting too good a deal. Twenty percent of all the land and first pick."

"You might think so. You're welcome to apply to fund the next colony. Of course, you'll need about twelve billion in cash to start it up, and about two to three billion a year for ten years to get it on its feet, although that two to three billion is partially offset by exports. We calculate that this year and next year will cost about one billion each. And you would need to have access to the jump gates and either pay for an expedition to find a planet or buy one from MacKenzies. What do you think?"

"You're still getting a nice deal."

"We hope so. We're still a ways from breaking even on this colony. Now any other questions?"

"How come you get all the mineral rights?"

"As you well know, that's not true. MacKenzie Discoveries owns twenty percent of the mineral rights for the entire planet. Twenty-five percent goes to the county government, fifty percent goes to the national government, and the landowner gets five percent."

"Still doesn't seem fair, you getting first pick and all."

"We were here first," Marc said. "I'm sure the second group of colonists is feeling that you're getting the better deal by getting to pick second. We have another wave of colonists coming in six weeks, and I'm sure they'll feel it's unfair that they have to select fourth.

"Okay, if there aren't any more questions, the lottery will begin in three days. Make sure you're ready to make your selection, you will only have five minutes once your name is called."

"Why only five minutes?"

"Because we have twenty-five hundred grants to go through. If each of you takes five minutes, we'll be here for eight days. We are hoping that you'll all keep up with the selections and make your decisions quite a bit faster than five minutes."

"You'd better make your decisions quick, or we'll be visiting you after the lottery!" someone yelled.

◆ ◆ ◆

The land grants were laid out in a grid. Each grant was 1km x 4km for farms and 1km by 8km for ranches. The rectangular layout was designed to minimize the cost of roads. There would be a major road along the short face of the properties where people would be encouraged to build their homes and barns. There would only be minor roads every ten kilometers along the long sides of the grants, twenty when it was ranch land. Then every one hundred kilometers there would be a major road to facilitate traffic.

Marc's hope was that people would set up small corner groupings in the corner of four grants along the major road. This would allow them to have reasonably close neighbors, and might even lead to small hamlets where farmworkers could live.

To encourage this more, the property tax was based on the frontage to the major east-west roads. And he made it clear that to start with they would only put in every other major road. So, for those families that would be getting two grants, if they kept farm or ranch to only one fronting on the road, they would cut their taxes in half for a few years.

The morning before the lottery, Cer Bachmann came to visit Marc. "What can I do for you, Madam Secretary?" Marc asked.

"I have some suggestions about parkland that I wanted to review with you. I thought it would only be fair if we made it public before the lottery tomorrow."

Marc was a bit shocked. "Already?"

"Yes, especially since this is the site of our first city, I thought it would be important to allocate some land in this area."

"Does that include part of what we've already indicated is available for the grants?"

"No, I'm smart enough to know better than that. Here, let me show you. I wanted to preserve this section of the coast," she said as she flicked a map up on the display.

Marc noted that much of the land she'd marked was along a very rough area of the coast, but it also included some tidelands and one especially nice area of beach.

"I realize that you were probably considering this area for a potential seaside town or resort area, but I wanted some beach area and it would be nice to have it contiguous to the rest of the park."

"Will the public be allowed to access the beach?"

"Possibly. We should wait until we understand what kind of marine life is there and how important the beach is to it."

"Okay, I don't see a problem with that. There are plenty of other coastal areas to develop when we get there. What else have you got?"

"I think we should make this area a regional park. It butts up against your ranch, which since you're the first governor of the colony, it feels like having a large park in that area would be appropriate. It also is one of the best areas for a view of those mountains and will have excellent fishing in the river here."

"Okay, anything else?" Marc was starting to regret appointing her Secretary of National Parks.

"Not for now. But I would like to set up a formal process to start surveying this continent and identifying what wildlife we should create reserves for as well as specific areas of forest or other habitats."

"Orion will provide you access to all the aerial survey data we have. Once you know where you would like to explore, we'll give you access to a Lynx. You should talk with Dr. Pramar and Dr. Teltar, they're our xenobiologist and xenozoologist, and they can help you start classifications. I'll see if we can find some biologists and zoologists to come out with the next group of colonists."

"Oh, thank you. I really think we need to be aggressive about this."

"I can tell."

The next day, they spent fourteen hours doing the lottery. It went faster than Marc had anticipated because so many of the numbers were for couples who picked both their grants at the same time.

"My wife and I want lots 1423 and 1424," Cer Guillemot said.

"Those lots are not in the lottery," Marc replied.

"Why not? Those are the ones we want."

"You do realize that there will not be any roads that reach that area for two years or more."

"We don't care. We like that location. The hills remind us of home! Is there a reason you're holding them back?"

"No reason. Does anyone have an objection if we allow him and his wife to select those lots?" Seeing nobody raise an objection, Marc assigned the lots to the Guillemots.

There were no other requests to go outside the designated lots. The lottery finally ended late in the evening. There were not too many arguments and only four fights. And the dealing to swap grants started long before they were done. Friends wanted to have places close to each other, and were making deals to swap their allotment another. Marc noted that most of the couples who were selecting city grants had taken his advice and selected a ranch or farm for their second grant, usually as close to the city, canal, or river as they could get.

◆ ◆ ◆

"You do know why Cer Guillemot wanted those two allotments?" Samantha asked Marc after the lottery finished.

"I had them marked down as a potential winery. I'm assuming he has the same idea."

"And you let him have them?"

"I wasn't going to run the winery. I'm sure they'll be shipping vines out on the next cargo load. It'll take a few years before they can produce anything. I'm just happy he's starting now since it means we'll have wine a few years earlier than planned."

"What do you think the others will say when they realize what he intends?"

"I'm sure he'll run some cattle on the ranch while he gets the vines established. I'm hoping everyone forgets before he starts picking grapes."

"Wishful thinking. You're probably hoping I'll agree to move to the next colony."

"It would allow me to run away from any of my mistakes."

"Keep dreaming."

Chapter 11 The Birth of Helike

"Cer Catie, I have a supposition I need to discuss with you."

"ADI, a supposition. Are you ill?"

"No, all the facts say that I am correct, but I cannot prove it."

"Okay, what is it?"

"The Helikens are Human."

"I don't get it."

"They are descendants from the people of Earth."

"How can that be?!"

"I do not know. But Dr. Moreau has run her DNA tests six times, she's recalibrated the equipment four times. And she is now having a technician take it apart, clean it, and put it back together. I do not expect her to reach a different conclusion. Their DNA is completely compatible with Human DNA. The probability of that happening and them not being from Earth is nearly zero."

"Okay, so say they're from Earth, what does that mean?"

"You mean besides the fact that you could marry Prince Charming?"

"Yes, besides that!"

"It would suggest that someone brought them here. I've also determined that their language shows all the characteristics of being derived from ancient Greek, so I would assume that they come from Greece."

"But their skin tone is darker."

"That would only suggest that some Humans from Africa or other areas were included in the group that was brought here. After a few hundred years, they would have all benefited from those genes."

"ADI, set up a call with Daddy, pick a time when we're both awake. Let Uncle Blake know that he's welcome to attend."

"Yes, Cer Catie."

"Hi, Daddy, hi, Sam."

"Hi, Sweety."

"Hey, Squirt."

"Uncle Blake! I wasn't sure you'd make it, now I wonder why I invited you."

"Because you miss me."

"That must be it. Anyway, did ADI brief you?"

"I did not, you didn't tell me to," ADI said.

"Oh, well here goes. Based on DNA testing, Dr. Moreau and ADI are convinced that the Helikens are Human and I agree."

"Human?" Marc asked.

"As in from Earth."

"How's that possible?"

"I don't know, but the data says that's true. Dr. Moreau also says that based on DNA comparison they would have forked off of the Human chain between fifteen hundred to three thousand years ago."

"Whoa, that's not that long ago when you talk about evolution. That means as far back as ancient Greece or as late as the Roman Empire," Blake said.

Everyone stared at Blake. "What, I studied ancient history at the academy for my minor."

"We're just shocked that you know about something besides sports, flying, or war," Marc said. "Catie, go on, what else have you learned?"

"Another thing ADI noticed is that their language resembles Greek. They use the same alphabet and have many similar words."

"That would indicate that they're from Ancient Greece, what else?"

"Well, I know that Helike's recorded history only goes back about twelve hundred years."

"That doesn't tally with Dr. Moreau's numbers," Samantha said. "And before one of you says it, I can do math in my head."

"But it would have taken time to move them here," Catie said. "I guess there might be more to those stories about alien abductions and alien visits than the experts think."

"Possibly, but we need to learn more."

"I can ask Captain Galanos about it. We've never really discussed their ancient history."

"Do that."

"But, does this change anything?" Samantha asked.

"I'm not sure," Marc said. "Probably not in the short term. But it does indicate that there is an advanced starfaring civilization out here somewhere that we and the Paraxeans don't know about. It would behoove us to learn as much as possible."

"I'll see what I can learn," Catie said, waving goodbye and laughing at Blake who was miming saying behoove over and over.

Captain Galanos had sent Catie to Ensign Nikitas, saying he knew more about their history than anyone she knew. Catie had been avoiding him since the night in his cabin.

She had invited him to join her for lunch in her day cabin, so she could ask him about the history of Helike.

"Hello, Princess. Captain Galanos tells me you would like to know more about our history."

"Yes, we've just learned a few things that make us curious about your history. What can you tell me?"

"What did you learn that makes you curious?"

"I'll tell you afterward. I don't want to bias your story."

"Okay, our records show us starting our civilization on the coast of Spitiva. Our archeologists have found no records of people living anyplace before that, which gives more credence to the myth about the birth of Helike."

"Myth?"

"Let me tell you more about our history before I tell you the myth. It will give you a better perspective from which to judge the myth."

"Okay, then go on."

"Anyway, the first city was named Helike; when we understood what a planet was, we then named the planet Helike after our first city. There were thirty-two princes of Helike at the beginning. They divided the city among themselves, but they quickly expanded their realms into the surrounding country. There was always land, so the princes kept moving farther away from the city so they could claim even more land. Each of them would have their loyal following, but would attract more people to their land by offering jobs, farms, or land to the people of Helike."

"That sounds like the feudal system we had on Earth in our early history. The people who lived on the lands controlled by the princes, we called them lords, were virtual slaves."

"Oh, that is not how it was on Helike. There was always a prince trying to attract more people to his lands, so they always treated their people well. They didn't exactly share their wealth, but they struck a good bargain where their people would have a good life in exchange for living and working for them.

"The princes built a huge network of roads between their lands to allow them to trade with the other principalities. Each principality specialized in just a few technologies so trade was essential.

"During our early history, the principalities were very strong, and their princes were absolute rulers. They were benevolent, but they set the laws and enforced them. The laws were similar among the various principalities, but varied based on the personality of the ruling family and the specifics of the technology from which they derived most of their wealth."

"That doesn't sound too fair."

"Not particularly, but remember, they had to rule with an even hand or their people would just move to another principality. When it was possible for people to move across the ocean to other continents, the power of the princes fell. They scrambled to establish themselves on other continents, but the flood of people made it impossible for them to gain control. Although they managed to acquire huge tracts of land on the other continents, those continents were so much larger than Spitiva that it was impossible for them to control all the land. At that time, they became more like elite citizens than rulers for the people. They still had incredible wealth, and that wealth continued to grow and stay clustered in those first families. They limited the number of children they had to limit how much their wealth was diluted. Most of it was inherited by the first son, but all the children were well provided for."

"Sounds like your society is sexist just like societies on Earth."

"If you mean by that that males were favored over females, then yes. Although we didn't have a history of heavy warfare between the principalities, there was still a sense of power that came with being a man. There were a few rare instances where there was no son to inherit and the principality passed to the daughter. But even then, it would pass to her first son."

"Figures."

"Yes, so our women point out today. Anyway, as our people expanded across the globe, they formed governments that were what you call democracies. The people chose their leaders, although it was rare for them to choose someone who wasn't of royal blood as governor or president. The original thirty-two families still wielded enormous power and that is true even today."

"How could they maintain their hold on power even when you migrated to other continents?"

"That brings us to the Myth of Helike -- the story of how our people just emerged whole on the shores of Spitiva. As I said, we have discovered no evidence of people before that time, not even on the other continents. Our archeologists have found no signs of primitive Helikens on the planet."

"Hmm, tell me the myth."

◆ ◆ ◆

"The myth tells of another Helike we came from, one that was destroyed. They say we were rescued by the gods and placed on the shores of Spitiva where we began again. But I get ahead of myself.

"There was a first city of Helike. It was a prosperous city. The people enjoyed a good life. They worked hard but benefited greatly from their efforts. It had a great harbor that allowed it to trade with other cities, so it became a wealthy place. Then tragedy struck.

"It was noon when the first tremor struck. People ran from their homes praying to the gods to protect them. Only a few hours later the first great earthquake struck. Many buildings collapsed, but the people were saved because the gods had sent the tremor to warn them. When the earthquake stopped, the people fled to the harbor to see if they could escape the city by boat. When they reached the harbor, they discovered that there was no water in it.

"Then they knew that Poseidon was the god they had angered. They prayed, they cried, they promised sacrifices. Then a great thundering was heard, and as they looked out to sea, they saw a giant wave bearing down on the city. It towered so high they could not see the top. On it came, thundering as it bore down on the city. Then Poseidon reached out with his great hand and sliced the wave in half. It collapsed, filling the harbor again. A layer of water rushed in and covered the city, a warning of what could have been. The people rejoiced. Then another tremor struck, and they despaired.

"In their despair they cried out to Poseidon, asking what they could do to appease him. At that time a great ship appeared in the harbor and opened up its hold. Another tremor struck, telling the people that Poseidon wished them to board the ship and flee the city.

"The people of the city ran into the hold of the ship, filling it quickly. As more people came, Poseidon made the ship larger so it could take them, also. Eventually, the entire city had found room in the ship and the people slept.

"When they awoke, they were here at Helike. They were against the shore and a moat had been dug around the place where they had slept. Poseidon had dug it to protect them. Even as they awoke, they were so weak from sleep that the greatest warrior among them couldn't have fought off one of the wild beasts that stalked the people from beyond the moat.

"As the people of Helike gathered to take stock of their new home, they saw among them other people that were not of Helike. These people spoke a foreign language. There were three different tribes of people and none of them spoke the language of the other tribes nor of Helike. Later when they learned our language, each told the same story: Their village went to sleep one night and woke up the next day here on Helike with us.

"One tribe had skin as black as coal. Their men were powerful warriors. Another tribe had dark skin, the color of sand. Their men were tall and lean and were great hunters. Their women knew how to make leather from the skins of the game their men brought home. The third tribe had skin that looked darkened from the sun. They were much like us. Their men were skilled craftsmen, they could build anything from the trees we cut down. Each tribe was only fifty to sixty people strong.

"In their weakened state, the warriors of Helike and the tribes could not fight each other. Instead, they chose to explore our new land. They found a great silo made of clay. It contained wheat like they had eaten at home. They also discovered a great well that was full of freshwater. But those were the only things they could find that reminded them of home.

"The next day they made spears to fight off the wild beasts. Many men had knives or daggers they had worn when they slept or when they fled the city. They made the spears using these. Once they were armed, they ventured across the moat. They were able to chase off the wild beasts, and as they ventured farther, they discovered game they could hunt. That night the people were fed on fresh meat and bread made from the wheat.

"The fishermen from Helike went to the shore where they found reeds and grasses like they had known at home. They used them to fashion nets and with those nets, they fished. Soon there was an abundance of food and the people rejoiced. They found their new home much to their liking.

"As they continued to explore, they discovered no other people on the land. They vowed to build boats so they could find their homes. Although they all agreed they would come back to their new home, but they missed the many things from home that they could not find on the shores of Spitiva. They wanted to discover their old home so they could trade for those goods.

"There were thirty-two great families that Poseidon blessed at the beginning. It was never proven, but it was clear that each family was blessed with special knowledge from Poseidon. It was said that each was given a book.

"The first family was given the secret of metals. They were able to make a new metal called iron that had never been seen before. It was stronger than the bronze and copper that they had used in their previous home. Later they made steel and even later they made a metal called aluminum that was lighter and stronger than steel. All advancements in metal have been derived from that family.

"The second was given the secret of brick making and masonry. They were able to make bricks far better than any bricks known before and in great quantities. They used this knowledge to help build the first city on Helike.

"The third family was given the secret of shipbuilding, for although they were shipbuilders before, now they were able to build great ships that could sail into the wind. Eventually, they built ships of metal that could power themselves. All the great ships of Helike were built by this family.

"A fourth family was given the secret of ceramics and pottery. They were able to make ceramics beyond anything anyone had ever seen. It is possible that it was of their own making, but the legend is they also had a book. Their recipes for ceramics are still used today.

"A fifth family was given the secret of power. They built Helike's first waterwheel. The people had never seen a waterwheel like that before. Their waterwheels drove the early industries of Helike. Later they built windmills. Years later they also developed Helike's steam engine. They became responsible for all sources of power, even the modern fusion reactor.

"A sixth family had the first recipe for cement and concrete. It was a new material and was used to speed the development of bridges, tall buildings, roads, and structures never before imagined.

"A seventh family was given the secret of glass. They developed receptacles for food and drink. They created the first glass windows, windshields for moving vehicles, even furniture was made from their glass. They created lenses that powered microscopes and telescopes so the people could study the stars or study the smallest living things on Helike.

"Another family were scholars. Their descendants made the greatest discoveries in science; although some of the equations were already known, they might have been forgotten without them. From them, we got the theory of triangles, the fundamentals of trigonometry. The law of logarithms. They developed calculus. They taught us to describe a space without regard to its alignment. They taught us about complex numbers. They first described gravity, taught us how to deal with vibrations. Eventually, they gave us the greatest equation of all time: $E=mc^2$. It is said that their book contained only twenty-five equations, but they have been the root of the most important scientific discoveries in our history.

"Another family were doctors. They were given knowledge of the body that allowed them to cure diseases, treat illnesses, mend broken bones. They gave us anesthesia which allowed them to operate on a person without causing them pain. Dentistry was another family and optometrics another.

"Another family was given the secret of language. They gave us a new alphabet, developed a process for making paper, gave us the first printing press.

"The list went on, electricity to one family. Agriculture to another, the secret of machines, with gears, screws, and more to another. The concept of refrigeration to another, how to breed animals for better production using genetics for another. A rack of beads for counting to the family that developed Helike's first computer.

"Clocks and chronometer, hot air balloons, metals casting, architecture, navigation with sextant and compass; that family built our first lighthouse and developed GPS. Chemistry to the family that made the first rubber tires, developed diesel. One family developed the concept of the modern sewer system and water treatment plants, another created the basis for weights and measures. That same family later developed Helike's first system of bookkeeping and also developed the modern theory of economics. The science of geology was handed down through another family.

"Modern Helike's banking system comes from the first family that formalized the lending of money.

"Helike's first spaceship was developed by the same family that produced the first rifle, then the first rocket.

"Those thirty-two families are still the wealthiest and most powerful families on Helike," Ensign Nikitas said as he finished the story.

"My god, that does tend to validate our theory. We believe that you were brought here from our planet by an ancient alien race. We don't understand why, but it's the only thing that makes sense," Catie said.

"Cers," ADI interrupted. "I have checked Earth history. A city called Helike was destroyed by an earthquake in 373 B.C. Your spelling of your world's name translates to the same name."

"But how does that explain Helike? Our history is only twelve hundred years."

Catie patted him on the shoulder. "They would have had to transport your people here. If they put them in stasis, then they would have gone to sleep and awakened a thousand years later. Maybe this ancient race of starfarers didn't have the ability to travel that fast. If they were only able to reach one-tenth the speed of light, it would have taken over a thousand years to get here."

"Why would an advanced alien race bring us here?"

"We don't know, but we would like to find out. We're wondering where they are now."

"So that means we're related."

"Yes it does, very distantly related." Catie gave Ensign Nikitas a light hug before she left the cabin. He was very huggable.

Chapter 12 Now We're Getting Somewhere

Marc was walking along the first road they'd built outside of the city. Its purpose was to give the farmers access to their farms from the city. Soon they would be building the roads that led to the ranches farther back in the hills. Following him were the farmers who had selected land grants along the road.

"Hey, why aren't there any bar ditches?"

Marc, a city boy, had to look up what a bar ditch was, 'a ditch alongside a road for the purpose of drainage. Dirt is borrowed from the ditch to crown the road.'

"Because the pavement is pervious."

"What the hell does pervious mean?"

"It means it's porous so water can flow through it. That eliminates most runoff so we don't need drainage ditches. It's safer too, ditches beside a road are just asking for an accident."

"Come on, what happens when it really pours down?"

"The road is sitting on three meters of decomposed granite; the pavement will allow over five centimeters of rain through per minute, so I don't think you have to worry."

"Won't that granite become waterlogged?"

"It's designed to allow the water to percolate down to the water table. If it's waterlogged, then all this land will be under water."

They continued to walk and finally arrived at a planned site for a mini-hamlet. Four families had agreed to build their homes close together so that they could share infrastructure. They'd also agreed to build four other houses each to create a small community. Those houses would be close to the corner, while their homes would be farther away, allowing for more privacy and larger homes.

"You said you'd give us the infrastructure for our hamlet if we created one."

"That's correct. Did you allocate the forty square meters for it?"

"Yes. So that means we get water and sewer, right?"

"Yes. We'll be using the small treatment plants that we designed for The Cook Islands. The water will be recycled, and a truck will pick up the dirt every week. That is unless you want it. Just let us know."

"Where's the water tower?"

"We're not using a water tower, we'll be using a weighted column," Marc said. "It will only be twenty feet tall, but the weight will generate eight hundred kilopascals."

"Huh?"

"About 110 PSI."

"Oh, that's good."

"What about internet?"

"There's a utility channel down the center of the road. We're running fiber through it and electricity, so you'll have internet and power. We have junctions every two kilometers."

"Comm coverage?"

"We have cell towers every fifty kilometers. You do know this is all in the handout?"

"Yep, just verifying."

"What about fire hydrants?"

"We only have those in the city. You'll have one in your hamlet, but if a fire breaks out, we'll use an Oryx to bring water to it. We can dump the water or run a hose down to the firefighters; the Oryxes will have pumps to make sure there's enough pressure."

"Okay, seems like you've thought of everything."

"I'm sure we'll eventually discover something we forgot. Do you plan to build a schoolhouse?"

Orion, the planet's AI, would be in charge of the children's education, but the Delphineans had learned that it worked better with an onsite coach to work with the children. The older children would be bussed to Orion City two days a week for their education and study remotely the other three days. But the younger children needed coaching every day, so the schoolhouse would be multi-grade classrooms for children from K through the sixth grade. They were allocating coaches for the onsite school based on the number of children and were planning on a twenty-to-one ratio.

"Might as well, you're paying for it," one of the farmers said.

Catie and Morgan were working on their aikido. Cristina was on duty, so couldn't join them.

"Morgan, what do you think about Tina taking over as my bodyguard when you and Tracey move to Colorado?"

"You mean, taking my job?"

"Yes."

"She'd make a good bodyguard, but I think she's too young to run your security detail."

"What do you mean, too young?"

"I think she's only eighteen or nineteen; I'm pretty sure she lied about her age when she joined up."

"What's wrong with being eighteen?" Catie was almost eighteen and wasn't too happy about having her age group disparaged.

"Catie, you can't judge everyone by comparing them to yourself. When you do that, it's called self-centered referencing. Most people do it, but it's a bad habit. Unlike you, most people under twenty-five are a bit stupid. I don't mean dumb, but prone to doing stupid things like car surfing."

"Isn't that profiling?"

"Yeah, but if you do it right, profiling works. Now you wouldn't want to take a fact like sixty percent of clowns are short and decide that all short people are clowns. But lots of statistics show that it takes people until they reach twenty-five to work all the stupid out of their systems."

"What about Tracey?"

"She happens to turn twenty-five next month. Making up with her father would tend to show she's worked most of the stupid out of her system."

"What about her father?"

"Some men take a lot longer to work the stupid out of them." Morgan laughed, "I'm just glad Tracey has worked through most of hers."

"Why, you don't want to get punched in the face again?" Catie teased. Morgan had once tried to break up a bar fight that Tracey was involved in. When she'd grabbed Tracey, Tracey had looked at Morgan, then punched her in the face.

"That too. But if we're going to do this ranch thing, it'd be best if she is done behaving stupidly."

"Should we screen for that when we select our Marines?"

"No. Unfortunately, stupid and crazy are two sides of the same coin. And you need your Marines to be a bit crazy. It's crazy that makes people do brave things."

"True." Catie tried to slide in under Morgan's guard and throw her.

"No way, I'm getting wise to your tricks."

"Another reason I need a new bodyguard."

Chapter 13   The Shipyard

"Welcome," Captain McAvoy greeted everyone as the team gathered in her day cabin. She and Captain Galanos were waiting as Catie, Lieutenant Racine, and Kasper entered.

"Captain Galanos, please proceed."

"ADI has traced the mystery ship back to the asteroid belt, in fact back to a specific asteroid. Now we need to plan our next move."

Everyone nodded as they sat down.

"Let's review what we know. The ship in question left this asteroid five months ago. It had a significant lead on the Geraki since it was leaving from the asteroid belt and was on the same side of the sun as Adelfós, the gas giant, while the Geraki had to travel from the thirty-degree point in Helike's orbit."

"Captain, can you explain the timing of your deployment?" Catie asked.

"Yes, we were three months late in leaving Helike. We encountered several technical problems that delayed us."

"Were those normal problems?" Captain McAvoy asked.

"Not really. There was an accident on the space station where we were preparing to launch. It created enough chaos that we were delayed. An experiment in one of the labs caused a significant hull breach. It was discovered that the lab contained two chemicals which when combined are very explosive. They should never have been in the same location. The issue was traced back to a clerical error in the shipping docket."

"Sounds like it could have been sabotage," Catie said.

"That was suspected, but when the clerical error was discovered, everyone relaxed and quit thinking about sabotage. Looking back that might have been a mistake, especially since the accident made us miss the ideal launch window."

Captain McAvoy nodded. "That's why I asked. It surprised me to see that your launch timing gave up the velocity from the planet's orbital velocity as well as giving you an additional AU of distance to travel."

Catie leaned in again. "And that is what allowed the other ship to beat you to Stási by two months. I definitely vote for sabotage."

"I agree," Captain McAvoy said. "Captain Galanos, please continue."

"We now know that the mystery ship left Stási when it was rounding the planet; the angle of departure was well suited to a return trip to the asteroid in question. We also know from experience that it would have been impossible to build and launch the ship from Helike or one of its space stations without it becoming common knowledge. So, given all that, what should our next step be?"

Lieutenant Racine smiled as she leaned forward. "I'm assuming that since I was invited, it would have something to do with taking control of that asteroid."

"Not necessarily taking control, but we do need to know more about it," Catie said.

"That's why you're all here. We need to figure out how to accomplish that without alerting them," Captain Galanos said.

"We'll send a Fox to drop a probe close to the asteroid. That will give us information about what is actually there as well as what sensors and detectors they have in place."

"But they would detect your Fox."

"Not if it's coasting, and it has a very low energy signature when it's operating on gravity drives and pulling energy from its capacitors. The same is true of the probe, both their hulls absorb any EM energy."

"But how will your probe communicate with you without being detected?"

"Our quantum relays. They don't leave an EM signature."

"Of course."

"Any other suggestions?" Captain McAvoy asked.

The group looked at each other. Kasper shrugged, "I can have a Fox ready in an hour."

Captain Galanos nodded to Captain McAvoy, asking her to take charge.

"Then I suggest we meet again tomorrow when we have some more data, and I'd prefer that ADI fly the Fox. I think we want to minimize any discussion among our crew and between the two crews."

"Yes, Ma'am."

Kasper personally mounted the probe on the Fox. He'd simply explained to the crew that they were sending it out to have a look around. Everyone gave him a knowing nod; they all knew something was up, why else would they be all but coasting toward Helike, but nobody dared question his excuse.

Eight hours later, Catie and Captain McAvoy were sitting in the captain's day cabin watching the feed from the Fox as it approached the asteroid belt. ADI had taken it above the ecliptic since most sensors were aimed within the ecliptic plane. Then she'd had it coast by the asteroid, launching the probe at one thousand kilometers.

"I would guess that it's been hollowed out," Catie said. "I suspect it's an abandoned mine. The metals they wanted were at its core, so they just burrowed in to get them. You can see the main shaft here."

"I agree," ADI added.

Captain McAvoy laughed. "How do you deal with it, her always being there and popping in at any time?"

"I do not pop in."

"Oh yes you do. And I'm used to it. She's always careful not to do it when it might cause me a problem. That is unless she's trying to get even for something."

"And where did I learn that from?"

"Back to the asteroid. Do you think they built the ship inside it?"

"It looks big enough."

"Cers, it is forty meters by twenty by twenty-eight. The ship could easily have been built inside of it."

The probe coasted in close to the asteroid and circled, showing an array of antennas and other sensors on each side of the asteroid. "They're certainly set up to detect any visitors," Captain McAvoy said.

"A lot of hardware for an abandoned asteroid. We need to get inside."

"We'll talk about it tomorrow. Might as well get a good night's sleep. Things continue to get more interesting."

The next morning, everyone had coffee while they watched the video feed again. The probe picked up some communication from the asteroid, but it was heavily encrypted. There was no sign of activity. Between the Fox and the probe, they had determined that the asteroid was one hundred thousand kilometers from any mining activity and from the space station that the miners used as a base.

Captain McAvoy opened the discussion. "Okay, so it's a nice quiet, out-of-the-way place where one could conceivably build a ship."

"Yes, and now that we have a better idea of what we're up against, are you still planning on stealth?" Lieutenant Racine asked.

"We should at least try. There has to be a way to get inside."

"They must be getting resupplied," Captain Galanos said. "That is unless it's abandoned."

"I think there's too much hardware there for an abandoned base; they would have salvaged those arrays. They must at least have a caretaker there. Remember, they were planning on that ship coming back."

"Then I suggest we put a team on a Lynx and go sit by it. We can send someone over to get a closer look at the door and see if they can find something. If a supply ship comes by, we can use it as a means to infiltrate." Lieutenant Racine clenched her fist as she sat back.

"Who will you send?" Catie asked.

"I can tell you have a preference."

"Cristina."

"Why?"

"She's familiar with the interrogation hood, the paralyzer, and the memory spray. As we saw in Mexico, a woman is easy to ignore if she plays her cards right. I think she would have the best chance to get someone isolated so we could interrogate them."

"I'm okay with that. I want to send at least six Marines. We can have them on standby in case things go sideways. And if stealth doesn't work, we have an assault team in the wings."

Catie nodded her head.

"I want to include Ensign Nikitas," Captain Galanos said. "Depending on what happens, we might want someone there who represents Helike. He's well known and he has trained for things like this."

"He has?" Catie was shocked.

"All the princes train for assaults and defense. Their fathers are paranoid about kidnapping, so they send their sons to a school where they're trained in various methods. He is also our best EVA specialist."

"Okay, Racine, pick your team, Kasper you fly the Lynx." Captain McAvoy smiled at Catie; she could tell she wanted to go on the mission. "Sorry," she mouthed.

Kasper was letting Merlin fly the Lynx. He'd asked ADI to fly it, but she'd told him that she was too busy. Kasper didn't fight it; he knew she was just making sure he was aware that she had a choice. And it wasn't that complicated a flight plan, so Merlin was doing just fine. It was going to take two days to reach the asteroid; unlike the Fox, they had to take it easy with a human crew. He walked to the back to take a shower. As he walked by Cristina, he could see she was interrogating Ensign Nikitas, asking him what a Heliken woman would say in different situations. Based on what he heard, it wasn't much different than what a woman from Delphi City would say.

Once he finished his shower, Kasper sat down beside Cristina. He'd only met her a few times, but he'd looked her up when she and Catie became close after the kidnapping attempt on Onisiwo. He could see why Catie had selected her to go undercover back then, and it made sense that she wanted her to be on this mission. The woman was one badass.

"Hi, Cristina."

"Lieutenant!"

"Sorry, should I call you sergeant?"

"No, Cristina's fine. Just being careful."

"You can call me Kasper, that's my call sign."

"Sure. Do you need something?"

"No, I wondered if you did. You're the one on the spot here. I'm not sure if you should be thanking Catie or cursing her."

"Oh, I live for this kind of stuff."

"You like the danger?"

"Not the danger, but having to rely on my wits, making a difference."

"Showing the men up?"

"That's a bonus."

"Cer Kasper, I detect a ship leaving the space station. It is on a vector toward the asteroid."

"Great. How much time do we have?"

"Six hours."

Cristina looked perplexed as she was only catching one side of the conversation.

"A ship's heading toward the asteroid," Kasper said, giving her the basics. "ADI, how hard do we have to accelerate to get there in four hours? And please share."

"You would need to do a 6-G acceleration."

"Can the grav drives do it?"

"No, you would need to use the space engines."

"Can we do that without being detected?"

"I can vector you above the asteroid so they don't detect the exhaust plume while you decelerate."

"Do it. Everyone, prepare for a hard burn. We'll be doing it for four hours. Ensign Nikitas, that means strap into your couch, the ship's AI will adjust its orientation to keep you from passing out. And zip up that shipsuit."

◆ ◆ ◆

Lieutenant Racine was checking Cristina's spacesuit while she gave her some last-minute instructions. "Okay, we're sending you and Nikitas out there. You have to be careful so you don't expose yourself to any cameras. Nikitas, you're to do whatever Sergeant Castro tells you to. You're there in case she needs some quick support but you're going to remain outside on the asteroid. Castro, you need to use that supply ship to get inside. You'll maintain radio silence unless you get into trouble, or you gain control of the station. We'll be waiting here to back you up."

"Got it, ma'am."

"Your HUD will provide you the vector to follow so you don't show up on their scanners. Be careful with your thrusters, if you use them too much, their sensors will pick up the gas. We'll give you enough velocity to get there, you'll be steering and slowing down the whole way."

"Got it."

"You clear on that, Ensign?" Racine asked.

"Yes, ma'am."

They were one hundred kilometers out from the asteroid and Racine had allocated one hour to get there. Their thrusters would be expelling gas at the speed of sound, so they would be slowing down at 2/1000 of a G, using up most of their reaction mass by the time they made it to the asteroid.

Cristina and Nikitas traveled side by side to avoid hitting one another with their thruster exhaust. Cristina was going through various scenarios in her head. She was confident she would be able to attach herself to the supply ship and use it to get inside, but what was she supposed to do after that? There were far too many possible scenarios to imagine, so she decided that she'd just have to play it by ear once she was inside.

When they were within a few meters of the asteroid, they cut their thrusters. Cristina reached out and grabbed a seam of Ensign Nikitas' armor and used it to push herself ahead of him. She didn't want them landing on the asteroid at the same time. Minimal impact was best, and she wasn't sure how good he would be at landing. She landed, bending her knees to distribute the impact over a greater period of time. She stood up straight and grabbed Nikitas with her arms, using them and her knees to slow his descent. When he landed, she realized she needn't have bothered, he bent his knees and his impact didn't even register on her sensors.

"Sorry," she said, using hand contact with his suit to allow transmission.

"No problem. I wouldn't trust me either."

Cristina removed her space armor and anchored it to the asteroid. Ensign Nikitas looked at her like she was crazy. Her shipsuit had been modified so that it looked like the ones the Helikens wore when they were inside a space station or spaceship. She was wearing her specs from the Onisiwo mission, they had been adapted to look like a regular pair of Onisiwoen glasses, and looked the same as what they wore on Helike. They weren't as effective as the wraparound style that Delphi used, but she needed to be able to fit in.

"I'm wearing a rebreather, it's small, so it'll be easy to hide. This armor would be too noticeable."

When Nikitas continued to stare, she added, "I didn't want to have to argue with Racine about it."

Nikitas nodded his head, that explained why it hadn't come up in the mission briefing.

"You wait here, I'll scream if I need help."

Nikitas nodded his head again, but he was pretty sure that there would be no scream unless it was one of the Helikens inside the asteroid.

Cristina crept along the surface of the asteroid. There was enough iron content in it that her boots would magnetically couple, at least enough to keep her from flying off into space. The probe had identified a large cargo door, it was covered with rock so that from a distance it just looked like the asteroid. She positioned herself beside the door and waited. The supply ship, really just a supply shuttle, should be arriving in twenty to thirty minutes; she could just make out its form as it flew toward the asteroid.

"Here she comes," Cristina thought as she finally got a clear view of the shuttle. *"Oops, wrong orientation."* Cristina realized that based on the shuttle's approach she must be at the top of the door, she definitely wanted to be along the bottom. She quickly started to make her way to the other side of the door. She needed to be well below it and the shuttle so she wouldn't be seen by the pilot when she pushed off from the asteroid.

She caught a glimpse of a laser pulse from the shuttle as it hit the asteroid's communication array. A brief reply laser beam came from the array. They were both tight communication beams. No EM transmission had been detected by her Comm.

Finally, she was in position. The shuttle was now close enough that she could get a good look. *"Now where is a hiding place for me?"* She looked over the shuttle, it had landing skids extending from its hull. Its engines were tight against the hull and toward the back, by now they were off as the shuttle was just using thrusters to maneuver. *"Perfect."* She saw a nook between the engine and the shuttle's hull that would be the perfect hiding place.

"They're getting ready to open the door." Cristina's feet sensed vibrations. *"Probably decompressing the bay now. Time to go."* Cristina pushed off from the asteroid, aiming at the center of the shuttle's bottom hull. She had one chance since without her space armor, she didn't have any thrusters. If she missed, she would have to call for help. *"How embarrassing, and Racine will rip me a new one too."*

As she closed with the shuttle, Cristina did a quick flip so she would land feet first. She needed to minimize her impact. Before her feet contacted the shuttle, she totally relaxed her knees, they bent as they absorbed her momentum, continuing to bend until her butt contacted the shuttle. *"I hope they didn't feel that."* Cristina reached out and grabbed the landing skid, using it to stop her slide toward the rear of the shuttle. Once she was stopped, she pulled on the skid to maneuver herself toward the back of the shuttle and the engine pod. After reaching the spot, she nestled inside the nook just as a sliver of light hit the shuttle. The cargo bay was opening. *"Idiots, they should have killed the lights."* Just then the lights went off. Cristina breathed a sigh of relief; she'd been counting on the bay being dark until the shuttle was inside and the door closed.

"Come on, land this thing!" Cristina was impatient with the shuttle pilot's overly careful maneuvers to line the shuttle up with the doorway, and his creeping forward motion. Finally, the shuttle settled down on the floor of the cargo bay. Cristina could feel vibrations of the door closing through the shuttle's landing skids. She rolled off of the engine pod and knelt beside the landing skid. The infrared view in her specs gave her a good view of the cargo bay as she started looking around for a hiding place. She needed to get to one before they turned the lights back on.

There was a row of cabinets and a bench along the same side as the control room; below the bench was just enough room for her, at least she hoped so. She launched herself toward it and slithered across the deck using her hands and toes to adjust her trajectory. She reached the workbench just as the lights came back on. Soon she could hear air being pumped into the bay. Once her Comm told her there was enough air she removed her helmet and rebreather and stashed them behind her.

"Kinsara, you're the slowest damn pilot we have," came from a speaker. "You know, some of us have lives to get back to."

"Sorry, Makata, but you guys got so pissed when I bumped the deck last time, I was being extra careful."

"Why don't you just learn to fly!"

The side door of the shuttle opened and a guy Cristina assumed was Kinsara was standing there with four others behind him. He motioned them toward the front of the bay and they hopped down and each walked over to a group of carts. Cristina could hear the click, click as their magnetic boots grabbed the floor.

"Hmm, zero gravity carts, I wonder how they work," Cristina thought as she watched the four push their carts back to the shuttle. Two other people in the shuttle were pushing boxes to the door.

The ones with the carts loaded the boxes on them and strapped them down. Then they rolled the carts to the front of the bay and through an open bay door. In a few minutes, they were back for another load. As they were leaving the bay, Cristina danced around the shuttle to the front where she grabbed another one of the carts, *"Magnetic wheels, clever."* Christina wheeled her cart to the shuttle's door and started moving boxes. Kinsara gave Cristina a 'who are you?' look. "Makata told me to help; he says you always take too long."

"I didn't know they had any women out here. No wonder he's in such a hurry to get back to his life, what an ass."

After strapping her load down, Cristina wheeled her cart through the door. She just followed the passageway until she saw the other carts lined up by a door. Two were empty and had been pushed beyond the door. Cristina put her cart in behind the two full ones and grabbed one of the empty carts and pushed it farther down the passageway. The passageway was cluttered with cabinets and junk, so she parked the cart on the other side of a passageway cabinet where it couldn't be seen from where the other carts were. She relaxed and floated next to the cart to wait.

It was another thirty minutes before Cristina heard sounds alerting her that the shuttle was getting ready to leave. Then it was fifteen minutes before she heard the sound indicating that they were closing the bay doors.

"He is slow and cautious," Cristina thought, shaking her head at how long the pilot had taken to fly the shuttle out of the bay. *"Okay, here goes nothing."*

Cristina rushed back to the cargo bay and pounded on the door.

"Hey what's up?"

"That idiot Kinsara left me. Call him back!"

"Not a chance. What the hell happened? You get lost?"

"I needed to use the ladies' room," Cristina said in case her voice hadn't been enough to tell him she was a woman.

"Well, Sweetheart, that little trip is going to cost you a couple of weeks out here with the boys. But don't worry, I'm sure we'll be able to keep you entertained."

"*We'll see who's entertained when I get your ass alone.*" Cristina waved at the guy through the glass. "How many of you are out here?"

"Just eight, but I'm the good-looking one."

"*Yeah right.*" Cristina leaned against the door of the control room. "You going to show me around?"

"Just a second, I've got to lock this place down first. Why don't you tell me about yourself?"

"I'm just a girl who missed her ride."

"Come on, there's more than that. We should get to know each other."

Cristina rolled her eyes. "*What a loser.* What do you guys have to drink out here?"

"Hey I've got some good stuff, just wait." Makata finally finished and opened the door to the control room. Cristina kneed him in the groin then snapped his head back with a palm strike to the chin. She pushed him back into the control room and slapped the paralyzer on the back of his neck. He looked at her in total shock. "Don't call me Sweetheart."

Cristina disarmed the alarm for the airlock then made a quick dash for her gear. When she got back, she put the interrogation hood over Makata's head and attached her spare Comm. It would record the full interrogation, but it wouldn't be until she could connect with ADI that they'd get all the information they wanted. For now, her Comm would be good enough to give her the basics.

Cristina reached up to scratch her ear but caught herself in time. Since they couldn't have any EM energy floating about, she had conductive strips that connected her earwigs and specs to her suit's wired network and her Comm. The damn conductors on her skin itched, she didn't know it if was real, or just her brain not liking the strange feeling.

She started studying the controls to see what she could learn on her own. They were similar to the controls in the Geraki that she'd studied with Ensign Nikitas to prepare for the mission.

"Hey, what's keeping you?!" blared from the speaker over her head.

"Keep your shirt on! I've got to fix a problem with the proximity alarms, they keep going off," Cristina replied, her Comm mimicking Makata's voice.

"We don't hear anything."

"That's because I silenced them. I could turn them back on if you want?"

"No, we're happy to let you deal with them."

Cristina disabled the proximity alarm and pulsed the communication laser twice to signal the probe that it could now move in.

"*Here it comes,*" Ensign Nikitas said as he saw the probe move in. He followed it to the communication array. When it landed, he made a few adjustments so that it was fully connected to the asteroid's internal circuits. The probe was equipped with a quantum relay, so it would give them an undetectable communication link to the station, and with the work that Cristina was doing, they would have access to the asteroid's internal systems. Then ADI could really get to work.

"Cristina, can you hear me? Over."

"Yes, I read you, do you have the probe in place? Over."

"Yes. How long before you're ready to come out? Over."

"Another hour. Out."

Cristina spent the time working with ADI to make sure that ADI had full access to the systems. "ADI, do you know why the guys were calling for Makata?"

"Cer Cristina, I've just reviewed the video. They are playing some kind of card game. When he didn't arrive, they got someone else to join them. It appears that they are quite content at this time."

"Good. Anything else you need me to do?"

"Yes, remove the panel I'm highlighting for you. I need you to bypass a circuit for me."

◆ ◆ ◆

"Cer Cristina, I have completed the interrogation."

"Great." Cristina took the hood off of Makata and stowed it back in her bag. "ADI, is the coast clear?"

"Yes."

Cristina pulled Makata out into the passageway and took him down to where she'd left the cart. She thumped his head on the edge of the cart, then floated him upside down over it. She then sprayed him with the memory eraser aerosol. She pressed her fingers on his carotid artery until he passed out. She didn't want him to wake up and cause any problem. She pulled the paralyzer off and left him hanging upside down in the microgravity. It would be about ten minutes before he woke up and started wondering what had happened. Cristina was sure he'd make up a story for his friends, but he would have no memory of the last four hours. Just a sore head and sore groin. Maybe she shouldn't have kneed him, but nobody called her Sweetheart.

"I'm ready," Cristina announced as she reached the airlock. She was communicating with ADI by placing her hand on one of the shipyard's control panels so her suit would transmit through the metal. They were still avoiding any EM transmissions; even though ADI could erase them from the system's memory, they couldn't be sure that there weren't other portable or isolated detectors.

"The alarm is disabled. You're good to go."

Cristina put on her rebreather and cycled through the airlock and crawled out onto the asteroid. It took her a moment to get oriented before she could head back to where Ensign Nikitas waited.

When she reached him, they touched heads so they could communicate. "Did everything go okay?" Ensign Nikitas asked.

"Perfect. Let me get my armor on and we can head back to the Lynx."

Once she had her armor on, Cristina flashed a laser toward where they had agreed the Lynx would wait for them. A small laser flash replied.

"Okay, they're there. Now we have to push off hard or they'll have to send someone to get us." Cristina bent her knees deep, then pushed toward the hidden Lynx. She was happy to see that Ensign Nikitas was right beside her, she was pretty sure they had enough momentum to reach the Lynx. They'd used up most of their thrusters to decelerate for a landing on the asteroid, so they needed to reach the Lynx with the energy from their push off. The Lynx would match their vector so they would only need enough from their thrusters to guide themselves to the hatch.

Lieutenant Racine was hanging out the hatch as they approached. She reached out and grabbed Cristina's hand and pulled her in, gave her a pat on the head to tell her she'd done well, then turned back to grab Ensign Nikitas.

Cristina cycled through the airlock. As soon as she was in the main cabin, she pulled her helmet off and yanked the earwigs out. "Damn, those things itch!"

"Earwigs?"

"No, the conductors that they had to run from them to my suit."

"Oh, never had to do that. Do you need some water?"

"I'll have whatever the Lieutenant allows me to have once we get underway and have gravity." Cristina continued to scratch around her ears to remove the conductor traces.

Lieutenant Racine pulled Ensign Nikitas into the Lynx's bay. She took the opportunity to pat him on the butt to let him know he'd done a good job.

"Lieutenant!" ADI admonished her.

"Sorry, I couldn't help myself. Wanted to know if it was as firm as it looks. Don't tell on me."

"I'll think about it."

Lieutenant Racine let Ensign Nikitas cycle through the airlock first, then followed. The Lynx was already moving back toward the Merlin so they had gravity and could move about easily.

"ADI tells me it was a complete success," Lieutenant Racine said after she pulled her helmet off.

"It looks that way. I just had to deal with one guy. We'll see if they notice anything, but I don't expect they will."

"Alright, you're off duty as of now, so have a drink. Catie sent a bottle of Scotch along."

"Hey, are we off duty?" one of the Marines asked.

"No! Just Ensign Nikitas and Sergeant Castro. You guys will have to wait until we get back to the Merlin."

There was a whisper of grumbling, but not much. Racine wasn't noted for putting up with much.

As soon as the Lynx docked in the Merlin's flight bay, Catie, Morgan, and Captain McAvoy went out. They were wearing small rebreathers so they could be there as soon as the Lynx's hatch opened.

Catie pulled her helmet off just as the hatch started to open, knowing that also signaled that the bay was now pressurized. Cristina was the first to emerge. "Tina, how'd it go?" Catie asked as she pulled Cristina into a hug.

"I'm sure ADI told you all about it, things went fine."

"She did, but without communication, we couldn't be there with you, and the video ADI pulled from your Comm wasn't all that great. Come on, you have to tell me every detail."

Ensign Nikitas and Lieutenant Racine emerged next, just in time to see Catie and Cristina enter the airlock. Ensign Nikitas looked confused.

"What's the matter, you feel like last night's leftovers?" Racine asked.

"I guess."

"The Princess misses being in action."

"In action?"

"Yeah, during the war with the Fazullans, she was captain of the Roebuck."

"Aren't the Fazullans those albino-looking guys with the sharp teeth?"

"Yes."

Racine thought Ensign Nikitas still looked confused.

"She was heavily involved in the war. Then they sent Captain McAvoy out to take over command so the Princess could assume command of all of our forces and act as ambassador to Onisiwo. She would have rather stayed in command of the Roebuck; she likes getting close to the action."

"How close?"

"She'd have been in the boarding parties if her uncle would have allowed it. She's a tough cookie."

"If you say so."

"Come on, I'll buy you a drink and show you some videos."

Chapter 14   We Need a Plan

Captain McAvoy, Captain Galanos, Kasper, Commander Petrou, and Ensign Nikitas were meeting with Catie in her day cabin.

"Daddy, Uncle Blake, are you listening in?" Catie messaged.

"We're on. We'll follow your suggestion and let Captain Galanos run the meeting."

"Yeah, I'll believe that when I see it," Catie thought. "Captain Galanos, Commander Petrou, and Ensign Nikitas, on the video link we have my father, Marc, the Monarch of Delphi, and my Uncle, Admiral Blake, the head of our armed forces."

"We're pleased you could join us. Again, I wish to express my thanks for all the help you've given us."

"We're happy to help."

"We should get started," Catie said. "ADI, review what we have learned."

"About one-third of the data we've gotten from the asteroid shipyard was encrypted. But from the unencrypted files, here's what we know: it took eighteen months to build the shipyard and the ship; they were built in parallel. They are being resupplied bi-weekly while they wait for the ship to return. And, they are mostly in the dark about the mission."

"Do they know that the ship was destroyed?" Blake asked.

"I knew Uncle Blake couldn't sit back," Catie thought.

"Cers, the shipyard and facilities in the belt all experienced the EM pulse. It was significantly degraded by the time it reached the asteroid belt, so it did minimal damage. But they suspect that the pulse could have damaged the ship. They have been told to continue to wait for it."

"What about the base?"

"As I said, the people in the shipyard do not know about the mission. They are aware that something happened to Stási since it is no longer sending messages to Helike or the space station in the asteroid belt, but that is all."

"Do we know who built the shipyard and the ship?" Catie asked.

"All evidence points to Polemistia. Although there is no definitive proof, all eight men in the shipyard are from Polemistia, they appear to be long-term colleagues. All the communication that has been delivered to them on the resupply runs appears to come from Polemistia."

All three of the Helikens drew in a deep breath when Polemistia was mentioned a third time. Captain Galanos and Commander Petrou both turned toward Ensign Nikitas.

"Is there something significant about Polemistia?" Catie asked.

"My uncle is their constitutional monarch," Ensign Nikitas said.

"Not your father?"

"My uncle is my mother's brother. My father's family is from Spitiva. My uncle's family controls much of the chemical industry, which is now mostly located in Polemistia."

"Would you tell us more about him?" Captain Galanos asked. She took her position as the lead investigator for Helike seriously even though she knew that they were dependent on the Delphineans to accomplish much.

"He is very aggressive in his politics. He would like to become the true monarch instead of just a symbol. He spends a lot of money and time promoting a return to a true monarchy. He thinks that Polemistia has lost much of its prestige and influence when the monarchy's power was taken away."

"Do you think he could be behind this?"

"It is possible, he would have the kind of money to back such a move. But it is very aggressive even for him. I'm not sure he would be able to convince enough people to support such a move. And what is its purpose anyway? How would this benefit Polemistia?"

"I have heard that he is ruthless, but would he go so far as to kill everyone on Stási?" Captain Galanos asked.

"I'm not sure he would go that far. And it would undermine his position. Why would he take such a risk?"

"Can you get close to him?" Catie asked.

"I know him well enough to call him and ask for a small favor. I have stayed in his palace when visiting Polemistia and he has stayed at my father's palace when visiting Spitiva."

Captain Galanos gave Ensign Nikitas a hard look. "If he is responsible, are you willing to help uncover his actions?"

"First, we need to know why this was done. But I will fight for Helike."

"We have reviewed the data enough, now we need to make some decisions," Captain Galanos said. "We must decide when we will contact Helike and when we want to arrive."

"And do we tell them about the Delphineans?" Commander Petrou asked.

"Yes, our arrival time will depend on that. Without your help, Captain McAvoy, we would be months away. We would have had to collect reaction mass from Adelfós, the gas giant. Then it would have taken six months to return to Helike."

"I do not think we can afford to wait six months," Ensign Nikitas said. "Once they round the sun, they will soon be able to confirm that the moon has been destroyed. From that, they will not have far to go to assume their ship has also been destroyed. Whatever plans they have, they will have to decide whether to move forward or start over. My uncle is not a patient man."

Captain Galanos looked at Catie. "Princess?"

"It's up to you. I tend to favor acting early over long waits, but it's your home."

"What do we tell them about you?"

"You should say that we were behind Adelfós when the moon was destroyed. We picked up your distress call and came out to help you."

"But we were still two months out from Stási when this all happened. How will we explain that you reached us in only two days, much less the fact that your spaceplanes cleared the debris for us before it destroyed our ship."

"But only your officers know about the Foxes, so we don't have to tell them about that. We can just pretend that we reached you at the same time as the shuttle, so it doesn't show our acceleration capabilities. We've been doing 0.2Gs since we started out."

"But the crew?"

"You don't know whom you can trust?"

"I can tell you whom to trust," ADI messaged Catie.

"We can do a profile to help you decide."

"There is only one member of the crew that I am concerned about. But I'm not sure about the scientists. What would we do with them?"

"Hold them on the Merlin until you conclude your investigation."

"Under what pretense?"

"Tell your command that they have medical issues which confine them to sickbay, or tell them that they were killed when your ship was disabled."

"Captain," Ensign Nikitas interjected, "it would make sense that only the bridge crew and engineering survived. The bridge and engineering have separate backup environmental controls. It would simplify any questions. And the fewer people involved, the longer we will be able to keep our plans secret."

"I like that plan," Blake said. "A famous man from Earth once said that three men can keep a secret only if two of them are dead. We have to be prepared for leaks."

Captain Galanos grimaced. "I will agree to this. It is not much of a hardship to be confined to the Merlin."

"Okay, then when do we contact Helike?"

"Tomorrow."

Chapter 15   Helike

Catie met Captain Galanos in the command center on the Merlin. It had a duplicate of each console from the bridge. Captain McAvoy was going to listen in from the bridge. Petty Officer Fotopoulos joined them so that the communication would appear consistent with Captain Galanos opening communication from the bridge of the Geraki.

"Mission control, this is Captain Galanos of the Geraki. Over." The delay was an hour since they were still six AUs away, two weeks at their 0.2G deceleration profile.

"That's all you're going to say?" Petty Officer Fotopoulos asked.

"We don't know who's listening. We need to know more before we share what we know."

"Thanks for explaining, ma'am."

"Geraki, this is mission control. What is your status? Over."

"We were disabled by an EMP event. We have initiated repairs and are returning to Helike. Over."

"Geraki, your communication delay indicates that you are within six AUs of Helike, please explain. Over."

"We required assistance with our repairs. An alien starship was entering our system and came to our aid. They have been very supportive. They have provided a tow back to Helike while we work on the repairs. As you can tell, they have advanced engines capable of constant 0.2G acceleration. Over."

"Geraki, please standby, we'll recommence communications in two hours. Mission control out."

"Not very chatty are they," Catie said.

"I think advanced alien starship might have been too much."

"Do you think they mean two hours after we received the message or after they sent it?"

"Who knows?"

"Geraki, this is mission control, please provide more information on the aliens and include command codes. Over."

"Ah, they now want to make sure I'm who I say I am, and that you are not holding a gun to my head." Captain Galanos typed the codes into the communication console. "Codes transmitted. These aliens appear much like us. They belong to a league of planets that engage in interstellar trade. They have only shared a little about their technology, but it appears to be well advanced of ours. They also appear to be quite friendly. Over."

"You forgot charming."

"Ah, maybe I will add it next time."

"Geraki, this is mission control. Please provide the force composition of aliens. What is your arrival time here in orbit? Will the aliens be accompanying you to Helike? Over."

Captain Galanos looked at Catie. Catie nodded, letting her know they were still on plan.

"Mission control, this is Captain Galanos. The alien starship is called Merlin. It is one hundred fifty meters by seventy meters, ellipsoid in shape. We have little data on their arms. I have seen one shuttle, twenty-four meters in length, and several fighters, thirty meters in length. The fighters appear to be armed with plasma cannons. We will arrive in two weeks and the aliens will accompany us into orbit. Over."

"Geraki, mission control. We ask that the alien starship orbit at 50 thousand kilometers, over."

"That puts you above our geosync orbits and all of our satellites."

Catie nodded. "That's only a three-hour flight for us to land; add another twenty minutes to the trip when we're traveling up from the surface; we can manage that."

Captain Galanos was surprised that they could reach 50 thousand kilometers in just three hours and twenty minutes. Shaking her head, she replied, "Mission control, Captain Galanos, the aliens have agreed to that orbit. They will park their starship at fifty thousand kilometers over the North Pole. Over."

"It will be interesting to see how they deal with a non-orbital parking."

"Geraki, mission control. Explain 'park'. Over."

"Mission control. Park is a geostationary orbit. Over."

Catie had insisted that Captain Galanos use park for geostationary. She suspected they were still struggling with a geostationary position above the North Pole; that meant they would not be orbiting the planet, so they would have to counter its gravitational pull with their engines. She wanted it to sound like something they commonly did, which it was. But now mission control knew it.

"Geraki, mission control, acknowledged. Out."

"That's it?" Catie asked. "No more questions."

"I'm sure they'll spend the next two weeks thinking some up."

"Alright, now we're ready for phase two."

"Catie, I'm still not comfortable with this," Marc said. Everyone was in Catie's day cabin to review the plans. "What about viruses and germs?"

"Dr. Moreau has given us a shot to boost our immune system. And she's loaded us up with Dr. Metra's anti-virus nanites. We're going to keep as much distance as we can between us and any other Helikens. It's a small risk for the week we'll be there. We'll get a full scan when we get back."

"But why you?"

"Daddy, who else could pull off this look?" Catie was dressed in blue capris pants and a peach blouse. Dr. Moreau had done some mild cosmetic work to make her look even younger than her seventeen years.

"Why is it necessary to have someone who looks like a teenager?"

"Because everyone ignores teenagers, even the Helikens."

Marc just shook his head. He didn't like Catie taking chances, but there was nothing he could do about it without destroying their relationship. "Morgan, Cristina, you'd better keep her safe!"

"We will." Morgan was her normal self, but Cristina had also had some minor work done. Unfortunately for Morgan and Marc, it only brought her apparent age down to eighteen, if you were being gracious. Nothing could soften the hard look in her eyes.

"You're sure you can make it in without being detected?" Captain Galanos asked.

"Yes. Don't worry, we'll have Ensign Nikitas back to you before you make orbit."

"Do you have everything you need?" Captain McAvoy asked.

"Yes," Catie patted her duffle bag. "Now, everyone knows the plan. We'll establish communications with you one or two days after we arrive. We should complete our mission within a week and we will rendezvous with the Merlin just before you park at the North Pole."

Catie nodded to everyone and headed for the Lynx, followed by Morgan, Cristina, Ensign Nikitas, and Lieutenant Racine. At the Lynx, they were met by Lieutenant Racine's four handpicked Marines. They would provide backup if things went south, but otherwise, they would have the joy of spending two weeks in the Lynx.

"What's with the big bag?" Lieutenant Racine asked as they climbed aboard the Lynx.

"Just some toys I had made up, plus what we need to tie ADI into their communication network. I'm trying to plan ahead."

"Do you want to share anything about your toys?"

"Not yet. I don't want to influence anyone's thinking about how we should handle things until they've had a chance to form their own ideas."

Morgan laughed and gave Lieutenant Racine a smile. *"Just go with it. She'll share when she's ready,"* Morgan messaged.

"You're going to fly this thing?" Ensign Nikitas asked as Catie headed to the cockpit.

"Yes. Do you want to join me?"

"If you don't mind. It would be interesting to see how one flies one of these, I never got a chance to see when we went back to get Dr. Rubis."

"Then come on, there's plenty of room."

Morgan winked at Cristina as Ensign Nikitas and Catie disappeared into the cockpit.

Catie piloted the Lynx out of the flight bay. It would take just over three days to reach Helike, giving them ten days to investigate without anyone knowing they were on the planet other than Ensign Prince Nikitas's close friend who was going to let them use his beach house. Of course, the friend didn't know that yet.

Even though ADI was perfectly capable of flying the Lynx, Catie couldn't resist taking the opportunity to get some flying in. It wasn't a dogfight, but at least it was an unusual flight plan. She took the Lynx well below the ecliptic so she could approach the South Pole of the planet on a steep descent. It was weird to fly the Lynx top first instead of like a plane, but that at least gave everyone gravity for the trip. Catie enjoyed having Ensign Nikitas beside her during the flight. They chatted more about how they'd both grown up as well as what they like to do for entertainment.

"It just looks like a small, blue marble," Ensign Nikitas said once they were in view of Helike.

"Yeah, we're still a long way away. We'll be closing in from above the South Pole, so I'm not sure if it's going to be much of a view."

"It won't. We'll see the icecap, but most of the landmasses are toward the north. But we should get a better view once you start flying north."

"Nope, by the time we get close to the shore, we'll be flying twenty meters above the deck."

"Oh, I thought you were invisible to radar."

"Mostly, but we don't want to take a chance on a small radar blip alerting someone, nor do we want to risk a visual sighting."

"I was hoping to be able to show you my beautiful planet."

"You can when we come back on the Merlin. Then we'll be trying to be seen."

Ensign Nikitas sat back in the copilot's seat and sighed, "What a mess."

"We still don't know what's behind all this."

"I know, and that's what worries me. It's easy to fight the enemies you can see, but the ones you can't and don't even know exist are tough."

"We should go back and get some sleep. ADI can fly us. We want to be well-rested when we land tomorrow."

They both moved back into the main cabin. Morgan waved at Catie and messaged, *"Were you two making out up there?"*

"Morgan!"

"Just checking. LOL."

"Wait until our next sparring session!"

"My knee already hurts."

◆ ◆ ◆

Morgan had volunteered to be the cook since, besides Catie, she was the only one familiar with the Lynx's galley. Of course, anyone could have reheated the prepackaged meals they were eating.

"Are you practicing for your next career?" Cristina asked.

"You want your meal with or without spit?"

"Without. Come on, you'd make a good flight attendant."

"I thought you said without."

"Sorry, touchy subject?"

"Not really, just coming up on a change. I'll talk with you later. Ensign, here's your meal."

Ensign Nikitas lowered his tray table and moved to allow Morgan to put his meal down. "You people sure know how to travel. This is as nice as being on one of our airlines. It's nothing like the Geraki."

"Were the meals that bad?" Catie asked.

"Not bad, just boring. Eating the same twelve meals for four months wears on you."

"I can imagine."

"Okay people, eat up. We've got four hours before we land. You need to be ready to go by then," Lieutenant Racine barked. "Although only our four operatives are going to leave the Lynx, we have to be prepared for anything, and I don't want any last-minute issues to delay our response time. I expect you to be geared up and ready at any time.

"Princess, that goes for you, too. We want you four to be out of the Lynx as soon as you dock her. We need to minimize our topside exposure," Racine messaged Catie.

"Yes, Ma'am!" Catie messaged back, giving the Lieutenant a salute as she did.

Catie had the Lynx start a slowly expanding spiral as she brought it down over the South Pole of Helike. She started their descent with zero velocity to minimize any friction against the Lynx's hull. She wasn't worried about the heat but wanted to avoid any light show that could be spotted from Helike. Three hours later they were approaching the surface of the ocean.

Catie leveled the Lynx off and starting following the course she'd worked out with Ensign Nikitas. The high-power telescope in the Lynx's nosecone provided a view of where they were going, and its passive radar was taking advantage of the EM energy from the various Heliken radio broadcasts and radar installations to provide a view of what was in the air around them. All that information and the fact that they were in the least populated area of Helike allowed Catie and ADI to avoid any detection by the few craft that were in the sky in their general area.

Catie kept slowing them down and lowering their altitude as they closed on the shores of the continent Spitiva and the border of the state of Helike.

"Prepare to launch the surveillance probe," Catie ordered as they entered the bay where Ensign Nikitas's friend's shoreside villa was. They wanted to get a probe in the air where it could provide guidance and surveillance before they took the Lynx beneath the surface.

"Probe ready!"

"Launch it."

"Probe away. . . . We're sealed up again."

"Everyone strap in. It might get a bit bumpy."

Catie gave them two minutes to get back to their seats before she took the Lynx down to the surface. The ride was a bit bumpy as she slowed the Lynx down on the surface of the water. Finally, it had slowed enough that she could submerge it. The ride immediately smoothed out.

"All right. We've got one hour before we dock. Last chance to hit the head," Lieutenant Racine called out.

ADI had printed them three sets of IDs each. The first set was for Spitiva, Ensign Nikitas's home, using his ID as a sample. They also had a set for each of their prime suspects, Polemistia and Agriosa. These were made using IDs from two of the scientists from the Geraki.

It was midnight when the Lynx surfaced next to the private dock of Ensign Nikitas's friend. The surveillance probe had led the way in and showed the surrounding area was quiet. Only a few lights glowed from the villa and it was quite a distance along the shore before the next villa's dock.

Morgan and Lieutenant Racine had argued about how to best case the villa; eventually, they agreed that the smallest footprint was best. So

Cristina and Morgan scoped out the area while Ensign Nikitas and Catie went to the back door to gain entrance.

"Here goes nothing!" Ensign Nikitas said as he entered the code into the security system. He could only hope that his friend hadn't changed it since he'd last visited.

Beep, Beep.

"We're in!"

"Check it out. Drop a few pucks and keep in touch, we'll tell you when we're finished with the outside," Morgan messaged.

"I remember," Catie messaged back.

"Good, then do it!"

It took twenty minutes for Morgan and Cristina to finish casing the outside of the villa. By the time they were ready to come inside, Catie and Ensign Nikitas had covered the interior.

"Okay, take a rest," Morgan said. "I'll take the first watch."

"I can do the second," Catie said.

"No, Cristina and I will handle the watches. You two have to be fresh in the morning, no yawns when you're out buying the cellphones."

Reluctantly, Catie agreed with Morgan's logic and headed to the bedroom she'd selected for herself. Ensign Nikitas had picked the room across the hall. Morgan and Cristina had rooms on each side of Catie's.

"Time to go," Morgan announced after cleaning their breakfast dishes. She noticed that Catie had opted to sit right next to Ensign Nikitas.

"Are you sure all four of us should go?" Catie asked.

"Yes," Morgan replied. "It's either all four of us or just Nikitas and Tina." Morgan knew Catie really wanted to go. But she wasn't going to allow her to go without backup.

"Okay."

"Do you think it will look weird if there are three women riding with him?" Cristina asked.

"That's not unusual," Ensign Nikitas said.

"Maybe not, but do you have the chops to have three good-looking babes like us riding with you?"

Ensign Nikitas blushed and stuttered.

"Leave him alone," Catie messaged in his defense. "We should go now."

They followed Ensign Nikitas out the door. There was a nice, silver sedan in the garage. "Kind of looks like a big Mercedes," Cristina said.

"It is a nice car," Morgan replied as she examined it. Then she placed one of the larger surveillance pucks in the middle of its roof.

"Won't that fall off?" Ensign Nikitas asked.

Morgan shrugged and nodded her head at the puck, indicating that he should see how well it stuck. Ensign Nikitas reached over and grabbed the puck, tugging at it to try and break its grip on the roof of the car.

"Will it ever come off?"

Morgan smiled at him and reached over and tapped the puck, then picked it up. She placed it back on the roof and checked the four cameras in her HUD. They had decided that wraparound sunglasses were not that unusual so had opted for the better specs while on Helike. Morgan nodded to herself as each camera showed a reasonable view around the car.

"You don't think a big black puck in the middle of the silver roof will look odd?"

"Naw." Morgan keyed in the command and the puck changed color until it matched the roof of the car.

"Oh, you could have told me it could do that."

"What fun would that be?" Okay, let's get this show on the road.

"I should have asked; do you want to drive?" Ensign Nikitas asked.

"I don't know how," Catie answered.

"What? Delphi doesn't have some stupid law against women drivers, do they?"

"*No*, but since I was thirteen, I've either lived in a floating city where cars aren't allowed, on a space station, or on a starship. I did once drive jeeps in the desert, but there weren't any roads and only one other jeep to worry about."

"Maybe I can teach you."

Morgan interrupted, "Not on this mission. We don't want anything drawing attention to ourselves."

"I guess having a wreck might be a problem," Ensign Nikitas said, laughing at the thought. Knowing how to drive wouldn't be enough since that didn't mean that one knew the details of driving a strange car on a strange planet with unfamiliar rules of the road.

Catie started to get into the passenger seat next to Ensign Nikitas. "No, Catie, you're in the back with me. Cristina, you're in front with Nikitas."

"Let's go. A nice busy mall is what we want."

"Okay." Ensign Nikitas put the car into gear and backed out of the garage. He keyed it closed and then turned the car so they went around the circular driveway and onto the road.

"This is a private community, there are only twelve villas here along the coast, so it's very secluded. The coastal road runs by it. We'll take it down to the town where the mall is. You'll get a nice view of the coastline just before we reach the town."

"Who else lives in the community?"

"They're all vacation homes. It's a bit cool right now, so I suspect that nobody, other than the caretakers, is in the homes."

"Why wasn't there a caretaker at your friend's villa?"

"He only has his come in once a week to clean and check things out. I've left a note on the mailbox telling them that we're visiting and will take care of ourselves."

"Won't that be strange since you're supposed to be in space?"

"I used my brother's name. They won't ask any questions; they'll get paid anyway."

They'd turned and were heading south on the road. There were trees on both sides creating a feeling of seclusion.

"No traffic?"

"Not much around here. There's a big highway just two kilometers to the west, most people use that road unless they're staying in one of the villas. There are three more private communities up north of us. This area is a state park, and in winter it's not too busy. Get ready, we'll exit the trees in two hundred meters and you'll get a view of the beach and coastline."

"Nice view," Cristina said as they exited the trees. "I could see living here."

"Yeah, like you could afford it. What does one of those villas cost?" Morgan asked.

"Twenty-five million." Their Comms had translated the cost into dollars.

"Oh, I guess I won't be moving in anytime soon. But Catie, you could, and I could come work for you."

"I'm not moving to Helike."

"Damn."

"Hey, you live in a floating city, with a private beach area. Why is this any better?"

"It's more exclusive."

"Come on?"

"Just dreaming. I'd never move Tiff, so it can't happen."

"Who's Tiff," Ensign Nikitas asked.

"My baby sister."

"Why would you have to move her?"

Catie nudged the back of Ensign Nikitas' seat to let him know he was entering forbidden territory.

"No parents, we're all we have."

"I'm sorry to hear that. But she's lucky to have you."

"This town was originally my 4th grandfather's vacation estate. They moved farther south where the weather's warmer and opened it up for some of the wealthier citizens of Spitiva to live here. The town was established around one hundred fifty years ago. It really hasn't grown much since then. Most of the houses were originally part of the estate. The main house is now a hotel that caters to wealthy people on vacation. The mall is the only recent addition, it was added fifty years ago. It's bigger now, but not much."

"It's quaint," Morgan said. She had been barely listening as she kept scanning the four camera views in her HUD. Cristina was watching what was happening in front of the car from her vantage point in the front seat. They were a bit more nervous now that there were two lanes and a car was driving next to them. Morgan gave a sigh of relief when Ensign Nikitas slowed down letting it drive on by them. He'd picked up on Morgan's tension and was now driving a bit more like a security guy, keeping distance between their car and the neighboring cars.

"Okay, here we are," Ensign Nikitas said. "Is this good for parking?"

"It's fine," Morgan said. "Catie, let Cristina and me get out first."

"Okay."

"Do we want to shop for the phones first or clothes?" Cristina asked.

"We'll have to go to four places to get the phones, it would look weird to go in one place and buy phones for four different carriers."

"Right. Then we'll just mix them in. Let's go get the first one now, there's a kiosk right over there."

"We also need to get money," Catie reminded Morgan. "We're supposed to sell those gold coins ADI had made up. We're lucky she found a show that talked about them so she could copy them." ADI had recorded lots of the various broadcasts using the probes they'd sent out. She'd managed to find one that described in detail the gold coins minted in Polemistia twenty years ago. Since the coins weren't really collectibles, the buyer would only care about the gold's purity. They had decided to sell eight coins today, which would net them about five thousand dollars. Just enough to cover their buying spree on clothes and phones.

"Pay attention people, remember one of the reasons we're out here is to learn how to walk and act like native Helikens," Morgan messaged everyone. *"Catie, quit walking like you're on the flight deck. You're a slovenly teenager."* Their Comms translated Morgan's message into an audio rendition, matching her voice and tone almost perfectly.

"Yes, mother!"

"Cristina, don't look like you're on the prowl."

"Are you really trying to teach me how to infiltrate a community?"

"No, just reminding you that you're trying to play an eighteen-year-old girl, not a twenty-two-year-old hooker."

"You just wait 'til I get you on the mat!"

"That was a busy day," Morgan said when they finally got back to the villa.

"Hopefully we have what we need," Catie replied.

Ensign Nikitas pulled the car into the garage and keyed the door closed behind them. He and the three women exited the car and went into the villa.

"I'll make us a snack," Morgan volunteered and headed to the kitchen.

Catie sat down with her Comm and the four cell phones they had purchased. They were each from a different carrier. She unpackaged them and read the set-up instructions, well, ADI read them to her. Then she went to her room and grabbed her bag of tricks, returning to the living room where she set up her toys on the coffee table to work on the adaptors. They'd used the cellphones that the Helikens had had on the Geraki to make the appropriate connectors. Although they had been destroyed by the EM pulse, they had been useful. By dissecting them, the engineer on the Merlin with ADI's help had been able to make the necessary parts to help ADI link into the local cell network and eventually the internet.

"Okay, ADI, you're connected. Let me know if you need anything else."

"I will, Cer Catie. Enjoy your snack."

"How are you communicating with her?" Ensign Nikitas asked.

"We have a link from our Comms to the surveillance probe outside. Then it has a link to the Lynx sitting on the bottom of your bay. The Lynx has a link to the Merlin, and the Merlin has a link to ADI."

"I see," he said nodding his head. "And where is ADI?"

"She's everywhere," Catie said.

"Never mind."

"Here we are," Morgan said as she brought a bowl of chips and some kind of dip into the room. "Water and sodas are on the counter."

"No beer?" Cristina asked.

"Not while we're on the mission. We need to stay sharp."

"Ahh, the sacrifices we have to make. What is this dip?"

"Something like guacamole," Morgan said. "It was in the refrigerator. Premade stuff, but it should taste good."

The four of them sat around the coffee table, with the chips and dip placed on the side away from Catie's construction with the phones.

"This must have a lot of fat in it, it tastes so good," Cristina said.

"Well, you could use a little fat on you," Morgan said.

"You think? I wonder if gaining a few pounds would make my breasts bigger?"

"The doctors already made them as big as they're going to get with fat," Catie said.

"What?" Ensign Nikitas looked surprised.

"When Cristina went undercover on Onisiwo, the doctors made her look like an Onisiwoen and they also made her breasts bigger so she'd be sexier. When they changed her back, she didn't let them reduce her breasts."

"So they can make them bigger using fat?"

"Yes, it's pretty natural. Mommy says she carries two extra kilos because otherwise, her breasts would shrink."

"She does, does she? Why doesn't she just have them enlarged?"

"I'm going to go to my room and read," Ensign Nikitas said.

The three women laughed as he walked away.

"He's lucky we weren't talking about our periods," Morgan said.

"What periods," Cristina said. "Oh, did we tell the Heliken women about the nanites?"

"Dr. Moreau took care of it. She got them to swear to secrecy. It wasn't a problem, especially since Captain Galanos was getting ready to start hers. She was really happy to avoid that," Catie said.

"Good, now back to breast size. Your mother hasn't had hers augmented?"

"No, she could but she says Zane likes her soft curves, so the extra two kilos works out."

"But can our doctors augment them?"

"Sure, I heard Mommy and Dr. Metra talking about it once. They can give you a treatment that tricks your body into storing fat in your breasts, which is good for about half a cup size. That's what they did for Cristina."

"What if you want more?" Morgan asked.

"Come on, Morgan, you can't want bigger breasts."

"Not me, Tracey."

"Does Tracey want bigger breasts or do you want Tracey to have bigger breasts?"

"She does. She's barely an A cup and is very self-conscious about it."

"Well, they can use nanites and stem cells to add breast tissue, that can give you a full cup size difference, but it takes two months, otherwise you get stretch marks."

"And if you want more?"

"Morgan?"

"Now I'm just curious."

"I think they'd send you to a shrink first," Catie said. "I think they can do two cup sizes, but it takes a long time."

"And more?" Cristina asked.

"Then they'd definitely send you to a shrink. I don't think they'll go over a C-cup. Maybe a D if you were a really big woman."

"So aspiring porn stars aren't going to be running to Delphi City for boob jobs?"

"I'm pretty sure that won't be happening."

Morgan made them a nice meal for dinner, then they all hit the sack. Who knew what ADI would come up with for them to deal with the next day?

Chapter 16   The Search Begins

"ADI, what have you learned?" Catie asked the next morning over breakfast.

"I have located two places where you need to tap into their networks. The first is twenty-two kilometers from here, the second is eighty-four."

"Where are they located?" Morgan asked.

ADI brought up a view of the areas. "This is from their global mapping, like Google Maps. It's a year old, but it should give you an understanding of the areas."

"So where do we need to tie in?"

"I think it would be this cell tower," Ensign Nikitas said as he pointed to a large, palm-like tree. "The tree is fake; we make them disguise the towers so they blend in."

"Okay, so that means we have to scale the tower?"

"I don't think so. ADI, do you want us to tie into the fiber optic cables linking the tower, or into the cell transmitter?"

"The internet link would be best. But to do that you'll need to purchase some hardware."

"What hardware?"

"I've sent you the list and the closest place to buy it. It is two hundred kilometers away."

"Road trip!" Cristina yelled.

"Did you include the tools we will need?" Catie asked.

"As if you need to ask."

"Okay, we go get the tools, find a place to make the hardware we need so all we have to do is attach it, then we'll hit the towers on the way back. We'll need to time things so it's dark when we get to the first tower."

◆ ◆ ◆

They stopped at another coin store to get more cash, exchanging eight more gold coins. After that, they picked up all the parts and tools they needed from Helike's version of Radio Shack, a nerd's paradise of computer parts and electronic components.

"Where can I work?" Catie asked.

"You can't do it in the car?"

"No way!"

"We can rent a motel room," Ensign Nikitas said.

"Oh, look who's trying to establish a reputation. Three women in a motel room," Cristina teased, breaking into a fit of giggles.

"I'm . . . ah . . ."

"Just ignore her. Responding just encourages her," Catie said as she punched Cristina on the shoulder.

"Come on, you have to admit he's going to have to pull this off."

"He can rent two rooms," Morgan said. "Now can it, we've got work to do."

"Did you see how red his ears turned?" Morgan messaged Cristina to take the sting off her rebuke.

"Come on, Tina. Lighten up. You're going to get him so flustered he'll wreck the car," Catie messaged.

"Okay, I'll restrict my comments to times when he's not driving."

"There's one around the corner," Catie said.

Ensign Nikitas drove into the motel's parking lot and parked in front of reception. "Anyone coming in with me?"

Catie started to open her door. "Catie, stay; Cristina, you go."

"Why?!" Catie demanded.

"Because you look sixteen, we don't need someone calling the police on our good prince here."

Catie sat back in the seat with a huff while Cristina gave a big smile, then crawled out of the car and followed Ensign Nikitas into the lobby. Ensign Nikitas walked up to the counter and rang the bell. It took a minute before the clerk came out of the back office. The guy leered at Cristina.

"Ugh, . . ."

"Two rooms," Cristina said, careful to hide her mouth from the clerk since her Comm was doing the talking.

"What do you need two rooms for?" the clerk asked, grinning at her.

"Because we want two rooms. Do you have them available?" Ensign Nikitas said, finally waking up.

"Sure."

"And can we have two that have a connecting door?" Cristina added.

"Yeah. How many nights?"

"Just one."

"Eighty dracu."

Ensign Nikitas paid cash and received the two keys.

"They're around the corner. Just leave your keys in the rooms when you leave."

They left the office. "What a jerk," Cristina said. "Did you see the way he looked at me?"

"Yeah, maybe we should have picked a nicer motel."

"No, he didn't even ask for ID; this place is perfect. Just be careful what you touch."

◆ ◆ ◆

Catie cleared everything off the desk and set up to work.

"Why do you have to tie into the network, can't ADI just use the phones?" Cristina asked.

"No," Catie rolled her eyes. "The data we got from the phones lets her access the network but the phones are traceable. These have quantum relays in them so she can have direct access through Merlin. We don't want anyone to be able to determine that one person is doing all the hacking she'll be doing."

"I do not hack! I'm an *artiste*."

"Hacking?" Ensign Nikitas asked.

"Accessing the network and data through unconventional means."

"How long will it take?"

"Don't know. ADI has to have Merlin do a lot of the work since she has limited bandwidth."

"Why can't Merlin do it for her?"

"Because Merlin is an AI, while ADI is a DI. AIs have to follow specific directions, while a DI is autonomous, it can make decisions. ADI is very independent."

"Isn't that dangerous?"

"No. ADI still has to follow certain rules. They're like laws. So it limits how independent she can be."

"If she's autonomous, can't she ignore the rules?"

"No. Her programming has very hard constraints around the few rules she has."

"Like what?"

"Like if I tell her I want privacy, she cannot access the recordings made of me by the surveillance pucks, or cameras, or my Comm."

"Why don't you just turn off the recording?"

Catie sighed. "Because everything is recorded and analyzed to make sure there isn't a danger to me or Delphi. If the analysis trips an alarm, then a more sophisticated process is set up to review the data. If that process determines that there is a threat, then ADI or Merlin can look at the data and decide what needs to be done. If it's a false alarm, then they have to forget what they read and store the data in a protected area of memory."

"Sounds complicated."

"It is, but it works and helps keep everyone safe. Your world has cameras all over the place; what constrains who can access them, and for what reason?"

"We have laws."

"Just like us, but we have the advantage of automatic analysis to alert us if something is happening."

"So, if someone is breaking the law, they'll automatically get arrested?"

"No. Unless it involves murder, rape, or kidnapping, or an immediate threat to the safety of the ship, city, or space station; a warrant is required to access any recording."

"Why?"

"Stop; all three of you go into the other room!"

"Why do we have to leave, he's the one asking all the questions?"

"Because I can hear you two making comments. I need to concentrate."

"Jeez, I forgot she was a princess," Cristina whispered to Morgan.

"I heard that!"

That evening they started their return trip. They stopped twice to connect the new hardware into the relay connections in the comm towers. ADI started work immediately.

"ADI, should we move to Agriosa?"

"I recommend sending Lieutenant Racine and her team to put our network taps in Agriosa. I've identified two remote towers that will give me the access we need. They should be able to fly the Lynx into the areas and make the changes without being detected. You should go to Polemistia, that will maximize our time where we believe the most likely suspects are from."

"Okay, we can have Racine drop us off before they head to Agriosa."

When they joined Lieutenant Racine on the Lynx, she wasn't happy.

"I don't like the idea of you being out there without backup!"

"We'll be okay. We won't do anything but get ourselves established in a hotel until you're back."

"To do that, you'll have to use your IDs, that exposes you."

"We'll only use one ID. That will minimize the exposure. And ADI is confident that the IDs are good."

"I know, but what . . ."

"Lieutenant, you're not going to win," Morgan said. "Why don't you focus on being as fast as you can. Tina and I will watch after Catie. We'll make sure she's safe."

Lieutenant Racine clenched her jaw but nodded her head. "No unnecessary risks!"

"That's always my motto, ma'am."

Chapter 17   Into the Lion's Den

The Lynx dropped the team off at a deserted fishing pier on the south side of the capital city. They would have to make their own way into the city.

"No unnecessary risks!" was Lieutenant Racine's last comment before the Lynx sank back beneath the water.

Morgan just waved to her, then set the surveillance probe to follow her at forty meters altitude. Once she had reviewed the area via the probe's infrared cameras, she decided it was safe to proceed. "Let's move it."

"Bossy, isn't she," Ensign Nikitas said. He was apparently getting more comfortable around Morgan.

"Yeah, and she's just a sergeant. I'm a full lieutenant and a princess, and she still bosses me around."

"And you're about to get my foot in your ass," Morgan growled.

"See!"

"The communication tower is just down the road, fifty meters," ADI informed them. She also let them know that she was now able to access the probe's quantum relay and that their Comms were tied into it.

"Do we just need to do the one?" Catie asked.

"For now. I'll know soon if we have to do another."

The team lugged the baggage the fifty meters to the tower. It was far enough off the road that Morgan felt comfortable having Catie and Ensign Nikitas take care of inserting the tap while she and Cristina covered them from the road.

Once they had the tap installed, Catie and Ensign Nikitas joined Cristina and Morgan by the road.

"Okay, how are we going to explain our luggage and being out here in the middle of nowhere?" Cristina asked.

"You're the undercover operative, what do you suggest?"

"Catie, what is the surveillance probe telling you about the area?"

Catie was now watching the probe's feed along with ADI so that Morgan and Cristina would be able to maintain situational awareness and avoid attention tunneling.

"There's not a lot around us."

"Any houses that are dark?"

"Two houses, one just up ahead about three hundred meters," ADI informed them.

"Good, then we'll go there, call a cab, and have him meet us out front."

The group carried their luggage down the road and set up at the end of the driveway for the house. Ensign Nikitas called a cab and they waited.

When the cab arrived, they loaded up their luggage and he gave the cabbie the name of the hotel they'd agreed on. The three women crowded into the back seat while Ensign Nikitas sat in front with the driver; this insured that their need to use their Comms to speak wouldn't be noticeable.

"Why are you going to a hotel, you're not that far out of town?" the cabbie asked.

"We're going to a convention. We don't want to have to make the trip every night. You know how late the parties go."

"Yeah, I've heard that. What's the convention about?"

"It's a sales convention."

"For what?"

"Luxury condos."

"Must be good money selling those."

"Yep."

"He's asking for a big tip!" Morgan messaged.

"You all four live back at that house?"

"No. We're from up north. It's my uncle's house. We got in early so we could see the sights before the convention."

"He's asking a lot of questions. Should we dose him?" Catie asked.

177

"He's just trying to be friendly, working on that tip," Morgan messaged back.

"Have him drop us out front, not at reception," Cristina messaged Ensign Nikitas.

After a few more minutes of inane chatter, they arrived at the hotel. The driver dropped them at the corner just before the ramp to reception. Nikitas gave the cabbie a good tip and waved him off.

"Why here?" he asked.

"Just wait." Cristina left her luggage with the others and headed up toward reception. She looked around and spotted the bar. She walked into the bar and checked out the crowd. It was late, coming up on midnight. There were quite a few patrons still in the bar seated at various tables. But what Cristina wanted was one sitting at the bar. Finally, she saw what she was looking for and moved up beside the guy.

"Hello," her Comm purred for her.

"Hel...lo," the guy slurred back.

"Are you meeting someone?"

"I'm mee...ting you."

"Are you staying here?"

"No, I, *hic,* was just here for the con...vention. I'm supposed to go home now."

"Why don't we get a room?"

The guy looked at her with glazed eyes. He wasn't sure he'd heard her right, but he didn't want to upset the arrangement. "Sure."

"Come on. Let's go." Cristina led him to the reception desk.

"We need a room," she said. "A suite if you have one?"

"Sir, are you alright?"

"...course I am."

"Give him your ID and credit card, honey."

The guy dug out his wallet and enthusiastically handed the clerk his ID and credit card.

"How long will you be staying?"

"Three days."

"Very well." The clerk ran the guy's credit card.

"I'm not sure if you're okay with this, but I left my purse in the car. Can I pay with these; he doesn't want any charges to show up on his card?" Cristina asked as she put four gold coins on the counter.

The clerk's eyes went wide. "Certainly, ma'am. Those are good anywhere."

"I think they're worth eight hundred each." Cristina intentionally undervalued them by almost one hundred each.

"Of course. I'll credit you thirty-two hundred to your suite. Here's your key."

"Greedy bastard!"

Cristina took the key and messaged Morgan to meet her at the door to the lobby. When they got there, she handed the guy over to her.

"Dose him and dump him in a cab."

"Do we even need to dose him?"

"Better safe than sorry. We're in 1283, I'll go up and wait for you."

◆ ◆ ◆

"Good move with the drunk," Catie told Cristina. "Racine will be proud of you."

"Maybe, but more likely she'll ask me why I didn't think about it during the planning session."

"She is hard to please," Morgan said.

"Nice digs. How are we going to split up?" Catie asked.

"You're in that room, Tina or I will bunk with you when we're not on duty. The ensign gets his own room."

"I'm willing to bunk with him if that simplifies things," Cristina said.

"Tina!"

"Hey, he's not driving."

"I think my plan's the best." Morgan glared at Cristina. Out of the corner of her eye, she could see Ensign Nikitas blush.

"Just trying to help."

"We can tell. Now, what's the status on the room?"

"I put thirty-two hundred on account, the room is six hundred a night. Which reminds me, I had to use gold, so we need more cash."

"There's a coin dealer just around the corner. I'll go over there and get us some cash in the morning," Ensign Nikitas said. "I should be able to do ten coins since this is such a big city."

"I'm hungry, do we go down to the restaurant or do room service?"

"Room service." ... "Restaurant." ... "Room service." ... "Restaurant."

Morgan looked at Catie and Ensign Nikitas, the two who had voted for the restaurant. "Cabin fever?"

"It would be nice to get out. And won't it look weird for four of us to order room service?"

"Not really. That's why people reserve suites. But sure, let's do the restaurant. But remember, you need to be discreet when you're talking, I'll be watching."

"So will I," ADI added.

They had to eat in the bar, the restaurant had closed at 0100. They managed a table in the corner. Morgan gave a subtle shake of her head when the waiter asked if they wanted a wine menu. *"No alcohol,"* she reminded everyone.

The menu was nice. Instead of just bar food, it was a shortened version of the restaurant menu. Once everyone had ordered, the three women made a beeline for the restroom, leaving Ensign Nikitas to hold the table and his bladder.

"Kozma, tell us about the city. How often have you been here?" Catie asked Ensign Nikitas.

"I've been here quite often. We used to visit my uncle once or twice a year. Of course, I wasn't quite as free to move about back then."

"Do you mean you had some head of security following you around and spoiling your fun?" Catie gave Morgan a wicked smile.

"You could say that. What I remember most was sailing on the bay. We would race our yacht. It was very exciting. Have you ever been sailing?"

"Not really. We have a big motor yacht we spend a lot of time on, but I've only been on a sailboat once. Actually, it was a four-masted schooner."

"Oh, Academy exercise?"

"Yeah. It was interesting, I'm not sure I'd say it was fun. We had to figure everything out for ourselves."

"Wasn't that dangerous?"

"Not really. There were four experienced sailors on board, but they wouldn't help. They were there to make sure we didn't wreck the boat or get anyone hurt."

"How did you manage?"

"I was the navigator; I'd done that on our yacht. But I was really impressed with my friend, Miranda. She was the cadet commander, and when the sailors told us we were on our own she took charge. The first thing she did was ask who had experience. It was interesting to see someone who didn't know what to do, take charge, and get everything lined up and organized by using the people around her that did know."

"Tell us more about the city?" Morgan asked.

That night Morgan took the first watch, so Catie and Cristina went into their room to get ready for bed.

"Tina, do you have to keep teasing Kozma?"

"He knows it's just fun. And someone needs to toughen him up. He's obviously led a sheltered life, not unlike you. He's got to learn to take it. You just watch, after another day or two, he'll be giving as good as he gets."

"I hope so."

◆ ◆ ◆

Later that night, actually the next morning, Morgan pinged Cristina's Comm to let her know it was her turn at guard.

"You know he's totally hot for her," Cristina told Morgan when she came out of the room.

"I know, and she's totally hot for him. Sometimes I think they're going to explode."

"That'd be funny to watch."

"Girl, you be nice."

"I would never do anything that would hurt Catie."

"Right, but remember she's emotionally vulnerable. You know she's never had a successful romantic relationship. So don't mess this one up."

"What should we do?"

"I keep vacillating between making them both take a cold shower each morning and locking them in a room so they get it over with."

"I vote for the room. That is unless I get to be the one that makes sure he takes his shower."

◆ ◆ ◆

The next morning everyone was anxious to learn what ADI had discovered in her foray into the Polemistian internet.

"ADI, what have you learned?" Catie asked, starting off the morning briefing, well, the mid-morning briefing.

"I'm making progress, but it's slow. It takes a long time to figure out how to get into the systems. I don't have that much access yet, but I'm getting there."

"How are you doing this?" Ensign Nikitas asked.

"I'm working my way up the chain. I start with the small players and work to get into their systems. I can be aggressive, accessing their social media, pretending to be someone else, and eventually, I figure out their passwords. Then I use their systems to spy on more important people. When they have their phones out at work, I can grab the camera and spy on the people around them."

"But it's slow?" Catie asked.

"You can't start a relationship and get much done in just one night. Humans are so slow, you take a few hours, or even days. But I'll be able to access what we need within a week."

"Should we go back to the Merlin?"

"No, I have detected some things I'm interested in."

"Please, explain."

"This building has a very high bandwidth connection and I detect an extreme amount of traffic. But that is inconsistent with its stated purpose." ADI brought up the image of the building in question.

"That's the Ministry of Trade's satellite office," Ensign Nikitas said.

"I know. But its architecture plans on file do not match the building; it was expanded during construction and the plans were not updated. Its power consumption would indicate a huge computer complex, far larger than one would expect at the Ministry of Trade. It also appears to have very tight security."

"Oh, that is interesting. Should we go check it out?"

"Yes, but be careful; I suspect it is much more than just a satellite office."

"Where is your probe?" Ensign Nikitas asked.

"It's hiding up on the hotel roof somewhere," Catie replied.

"Can we use it to surveil the building?"

"Not until tonight, there's too big a risk of it being detected if it flies around during the day."

"So we should do a recon walk by."

"You've got it in one," Cristina said. "It's nice to know you've got more than just good looks."

"Cristina!"

"Not driving!"

◆ ◆ ◆

"Okay, here's the building just ahead. Cristina, you and Kozma pair up and go ahead. Catie and I'll watch the feeds from your specs, then we'll follow and try to cover what you miss."

"I'll let you know how to turn your head," ADI added.

"Kozma, that's a nice ass on that woman, why don't you stare at it for a while."

"What? . . . oh!" Kozma figured out what Cristina wanted. He started to stare at the woman's ass as she walked in front of them. He continued to stare, turning his head to follow her as she walked up to the building.

"Good boy."

"You could have explained?" he whispered.

"Then you wouldn't have shown the proper level of embarrassment for looking at another woman's ass while walking with me."

"You're a tough cookie," Ensign Nikitas whispered. He didn't have the advantage of the tailboards which allowed the three women to type messages without looking or even trying very hard.

"And don't you forget it. We'll turn the corner here and get a view down the side of the building."

"Okay, ADI, did you get what you need?"

"Analyzing. Catie, could you find a guy with a nice ass to stare at? I need to get a different view of the door, so please stay farther behind him so you're at an angle when he goes in."

"ADI!"

"Hey, I'm learning from the best."

◆ ◆ ◆

"We need to get a view inside of that building," ADI said when they were back in the hotel room.

"I've got it covered," Catie said. "We'll go back tomorrow early and take care of it."

"How are you going to do that?" Cristina asked.

"We're going to send a spybot in." Catie pulled her bag of tricks out of her suitcase and set it on the table. "But first, I need to program these."

"What are those things?" Ensign Nikitas asked Catie.

"Microbots."

"What?"

"They're little bots. See, they look like small insects. And they can fly."

"What can they do?"

"They can follow limited instructions, just enough to get to the place you tell them to go."

"Then what good are they?"

"Ah, that's the beauty of them. When you get a bunch of them in one place, say like ten, then they assemble themselves into a bigger bot. That bot can do a lot more. And when you get a bunch of those bots into one place, they can make an even bigger bot."

"That sounds cool, but if they can only follow a limited set of instructions, then what can they do when you assemble them?"

"Each microbot carries the part of the code for more complex instructions; when they're assembled, those processes run in parallel and can do more complex stuff. So they can do a lot."

"So you think they will get by the security here?"

"That's the plan. They're so small that they won't trigger the sensors."

"But how are you going to get them inside?"

"On people who are going in. They'll attach themselves to their clothing until they're inside the security zone, then they'll fly off and collect up in the crawl space, where we'll have them assemble into a bigger spybot."

"How did you come up with these?" Cristina asked.

"You know the boarding actions we use to train our Marines how to infiltrate a ship or space station?"

"Yeah, I've done a couple."

"Well, they kept getting Marines killed when they tried to access the engineering spaces so they could get into the ship systems. So they designed spybots that they could release into those spaces instead of sending Marines into them."

"Marines got killed?" Ensign Nikitas asked, shocked at the ruthlessness of the training exercise.

"Only fake killed. It's practice."

"Good. So how did microbots help?"

"Well, the introduction of bots into the exercises turned into an arms race. One side designed lasers and killer bots to attack the bots the enemy sent in to infiltrate their systems. The other side hardened their bots and armed them. It eventually reached a stalemate. I designed these so when I get to go through the simulation with Liz and the twins, we can win."

"The twins?"

"Prisha and Alisha Khanna, you can't tell them apart, so we just call them the Twins. They're amazing in microgravity and have been dying to get a chance to run through the boarding exercises. They're fifteen."

"You use fifteen-year-old kids in your Marines?"

"No. They just like to go through the training. They're the ones who got us to do organized microgravity training. We set up an obstacle course on Delphi Station; nobody can catch them."

"Crazy, so how are these microbots going to help you win? And I guess, how are they going to help us?"

"With microbots, they fly up to the crawl space and inch along until they find a laser or killer bot. They're too small to register on the sensors, so they can gather up slowly. Then they assemble themselves into a bigger bot, but where the laser or killer bot can't get to them. Once they're assembled, they can destroy the laser or killer bot. Then they disassemble themselves and go looking for the next target. Eventually, they reach the system they're supposed to link into, and they assemble into a spybot and do their thing, either install a tap or destroy the system. If it's a tap, then our DI, ADI, will dig into their system and shut down their defenses, then Liz, the twins, and I will walk in and win the bet. We'll do the same thing here."

"Back to the exercise, don't you mean, win the exercise?"

"That too, but we'll make a big bet with Kal before we do it. He's a sucker for bets like that."

"Don't you think Kal will review the footage from this mission and know all about your microbots?" Morgan asked.

"What footage?"

"Oh, you're going to erase it."

"Make it confidential."

"The things you'll do just to win a bet."

"Everyone needs to work with what motivates them."

That night when Cristina took over the watch, Morgan called Tracey. She was always careful to not abuse the privilege of using the quantum relays to communicate with Delphi City and Earth since most people on the Merlin didn't have access.

"Hi, Tracey."

"Morgan, when are you going to be home?"

"I still don't know. A couple of months, maybe."

"I'm missing you."

"I could tell by that nice hello I got."

"Oh, you're such a big baby. Kiss, kiss, Sweetie. Is that better?"

"Yes. How are you and your father getting along?"

"Great, it's like it was before I came out."

"Good."

"He says he can't wait to meet you. He wants to teach you how to ride a bronc."

"I'm not sure that sounds like he's going to be glad to meet me."

"Oh, come on, it'll be fun."

"If you say so. How's your search going?"

"Oh! I found the perfect ranch. Two hundred fifty acres with a three-bedroom house."

"How much?"

Tracey's face fell, "Two million."

"Ouch."

"Prices have really gone up lately. We'd have to go way east to find someplace cheaper. Do you think we could swing it?"

"I could see us managing the ranch, but then where would we come up with enough to buy any horses?"

"Yeah, that's the problem."

"Hey, you remember Catie?"

"You mean the princess?"

"Yeah, what other Catie would I be talking about?"

"Yes, I remember her. You introduced us on the Sakira when she was captain. Nice kid."

"Well, she's offered to partner with us."

"What?!"

"She's offered to partner with us. She'll put up the capital, we manage the ranch. She even said she'd set up a deal where we bring some of our horses to Delphi City. Lease them to the riding stable she owns there."

"Hmm, our horses won't be putting up with no English riding tack."

"She knows, or at least I think she does. Anyway, what do you think?"

"Do you think she'd make a good partner?"

"I think so. She owns a couple of companies. You know she's a major partner in ZMS electronics."

"They're the ones that make the Mini-Comms."

"Right."

"Wow, she must be getting rich off of those things, that is, if she wasn't already rich."

"Yeah. Anyway, Marcie Sloan runs the company. Catie just helps out with design and product ideas and mostly leaves the rest to Marcie."

"Let me think about it."

"No problem. It's just an option. Text me if you make a decision."

"Will you get the text before you get back?"

"Cer Morgan, you'll get the text."

"Yes, I've been told I'll get it when you send it."

"Okay, I'll sleep on it. *Bye, Morgan,*" Tracey said in her sexiest voice.

"Bye."

That morning as the group gathered for breakfast in the suite, Tracey texted Morgan, "I'm in."

When the waiter brought up their orders, he gave the group a strange look.

"What's his problem?" Ensign Nikitas asked once the waiter left.

"He's confused by how rested you look when you're sharing a room with three beautiful women. He wonders what's wrong with you."

"Tina, you know if you want to be more attractive to your friends, I would suggest that instead of getting breast augmentations, you consider a tongue reduction."

Morgan spit her coffee on the tray, while Cristina stared at Ensign Nikitas with her mouth gaping. Catie just giggled.

"Tina, close your mouth, it's unbecoming," Morgan said.

Cristina smiled and picked up a piece of fruit from the tray. SNICK, she'd pulled a knife out of nowhere and flicked it open. She sliced off a piece of fruit, "Look who's come out of his shell. Just remember, don't stick your neck out too far." She smiled at Ensign Nikitas as she slid the piece of fruit into her mouth.

Ensign Nikitas, remembering what happened to the guy at the shipyard, was trying to decide if he should protect his groin. Instead, he opted to salute Cristina with his coffee cup. She gave him a wink in reply.

"Okay, if you two are done sharpening your claws, we have to decide what to do today." Morgan had just finished wiping up her coffee spray when Tina pulled the knife. *"Damn, she's better than Liz with that thing. I'll have to get her to give me lessons."*

"ADI?"

"If you hurry, you'll be able to use the morning rush to select your bot couriers. Then we'll need to see what we learn. I suggest you minimize the number you send in this time."

"Okay, we'll go as soon as we finish breakfast." They'd actually gotten up at 0700 this morning since they had been able to go to bed at a reasonable time the night before.

Chapter 18   Bearding the Lion

Catie programed the microbots after breakfast while the rest of them reviewed what ADI could provide of the building's layout.

"A double door to get past reception," Ensign Nikitas said. "Strange."

"Yeah, it's like an environmental lab. Do you think that they'll pick up your bots?" Cristina asked.

"I don't think so. We'll send one in by itself to see. Then we'll send the rest in a bit later. We just need ten to get a good camera inside."

"How are we going to get a feed from the building? It's bound to be in a faraday cage," Cristina said.

"I know, but we should be able to send something out over their electrical feed. We'll put a tap on the powerline outside."

"How's that going to work?"

"It will send small pulses on the line, basically transmitting in the noise. The U.S. developed it for battlefield communication. You can't jam it."

"Won't they notice?"

"You have to have the formula for how it tweaks the noise level to tell. I wish we could get a quantum relay in there, but they're too big to sneak inside."

"You can't break it down like the microbots?"

"No, it has to be in a small isolation chamber or you'll disrupt the coupling."

"Are you ready?"

"I'm right behind you."

◆ ◆ ◆

"Who are we going to use as couriers?" Morgan asked.

"Drop a spybot off at the traffic light on the corner. Then as you pass the building send the microbots to the shrub right next to the entrance using whoever is going that way. Then can we use the spybot to identify who you want to courier the microbots through security," ADI instructed.

"Great. Cristina, take this and find the electrical access on the street for the building. Drop it. The microbots will disassemble and crawl down into it, then they'll reassemble and find the power line we want to use, and they'll attach themselves to it to provide our communication link."

"Kozma, you take the package. Cristina, I want you to provide cover. Let him know when it's clear to drop the package," Morgan countermanded Catie's order.

Ensign Nikitas gave Morgan a hurt look. He obviously felt he was capable of tracking and analyzing the situation.

"Sorry, I have to work with the tools I know. You're still an unknown," Morgan explained.

Cristina grabbed Ensign Nikitas's arm and dragged him off. "Come on, we can take care of this; then we'll get a table in the coffee shop and watch over Catie and Morgan."

Catie and Morgan proceeded to the front of the ministry building. Catie quickly picked a woman with a long skirt who'd just turned toward the entrance. She dropped all the microbots and had ADI guide them under the woman's skirt. When she reached the entrance, she had ADI have all but one drop off and crawl into the bush.

The two then walked to the corner and Morgan, on ADI's signal, flipped the spybot onto the traffic light's pole.

"Good job, so now where should we watch from?" Catie asked.

"Damn, that hussy Tina called dibs on the coffee shop. So what do you think?"

"There's a bakery just down the street."

They made their way to the bakery and found a table outside. It was a little brisk to be sitting outside, but that meant they had the section of the seating to themselves.

"ADI, no alarms from our first bot?"

"No, it made it inside, so we're ready to try some more."

"Okay." Catie picked a man who was wearing a long jacket to be the next courier. Then there was a couple of women wearing cinched trench coats. She slowly fed the microbots into the building until all ten were on the other side of the main door. Now they had to rely on their coding to finish the job since they couldn't transmit instructions to the bots inside the building.

The microbots each went to a light fixture in the ceiling. The first bot that Catie had sent in pulsed the light fixture's power line with a signal to tell the other bots where to gather. Slowly the ones that had chosen a different light fixture to fly to made their way over to the alpha bot. When all ten were gathered, they assembled to form a camera and dipped the lens below the fixture's edge to provide a view of the room. They were able to send the feed along the fixture's powerline to the bot that Ensign Nikitas had dropped in the power box.

After observing the bot's video feed for a couple of hours, Morgan commented, "Interesting setup. Other than the weird double entry, it looks just like a normal office."

"That's true so far," ADI said. "But now you should go have lunch while the bot and I map out the building's interior. It will take at least another four hours."

"Okay. Cristina, we'll meet you at that pizza joint by the hotel?"

"Are you sure you know what the Helikens mean by pizza?"

"ADI showed me. The way it's described pretty much sounds like pizza, that's why she translates it to pizza."

"Okay, we'll see you there in five."

"Hey, not bad," Cristina said after she finished her first slice of pizza. "But it would go better with beer."

"Quit whining. ADI, what do we have?"

"There is a second set of doors inside the office that leads to another area. It has the same level of security as the main entrance."

"Very cautious, these Polemistians. Do you need us to deliver another set of microbots?"

"Yes, this time I want twenty. I've learned that there is a second shift that will come to the office at 1530. That should allow us to get them inside. I want to keep one camera in the main office and have enough for a camera and possibly a tap for the inner office."

"Got it. We'll go back to the hotel after lunch and pick them up."

"I've got them, let's go," Catie said as she headed for the door.

Morgan quickly stepped in front of her to keep her from leading the way out of the room. "Wait, I think we should change things up a bit. Tina and I will take care of this, you two stay here. We don't want them to see the same group passing that building all the time."

"We should come with you. We can watch from the coffee shop."

"No, ADI can cover us. You stay here. Don't go anywhere."

Morgan took the package from Catie, almost having to rip it out of her hands. "It'll take us a couple of hours to get there, deploy them, and get back."

Morgan grabbed Cristina by the arm and pulled her from the suite.

"Are you sure it's a good idea to leave them alone?"

"I hope it's a bad idea," Morgan said with a giggle. "You've got them both primed so much, they're going to explode."

"I hope so."

"ADI, privacy please." Catie took Ensign Nikitas by the hand and led him toward his room.

"Do you know what you're doing?"

"I was hoping that you would know."

"Ms. Ludlow?"

"Yes, who is this?" Tracey asked.

"I'm James Bartle, Catherine McCormack has retained me to set up your corporation."

"She sure moves fast."

"So I've been informed. Could we meet? I can be in Fort Collins in two hours."

"Sure, any place special?"

"I've reserved a conference room at the Marriott."

"Okay, I'll see you there in two hours."

◆ ◆ ◆

"Howdy," Tracey said as she shook Mr. Bartle's hand.

"Pleased to meet you. Let us begin. Do you have a name that you would like for your company?"

"I don't know about the company, but I'd like the ranch to be called The Leopard Quarter."

"Then I would suggest we just add an INC after that for the company name."

"That's fine with me."

"Let me review the partnership agreement. Ms. McCormack will put up five million dollars while you and Ms. Blair will be responsible for setting up and running the ranch."

"Ohh," Tracey gasped at the amount Catie was putting in.

Mr. Bartle ignored her gasp. "You and Ms. Blair will receive a salary for operating the ranch plus you'll have free reign of the house. There will be a quarterly board meeting to discuss progress."

"That sounds good."

"There is a buy-sell clause should you decide you no longer want to be partners. Ms. McCormack would pay you fifty percent of the value of the ranch if you decide you'd rather sell. . . ."

"Ohh, I'm not sure I like that."

"I can understand. However, should you decide you'd rather buy than sell, then Ms. McCormack's value would be converted into a twenty-year note at prime rate."

"Oh, that's not too bad."

"I would think not. Ms. McCormack has been extremely generous with the terms. Do you wish to sign, or do you need some time?"

"Oh, I'm ready to sign."

"Sign, here, here, and here. There will be an account established at The Bank of Colorado. It should be in place by tomorrow with the necessary funds. I understand you have a property that you intend to purchase."

"Yes, I've found a place I like."

"Would you like me to represent you on the purchase? I can stay over."

"Give me a minute."

"Morgan, what's going on? I've just signed our life away and the lawyer is offering to help me buy the ranch."

"Let him do it. Catie only uses the best. Have fun."

"I'd be happy to have your assistance."

That night after an only slightly awkward dinner, everyone headed to bed. Cristina had the first watch.

"Catie, how was he?" Morgan asked once she and Catie were alone in their room.

"What?"

"How was Kozma?"

"What do you mean how was he?"

"Come on, I know you did it."

"Did what?" ADI asked.

"What?" Catie glared at Morgan.

"I can tell. I just want to know how he was?"

"I'm not telling you something like that, and how do you know? Did ADI tell you?"

"Tell her what?"

"No ADI didn't tell me. I can tell because you're more relaxed and you look more ... feminine. And I don't want details."

"I want details."

"ADI, be quiet. Catie, I just want to know if he was nice about it. Was he gentle?"

"Yes, he was."

"Good, that's all that counts. Loving and gentle. Otherwise, it's just exercise. Good exercise, but not special like it should be."

"Can you explain what you two are talking about?"

Morgan looked at Catie and shrugged.

"ADI, Kozma and I slept together."

"So . . . Oh, I see. Well, congratulations."

"Time to head back to the Merlin," Catie announced at breakfast the next morning. "ADI has rented us a car and mapped a route to a secluded cove just south of here. She thinks it'll be quiet enough this time of year that we won't have to wait until dark. We'll haul the surveillance probe along with us and launch it before we call for the Lynx."

"Okay, we'll get packed, do we need to check out?" Morgan asked.

"No, we'll let the clerk pocket the difference. He's a greedy bastard, but he hasn't asked any questions."

"Okay. One hour, where's the car going to be?"

"It'll be waiting at the valet under Ensign Nikitas's fake name."

Catie went into her room to start packing. Cristina came in right behind her. "I assume that since Morgan hasn't killed him that he was nice," she whispered to Catie.

"What?"

"Prince Charming. He was nice, right?"

"Do I have a sign on my forehead that says I just had sex?!"

"No, you have a sign on your forehead that says, 'I just made love with a sweet man.'"

Catie just shook her head.

"Just let me know if I need to tune him up," Cristina said.

"Please, just pack!"

"Okay we're ready to go," Catie informed ADI a few minutes later.

"Release the bot and give me ten minutes."

"What's with the bot?" Ensign Nikitas asked.

"It'll clean up any fingerprints and DNA that the cleaning staff wouldn't get. We don't want them to trace us back to here."

"What about the motel in Spitiva?"

"I ran it while you were loading the car."

"Oh."

It was a two-hour drive down the coast before they reached the cove ADI had picked out. It was only 0900 and early winter so the cove was deserted. Ensign Nikitas drove to the water's edge and they all unloaded the car. Then he drove it back to the small parking lot and parked it.

"One minute," ADI told him. She ran the small cleaning bot around the inside and outside of the car to clean any sign of them.

"What's going to happen to it?"

"I'll call the service tomorrow and tell them to come pick it up. Just grab the bot and you're good."

"Thanks, ADI."

"Thank you, Cer Kozma."

Ensign Nikitas ran back down to the shore. Catie had released the surveillance bot and it had called an all-clear. The Lynx was just rising out of the water. With its gravity drives, it was able to hover right over the bank so they could climb in without getting wet.

"Welcome back," Lieutenant Racine told them as they boarded. She closed the hatch and followed them back into the main cabin as the Lynx submerged again.

"Sergeant Castro, good move with the hotel. It would have been nice if you'd mentioned it during the planning meeting."

"Sorry, Lieutenant. Too much data at one time."

Lieutenant Racine smiled at Cristina, "Don't worry about it. Catie, are you going to let Merlin fly us home?"

"Yes."

"Good, then I declare us all off duty. There is wine and Scotch in the galley along with some snacks."

"Lieutenant, you're the best commanding officer I've ever had," Cristina said as she rushed to the galley.

"Just leave some for the rest of us!"

Catie thought that Lieutenant Racine had been giving her a strange look since she had boarded. "Is there something, Lieutenant?" Catie asked.

"I just want to say you're looking exceptional," Lieutenant Racine said as she gave Catie a hug.

"Geez!"

Chapter 19   Welcome to Helike

By the time the Lynx reached the Merlin, the night was over. Everyone had slept on the Lynx; alcohol will do that to you. Captain McAvoy asked them all to join her in her day cabin as soon as they'd showered and had breakfast.

"Catie, how did it go?"

"You've been getting daily reports and probably hourly updates from ADI."

"I know, but what's your opinion?"

"We accomplished what we set out to do, we got ADI integrated into their internet and communications network. Finding the Ministry of Trade building was a bonus. We're still waiting to see what's going on there."

"I have a report on that," ADI said.

"Oh, good; what did you learn?"

"You need to wait until the others arrive."

Catie rolled her eyes. ADI was being officious lately, being part of the board and on the investigation team was going to her head, or CPU, or whatever.

Once everyone was assembled, Captain Galanos asked ADI to report her findings.

"I am still working to gain access to the actual computer systems. I've managed to gain access to four accounts, but I haven't been able to access an admin account yet."

"Do you think you will be able to gain access to the admin accounts?"

"Yes, it's just a matter of a day or two. I'm getting close. But what is interesting is that the second environment in the Ministry of Trade building contains an extensive set of computers. I would estimate that it is one of the largest computer systems in Polemistia."

"That is interesting."

"Another interesting thing is that the computer system is completely isolated. They actually physically move the data between the outer environment's computer systems and the second environment's systems. There is a one-way link that allows the inner system to send messages and commands out, but there is no way for the outside world to reach the protected systems."

"I assume they've done that to prevent anyone from hacking into their systems," Captain McAvoy said.

"Yes. We employ a similar system in Delphi. We surround our core systems with a pseudo system that insolates them. Data and messages are handed off between the two systems. It has been very effective in preventing viruses from infecting our systems and prevents any attacks on our key systems."

"Where does the inner system send its messages and commands to?" Catie asked.

"I've been able to determine several locations. The palace and a collection of computer centers spread around Polemistia. Those centers appear to be part of the intelligence service and it appears that they are used to hack systems in other countries as well as spread disinformation on their social media platforms."

"All countries try to hack into the systems of other countries," Commander Petrou said. "It's pretty much spying 101 and to be expected."

"But the disinformation?"

"Some countries say it's spreading the truth, others call it disinformation. It depends on which side of the argument you're on."

Captain Galanos interrupted "Let's get back on point. We have what appears to be a central computer resource for their spying. Do we think it's used for anything else?"

"With that kind of investment, one would expect that they do a lot of data analysis, run scenarios, do planning," Captain McAvoy said. "We should focus our resources there and see if we can find a connection to the incident at Stási."

"I agree. We also need to prepare for our arrival at Helike tomorrow."

"We've managed to repair your air scrubber and give you control of your thrusters," Captain McAvoy said. "So, when we make orbit, we'll release your ship and you can guide it to your space shipyard under your own power."

"I appreciate that, it will look much better to our people. When should we move back to the ship?"

"I recommend tomorrow morning."

"Okay. We're scheduled to provide an update to mission control in two hours. Is there anything else we want to share with them?"

"I don't think so, we should keep as many cards in our hand as we can until things start to play out."

"They have been very impatient to talk with the princess."

Catie rolled her eyes. "All they want to do is talk about the reception."

"Of course, being the first alien civilization to visit Helike is a big deal. The government wants to show the people that it is still in control and to reassure them that you're a friendly people."

"Sure. I guess I should dress up."

"It would help."

"Mission Control, this is Geraki. Over."

"Geraki, this is Mission Control. What is your status? Over."

"Mission Control. We will reach orbit at 1500 tomorrow. We have thrusters and will be able to dock at the shipyard. Over."

"Very well, Geraki. Please contact us when you make orbit. Will the princess be able to talk with Ambassador Drakoso? Over."

"Mission Control. The princess is available to talk. We can set up a private channel to her cabin. Over."

"Please do so. Mission Control out."

"Princess, I am so happy you could make time to talk with me," Ambassador Drakoso said.

"My pleasure." Catie was dressed up in her princess uniform, with the fancy ribbons and her Delphi Cross prominently displayed.

"Our people are excited to learn about your existence and your arrival. We would like for you to meet President Tripino when you arrive. But we wished to discuss protocol with you."

"Of course." Catie resisted the urge to roll her eyes.

"Catie, you've been in meetings all day. How are you doing?" Morgan asked when Catie finally made it to her cabin.

"I'm doing fine. How about you? You've been in meetings, too."

"Just a few to discuss security. And I don't have to play nice like you do."

"Do you know how to play nice?"

Morgan made a threatening move at Catie, but then just smiled.

Catie had started to duck before she caught herself. "It's been crazy. We'll be reaching Helike tomorrow, so it's going to get even crazier."

"Oh, so the princess will have to go down and meet the poobahs of Helike. Have you unpacked your gowns and jewelry yet?" Morgan sent a quick message to Ensign Nikitas, *"Ensign, could you meet me in the princess's day cabin?"*

"Oh no. She must have found out. She's going to kill me," he thought.

"Yes, and no I haven't unpacked that stuff. I'll take care of it when we make orbit. I'm not looking forward to all the hoopla. It means there will be zero privacy. What a mess."

"It won't be all that bad. Have you decided when you're going to tell the planet that they're all Earthlings?"

"We're going to hold that card for a while. We still don't know what this mess is all about."

"Ensign Nikitas," the sentry announced.

"What's he doing here?" Catie asked, she couldn't recall anyone suggesting a meeting.

Morgan signaled the sentry to send the ensign in.

"You wanted to see me?" he asked Morgan.

"I'm bunking with Tina tonight. You two have the cabin to yourselves. ADI has made arrangements for the ensign to leave early in the morning." Morgan smiled and quickly exited the cabin.

"She knows?"

"Yes."

"Did you tell her?"

"No, she just knew."

"What about Cristina, she's going to wonder why Morgan is bunking with her?"

"She knows, too."

"Oh, Morgan told her?"

"No, she just knew."

"And ADI?"

"She overheard Morgan and me talking. *ADI, privacy please.*"

"*You're no fun!*"

◆ ◆ ◆

"Ensign Nikitas, it's time for you to return to your cabin," ADI announced.

"Already?"

"It is 0400, and this is the quietest time on the ship. You should be able to make it to your cabin unnoticed."

"You'd better hurry," Catie said as she gave him a kiss before shoving him out of the bed.

He gathered his clothes and hurried into the bathroom to dress. "You sure seem to be in a hurry to get rid of me."

"You hog the covers."

"I do not!"

"Hey, the blanket is mostly on your side."

Ensign Nikitas exited the bathroom and walked over to the bed to give Catie a kiss. "That's because you kept pushing them over to me."

"Yeah, right. I'll see you at the briefing. Now get out of here so I can get some sleep."

The Merlin made orbit early in the morning with the Geraki in tow. After several discussions with the Heliken Defense Ministry, they had agreed that the Merlin could take up position above the North Pole. They had also arranged for an official welcome for Princess Catherine accompanied by Prince Nikitas.

The event was arranged so that the shuttle would land in the arena and Catie would exit it, accompanied by her guard, and walk onto the platform where she would be met by President Tripino and Prince Demetrius.

"Morgan, I can dress myself!"

"I'm sure you can. But I want to make sure you've got your body armor on correctly."

"Arrr! This would be so much easier if I could just wear my uniform."

"A princess needs to be in a gown. Now put this on," Morgan tossed Catie the light armor she would be wearing under the gown.

Catie struggled into the armor. It covered her from throat to toe, but the last six inches of the legs were made of flexible transparent armor. Nobody would notice it unless they were standing right next to her. The yoke of the armor was also transparent, allowing Catie to wear a gown with a more revealing décolletage than the standard uniform. The sleeves were also transparent, from her shoulder to her wrist.

"I feel like I'm in a cocoon!"

"Then everyone will get to see the beautiful butterfly. Now put on the gown."

"Are you sure you don't have something else I need to put on first?" Catie huffed as she stepped into the gown. Morgan helped her pull it up and zipped it up for her. It was a dark blue gown with diamond beads and black pearls sewn into the embroidery. Catie adjusted the sleeves. "Am I going to have to wear gloves?"

"Yes, they're very flexible, you won't even realize you have them on."

"Right!"

"You're lucky you don't have to wear a bunch of petticoats." Morgan picked up the throat cover.

"Arr, you've got to be kidding?"

"Nope. It's not that bad, it's a lot better since they made it a separate piece. Now put it on." Morgan handed the transparent armor wrap to Catie.

Catie stuck her tongue out at Morgan before she wrapped the cover around her neck. She adjusted it so that the seam was in the back under her hair. Turning her head from side to side, she looked at herself in the mirror. "Gawd, I can't wait to go home."

"Why, do you think you won't have to wear this stuff there?"

"I never did before."

"We'll see. At least there we have total control of security and we know that nobody has a gun in the city or on the station. Here, it's stressful dealing with Helike's lax security protocols."

"Don't they worry about assassination?"

"Yes, but they're assuming classic threats. We're not willing to assume the enemy is that unimaginative. Now shoes."

Catie stepped into her shoes, they were low heeled. Since she was tall and the dress went to the floor, she'd opted for something that would be easier to walk in. The heel was surrounded by clear polysteel, so it looked tapered but had a firm base to stand on.

"Now, your jewels." Morgan brought the box with Catie's diamond tiara, necklace, and earrings. After brushing out her hair, she placed the tiara on Catie's head and stepped back to look. She made a slight adjustment before she Commed it to latch on. "ADI, are the cameras aligned correctly?"

"Yes, Cer Morgan, the cameras give me a clear view of the front and back."

"Good." Morgan put the necklace on Catie but handed her the earrings to put on herself.

"Oh, I get to actually do something myself."

Morgan stepped back to get a good view of Catie. "You're beautiful."

"How can you tell?"

Morgan grabbed Catie by the shoulder and turned her to the mirror. "Just look."

"Okay, I'll give you that."

"Prince Charming will swoon over you. He might even need a cane to walk, he'll be so weak in the knees."

"Morgan, thanks for the ego boost, but we should get this show on the road." Catie walked to the door and entered the shuttle's main cabin.

"Wow!" Kasper said. "I'm feeling underdressed." Kasper was wearing his dress uniform and would be acting as Catie's escort during the ceremony.

"We're five minutes from landing," Lieutenant Racine informed the group. She, Cristina, and Morgan would be Catie's main bodyguards, while four other Marines would back them up. They'd snuck a team of five Marines down earlier; they would be dressed like Helikens and mix into the crowd to help provide a view of what was happening as well as backup should something happen.

Catie reached up and adjusted the throat collar.

"Don't touch it. You'll leave fingerprints on it." Morgan took a wipe and cleaned the collar. "You can take it off once we get inside."

"Okay, I'm ready," Catie sighed as she shook out her gown and flexed her arms.

"We're down."

The shuttle had landed right next to the viewing platform in a display of Delphinean technological superiority that Catie had insisted on. With its gravity drives, the shuttle was able to land right next to the crowd without any downdraft, noise, or heat. To emphasize the point, it was hovering so that the boarding ramp would have a slight decline onto the platform, allowing Catie and her entourage to walk gracefully onto the platform.

"I'm ready."

The shuttle door opened and Catie walked out, flanked by Morgan and Cristina. Lieutenant Racine followed, flanked by two marines on each side. They would be able to quickly surround Catie should they need to.

President Tripino was waiting at the end of the ramp; he bowed to Catie and extended his arm. Catie took it, with Morgan moving to the other side of the president. They then proceeded to the center of the platform where Prince Nikitas and his father, Prince Demetrius, waited.

Catie smiled at Ensign Nikitas as he and his father bowed. Then the prince, the president, and Catie turned and walked out to the edge of the platform where the crowd and the news media could get a good view.

BZZZ

Catie was shocked when she saw several drones rise up.

"They're just camera drones. The news media uses them to get better views," Ensign Nikitas Commed to Catie.

Catie turned her head to view the crowd.

"The drones fired at them!" ADI shouted over the Comm.

Morgan and Cristina stepped forward and took out the six drones; they had a gun mounted on each wrist. The frangible rounds exploded as they hit the drones. The prince looked around him, stunned at all the activity. He rubbed his neck where he'd gotten splattered. The president turned to him and gave him a questioning look.

"What's going on?!" the president demanded.

"Those drones fired pellets at us!" Morgan shouted back. "The princess, you, and Prince Demetrius were hit."

"I'm not injured."

Catie looked down and saw some kind of liquid dripping onto her gown. Lieutenant Racine stepped in front of Catie and pulled out her polyglass shield. It expanded into a meter square barrier. The other four marines followed suit, quickly forming a wall around Catie.

"Don't touch it, I think it's poison," Racine shouted. Racine grabbed Catie's dress and tore it off of her. "Give her your jacket," she ordered one of the Marines. "You take this into the shuttle and give it to Dr. Moreau. Tell her it's probably poison."

"What happened?" Catie asked.

"Pellets, liquid capsules probably. Your armor dispersed the impact enough that it barely burst so you didn't get sprayed with it. The president and prince didn't fare so well." Lieutenant Racine handed Catie the jacket.

"What about Kosmo?"

"They didn't target him."

"We should get them into the shuttle. Dr. Moreau can probably help them." Catie pulled on the Marine's uniform jacket. Lieutenant Racine had picked a tall Marine to get the jacket from so the jacket hung down to Catie's thighs.

"Get one of those drones," Lieutenant Racine ordered the Marines who were embedded in the crowd.

One of the female Marines walked over to the drone that ADI identified for her. She stepped on the rotor's frame and ripped the body of the drone from it and then slipped it into her purse. She drifted back into the crowd to lose herself.

"Doctor, Racine says this is probably poison." The Marine handed the doctor Catie's gown, pointing at the liquid.

"Give it here. I'll get it analyzed right away." The doctor grabbed the gown and headed to the small medical bay at the back of the shuttle. She scraped off a sample of the liquid and put it into the analyzer.

"What is it?"

"Something new, but it's very poisonous." Dr. Moreau moved to another machine and entered a code. The machine whirled for a few minutes then spit out an ampule of liquid substance. "Here, take this syringe and have Catie injected."

"What about the other two?"

"You didn't tell me there were others. I need a sample of their blood. Quickly."

The Marine grabbed the ampule and syringe and ran back Lieutenant Racine. "The doctor says to inject Catie with this. She also says she needs blood samples from the other two."

"Castro, over here. You've got the princess."

Lieutenant Racine rushed over to where the prince and president were arguing with Morgan.

"I was not shot!" Prince Demetrius yelled.

"Sir, the rounds were gel pellets. They exploded and sprayed you with poison. Our doctor says it's very poisonous. We need blood samples from you so she can make an antidote."

"What kind of poison?"

"Father, trust her. Let her take the sample," Ensign Nikitas said.

ADI opened a channel with the lieutenant. "Lieutenant Racine, I've used the analysis the doctor did to identify the poison. It is called Hadrixa."

"Our analysis says it's Hadrixa."

The prince blanched. "Then we're dead. Our bodies just don't know it yet. There is no cure."

"I understand, but if you give us a blood sample, I believe our doctor can remove the poison from your system. You also need to clean it off yourself. I suggest you go into our shuttle; we'll provide you something to change into."

The two men, followed by their bodyguards and Ensign Nikitas went into the shuttle.

"Please remove your outer clothing. There's a restroom there where you can clean up. But first, give me a blood sample."

"What good will that do? There is no cure for this poison."

"I know, but we can program these microscopic robots, we call them nanites. They will scour your bloodstream and consume the poison. Then your body can eliminate it without it entering your cells. But we have to hurry."

The prince removed his jacket and handed it to his bodyguard. He ripped off his shirt since he could see droplets on it now that he was looking. He extended his arm to Dr. Moreau who pricked it with a blood sampler.

"That's all?"

"I just need a reference sample." Dr. Moreau moved over to the president and pricked his cheek. "Now go get cleaned up."

The two men removed the rest of their outer clothes and went into the head, where they were able to clean up. When they exited, they were each handed a clean shirt by one of the Marines. "I think the size will be close. We were able to clean your jackets, so you're free to get dressed."

"Just one second. I need to inject you." Dr. Moreau gave each man an injection. "You shouldn't feel much effect from the poison. The injection should remove most of it from your system. You'll want to get your doctors to give you extra saline and a little glucose each day for the next week."

"Does that mean we can continue with the ceremony?"

Dr. Moreau's eyes flared in shock as she was taken aback by the suggestion. "*I guess you could,*" she said incredulously.

The prince looked at the president.

"Why not?"

"What about the princess?"

"Someone ripped my gown off!"

"Hey, I can mend it," one of the Marines said. "She just tore the zipper a little and I can restitch this seam."

"Okay, then I'm game."

Five minutes later, Catie, the prince, and the president emerged from the shuttle to a confused and stunned crowd.

They made their way back to the center of the platform. Ensign Nikitas waited until they were at the center of the platform before he followed.

The prince waved the crowd down. "We apologize for the bit of excitement. The drones' rotors sprayed water over us. Our friends, the

Delphineans, immediately sensed a threat, and as you saw, dispatched the drones. If everyone will return to their places, we will continue the ceremony, without the drones, of course."

The ceremony progressed. Catie was presented with the Star of Helike, a bejeweled medal, in recognition of their saving the Spaceship Geraki.

Catie moved to the lectern for her speech. She wasn't sure what she should say, but she needed to defuse the situation and misdirect the bad guys so they wouldn't know their attempt had failed.

"I hope you'll forgive the over-exuberance of my security detail; they take their job seriously. In Delphi, we issue the cameras that the reporters use at events like this. I want to thank President Tripino for welcoming us to Helike and Prince Demetrius for hosting our stay. And I also wish to express our deep sadness at the loss of the members of the Geraki crew and the loss of your moon base. We are from a planet called Earth, but more importantly, we belong to a confederation of planets called The Delphi League. The Delphi League promotes trade and self-defense among its members. We facilitate the exchange of technology and preserve the right of self-determination of our member planets. We hope that we'll be able to convince the people of Helike to join us in our quest to settle the galaxy and to promote the wellbeing of all its citizens."

After a few more speeches, they moved on to the palace where they would be staying while they continued to negotiate with the Helikens about joining The Delphi League as well as to try to figure out what was going on with the conspiracy.

Chapter 20   Playing of Cards

"Okay, what was that assassination attempt all about?" Catie asked as she joined Ensign Nikitas, Captain Galanos, and Kasper in the library at the palace. Captain McAvoy, Blake, and Marc were tied in via video.

"It says things are getting dangerous," Marc said. "I think you should move back to the Merlin."

"Daddy, I can't. We're playing like nothing happened. Moving to the Merlin would cause an uproar."

"And just why are you guys pretending that nothing happened?"

"Because the poison they used takes two days before signs present, and then it takes three more days to kill you. We don't want the enemy to realize they've failed."

"And you thought that up on your own?"

"Not really; Prince Demetrius wanted to avoid the bad press, so he came up with the idea. It just seems obvious that we should keep that card off the table."

"I hate to say it, but I agree with her," Blake said.

"So do I," Samantha added as she joined the conference.

Marc glared at Samantha but gave a sigh, showing he would relent. "Now what?"

"Now we need to figure out what their end goal is," Catie said.

"Yes," Captain Galanos agreed. "They didn't do this just to assassinate the president and the prince. And they couldn't know that there would be an event with the president, Prince Demetrius, and the princess in attendance until last week. The plan had to be in the works longer than that."

"I think they are trying to create unrest for another purpose," Ensign Nikitas said. "The arrival of the Delphineans threw their plan out of balance. I think they were planning to assassinate my father, the prince. The president and the princess were added when they were scrambling to adjust their plan. Assassinating the princess would likely have the Delphineans leaving the planet, or taking retribution on Spitiva since we were hosting the event."

"I agree," Blake said. "So what is their end goal?"

"Returning Polemistia to a true monarchy."

"How would this achieve that?"

"It won't. There must be more to the plan?"

"I think I know," ADI said.

"Please explain?" Marc asked.

ADI projected a map of Spitiva on the wall, feeding it into the video feed for those not in the palace.

"I believe that this is their target." ADI highlighted a peninsula on the west coast of Spitiva; it hung down from the main continent like Spain did from Europe, except it was narrower and longer. "The Zakinthos Peninsula is one of the richest areas of Spitiva. A large part of their high-tech industry is located there. It used to be part of Polemistia until eighty years ago when it was ceded to Spitiva in exchange for land Spitiva controlled on Synoro."

"That is correct," Prince Nikitas said. "It would be a major coup for my uncle to reacquire it. But how?"

"I've seen a lot of activity on their social media over the last ten years espousing that they rejoin Polemistia. That activity has increased significantly in the last year."

"Oh, that makes sense," Prince Nikitas said, "but how would they accomplish that?"

"I would suggest that they will use the same formula that the Russians used to annex the Crimea. Large public protest and paramilitary movements supported by the Polemistia military."

"It would be easy to isolate Zakinthos, the peninsula is very narrow up here where it joins the mainland," Prince Nikitas said as he pointed at the map. "They could create enough problems to cut it off; it is very mountainous, and the roads go through narrow passages."

"How will they bring the Polemistia military into play?"

"They would have to send a naval force," Blake said.

"But Polemistia has a very small navy and few large ships; they are building an aircraft carrier, but it won't be ready for another six months."

"That is not true," ADI said. "My analysis of the systems in the Trade Ministry building shows that there are three aircraft carriers under construction."

"They were only supposed to build one."

"Nevertheless, they have been building three. The records I've obtained show a coordinated effort to make it appear that the carriers are further from completion than they are. It is possible that all three are finished now."

"Oh, that is big. Can you prove it?"

"To prove it we would need to get into the shipyards or use satellite photos. But the sites seem to be screened so that you cannot take images of them from satellite."

"I think it's time we brought my father in," Ensign Nikitas said. "He can help us decide whether we should bring the president in."

"How well does your father know the president?" Marc asked.

"They grew up together. My father has been one of his biggest sponsors whenever he has run for office, including his last campaign for president."

"Then why don't you brief him and we'll meet again tomorrow morning," Marc suggested.

"Our time!" Catie added.

"Of course."

◆ ◆ ◆

The next morning, they all gathered in the palace library again, with the others attending via video. Catie had given Ensign Nikitas a Comm for his father so he would be fully tied in with the members attending remotely.

Catie began the meeting. "Prince Demetrius, I'm sure you have some questions."

"I do; if it were not for the fact that my son has sworn to me that all this is true, I would be asking what asylum you have escaped from. But my concern now is how committed is The Delphi League to helping us with this problem."

Catie motioned to Marc, "Father?"

Marc nodded. "We are as committed as you want us to be. I know it is hard to accept help from an outside source, especially one that is not from your planet. The fact that we share a common ancestry is a minor factor given how distant that link is. We would like to have your planet join The Delphi League, but for that, it needs to be united in purpose."

"But is any planet or country truly united in purpose?"

"We understand there will be political differences. Our planet is not a shining beacon of unity, but we are working on it. But we need to see that a majority of the countries want to be part of the league."

"Very well, then I can speak for myself and the president that we want you to be involved. Lykaios Tripino, our president, had to return to the capital. But I will talk with him and gain his support."

"We would ask that you get a Comm to him first. Communication via our Comms is not traceable nor can someone tap into the line."

"But how will we communicate when he is hundreds of miles away?"

"The Comms use your network, but the encryption is unbreakable, and we have some methods of preventing them from being traced."

"Yes, Kozma mentioned that you installed some hardware into our networks." The prince did not look particularly pleased with that fact.

"It was unavoidable. We will remove it as soon as we can."

"Excellent."

"Your Excellency," Captain Galanos said. "We must decide our next move. We believe that there will be a military move against Zakinthos."

"I'm sure you're correct. There has been a lot of agitation in that region, and my agents tell me that it has been accelerating over the last few weeks."

"I think we need to decide when to show some of our cards," Samantha said. "When do we tell the people that the moon was destroyed? When do we tell them that we have survivors from the moon? And when do we show them the evidence that points to Polemistia?" Samantha asked.

"There is general knowledge that we have lost contact with the base and that we have lost the people there," Prince Demetrius said. "I think I should ask President Tripino to confirm this. But you do know that there are already conspiracy theories out there that claim that you destroyed the base?"

"We are aware of that," Samantha said. "We should let the opposition get behind those theories before we show what really happened and bring our survivors forward."

"The poison they used against us would be taking effect by tomorrow, what do we do about that?" Catie asked.

"A report that the president is feeling ill might make them reveal their next move."

"I will send him a Comm and suggest that he stay in bed tomorrow."

"Would any of you like a tour of the palace?" Ensign Nikitas asked once his father left the group.

"I would," Catie said.

"So would I," Kasper said. "Ouch, that is, I would if my knee wasn't so sore." Morgan had kicked his knee under the table as he was trying to stand up.

"I've been on the tour before," Captain Galanos said.

"Well, then it's just the two of us. Come right this way."

Did you have to kick me so hard? You could have just Commed.

Hey, you should have known better. I didn't have time to type out a message.

You do know that striking a superior officer is a court-martial offense?

I'm sure I could get a pardon from the princess."

◆ ◆ ◆

"This is the room where I took my classes." Ensign Nikitas began his tour with just Catie.

"Just you?"

"No, several other prominent families sent their children here. We had excellent teachers, and of course, it was secure."

"What about your sister?"

"She is five years younger than I, so she was educated by her governess while I was still here. I had left for the academy before she was taking classes that required advanced teachers."

"What did you study at the academy?"

"Military history, engineering, stuff like that. We get a pretty rounded education. My focus was computer science. What did you study?"

"Engineering. I got my master's in ship design while I was at our Academy."

"A master's." Ensign Nikitas sounded impressed.

"I had completed most of my undergrad requirements before I started. So what's this room?"

"This is the dining hall; we'll have dinner here tonight. Father will attend and it will be quite a production. I believe he's invited three other princes from Spitiva."

"There's certainly enough room." Catie surveyed the dining table. It could seat twenty-four people. "Your family must like to entertain."

"So much work gets accomplished during entertainment. The ballroom is through here. Father holds a ball four times a year. They're attended by all the major players in business and politics."

"I would think so. After all, he is the Prince of Spitiva."

"Yes. You saw the library, that's where all the big deals are made. Father takes people aside then drags them to the library for the talk. He can be very persuasive."

"How?"

"He controls a lot of business and a lot of money. Plus he has spies. So he knows things about everyone."

"You mean he blackmails them?"

"That is such an awful word. Let's say he persuades them that they have common interests."

"I *see.*"

"Out back is the formal garden. Would you like to see it? You'll need a wrap."

Morgan showed up with a coat for Catie. "If you're going outside, I'll need to keep you in sight."

Catie frowned at Morgan.

"Hey, I'm here to make sure nobody is watching you; I won't take notice of anything that the two of you might decide to do as long as you're safe."

Breaking news: "Prince Callistus, the director of the International Space Agency acknowledged today that Stási has been destroyed. It was widely rumored that something went wrong there when the Geraki had to be helped home by the Delphineans. The space agency had acknowledged that there had been an accident and our moon base on Stási was lost, but this is the first time they've admitted that the moon was destroyed. The director would not comment on how the moon was destroyed. We will continue to seek answers."

Tweet: "We all know that the Delphineans destroyed our base, why won't our government admit it? What private deal are they making with these aliens!"

Breaking news: "Our sources at the presidential palace tell us that President Tripino stayed in his bed all day. His doctors refused to comment other than to say he was resting after a long week."

Tweet: "The aliens have poisoned our president. Is he even in control of his own thoughts?"

Tweet: "People of Zakinthos, it is time to throw off the yoke of mediocrity imposed by Spitiva and rejoin Polemistia. Our destiny awaits."

Tweet: "People of Zakinthos, help us throw out the Spitiva oppressors."

Tweet: "Why is our government allowing a powerful alien starship to orbit our planet?"

Tweet: "Where is our president? Is Prince Demetrius in league with the aliens?"

◆ ◆ ◆

"I hate tweets and breaking news!" Catie screamed in her head.

Looking for a little normalcy Catie decided to call the triplets. Obviously, she was looking for normal drama, not normalcy.

"Hey, girls."

"Princesa!" The triplets quickly gathered around the display.

"How are you three doing?"

"Fine. We're on break from school now, so we have lots of time to play podball."

"Who are you playing with?"

"Prisha and Aalia have moved up here for the summer, so we play with them against other teams. There are five new teams now."

"The twins moved to Delphi Station?"

"Yes, silly. They sent you a message!"

ADI opened a channel with Catie, "Cer Catie, you received the message two weeks ago."

"Arrg, I can't believe I missed that! . . . So, where are they living?"

"They live one-eighth spinward of us, and we're on the same floor." The residents of Delphi Station had divided it into sections of a circle to define their addresses. Being on the same floor meant they could reach each other's cabin without having to use the stairs or an elevator.

"That sounds nice. How do they like living on Delphi Station?"

"They love it and . . . Prisha has a boyfriend!"

"Wow, she does? How does he know which one she is?"

"She cut her hair."

"She must really like him if she cut her hair and made herself look different than her sister. Is he nice?"

"We think so. He plays on our podball team."

"Who is he?"

"His name is Damon Marcelles. His father is a teacher up here and his mother runs the Solar Panel plant up here."

"Oh, I know her. How old is he?"

"Huh?"

"Cer Catie, he is sixteen."

"What does Aalia think of him?"

"She ignores him."

"Hmm, does she have a boyfriend?"

"No, but she does like someone."

"Oh, who?"

"We don't know his name. She just stares at him a lot."

"I see. Does she talk to him?"

"Not yet!"

"Do you tease her about him?"

"No, we'd get dinged for bullying if we did!"

"What?"

"I would not ding them for bullying if they only teased her," ANDI clarified.

"Oh, then we need to tease her!"

"Be careful, it's a fine line between teasing and being mean."

"We will."

◆ ◆ ◆

"Captain McAvoy, ADI says that her analysis of communication traffic from Polemistia indicates that they are likely launching their aircraft carriers. They have a small flotilla of ships operating along the coast.

She thinks that the carriers will rendezvous with the flotilla before they head east."

"Thank you, Princess, but why didn't ADI inform me?"

"Captain McAvoy, you were asleep when I completed my analysis. I asked Catie whether I should wake you since she was already up for her run. She suggested it could wait until your breakfast."

"Thank you, ADI. I should have known better than to question your motives. Princess?"

"I thought it might be a good idea to have a Fox shadow the fleet from high altitude. We don't have access to the Heliken satellite system yet, so that would let us track their movements."

"I've already discussed this with Kasper. I'll inform him that it's time to put that plan into effect."

"What do you think we can do against a naval fleet?" Catie asked.

"I'm not sure. ADI, have you completed your analysis of their weapons?"

"Yes, Captain McAvoy. They have standard surface-to-air and air-to-air missiles similar to Earth. The data shows that they can achieve velocities of Mach 3.2. They also have primitive lasers that they use in their anti-missile defense. The power rating is sufficient to destroy one of our missiles if they can get a three-second lock."

"What about their fighters?"

"Top speed would be Mach 2.6. An air-to-air missile launched from a fighter would be able to achieve a speed of Mach 4, but it would have very limited maneuverability."

"The speed of their ships?"

"Thirty to forty knots. I estimate that it will take five days to reach Spitiva once they rendezvous."

"How good is their armor?"

"Their destroyers and frigates would be very susceptible to our lasers, plasma cannons, and rial guns. But the new carriers appear to have advanced armor. They probably will be able to withstand all but a sustained plasma blast."

"Please review all this with Admiral Blake and Admiral Michaels. Copy President McCormack as well."

"I've recorded our conversation and will send it to them."

"Thank you, ADI."

"So, Catie, what do you think?"

"It might get ugly."

"We'll have to watch what they do."

"Yes, and we need to see if we can turn their people against this aggression."

"I'll leave that to you, Sam, and Prince Demetrius."

"Oh, thanks!"

"Captain McAvoy, Cer Catie, I've detected an unauthorized transmission from one of the Heliken scientists," ADI Commed.

"Which one?"

"It appears to have come from Cer Eliades's cabin."

"What did it say?"

"It was encrypted."

"We should be able to tell what he sent by reviewing the videos from the cabin," Catie said.

"Let's see them."

"Captain McAvoy, I need you to declare that Cer Eliades has violated his duty to the Merlin in order to break the privacy seal. You will have to order me to play the videos."

"I declare that the occupant of that cabin has violated our security and is in violation of standing orders. I order you to open the videos that were recorded around the time of the transmission."

The four videos of the cabin came up on Catie's and Captain McAvoy's HUDs. ADI combined the audio channels to provide the best sound. As she played the video, they could see Eliades dig into his bag and pull out a small device. He looked around then went into the head. He crouched on top of the commode and started talking.

"This is Eliades reporting. The aliens' starship is powerful but not as powerful as they want you to believe. We could only do 0.2Gs on the way here and they had to rest the engines twice. They are also taxing their engines to hold this orbit."

Catie signaled ADI to stop the video. "What would give him that idea?"

"Cer Catie, I believe he is misinterpreting something he overheard. He was in the mess when one of the crew was telling an engineer how much he was enjoying the reduced shifts that Captain McAvoy has put most of the crew on. The engineer told him that engineering wasn't getting a break. That he wished the captain would establish a normal orbit so they could rest the reactors. But as it is, they were all having to babysit them every hour."

"The chief engineer does refer to standing watch on the reactors as babysitting," Captain McAvoy said. "Please continue the video."

Eliades was continuing to talk. "They brought us over to the Merlin in a shuttle. It didn't look particularly aerodynamic or powerful. I believe they are not equipped to wage war. I'm sure they have weapons on their ship, but it doesn't look like it can enter the atmosphere. Our space station might be at risk, but I don't believe they can project force down onto the planet's surface."

"As you see, he then transmits the recording," ADI explained.

"What should we do now?" Catie asked.

"I want to search his room."

"But we know he didn't bring anything dangerous."

"Let's make sure. Should we interrogate him?"

Catie laughed. "Well, they say it's always nice to have a mole you know about. Then you can feed him misinformation. If we interrogate him, we can make him forget the interrogation, but he'll know he lost some time. I say we just watch him."

"Okay."

Breaking News: "Prince Xenakis has declared himself king and dissolved parliament. He says that only he can save Helike from the aliens. He is demanding that President Tripino give him control over Helike's military so that he can deal with the threat."

Tweet: "President Tripino is dying. His aides refuse to comment, but he hasn't been seen for two days."

Tweet: "Resist the invasion. Join King Xenakis and take Helike back."

Tweet: "Prince Demetrius has betrayed Helike. Join King Xenakis in restoring Helike to its former glory."

Breaking News: "Prince Xenakis is demanding that Spitiva cede Zakinthos to Polemistia."

"And so it begins," Marc said as he and Catie finished reviewing all the news and tweets from the last two days.

"Cers, the carriers have joined the fleet and they are steaming toward Zakinthos."

"Thank you, ADI. Catie, now what?" Captain Galanos asked.

"Now we call our council of war."

Blake and Admiral Michaels joined them on the video call. "Catie, you seem to find trouble wherever you go," Blake said.

"Uncle Blake, trouble finds me. Now, quit teasing and help us figure out what we should do next."

"Admiral Michaels, since these ships are on the water, this is more your bailiwick."

"Thanks," Admiral Michaels said as he frowned at Blake. "We've reviewed the data ADI sent us. It seems that their frigates, destroyers, and support ships are the only ones that are vulnerable to our weapons. We should focus on paring down the size of their fleet. It's possible that if you eliminate enough of their support vessels they would be forced to turn back home. They're still four days out."

Breaking News, the truth about Stási:

"Hello, I'm Dr. Phillipa Rubis. I was one of the scientists at Stási before the base was lost. I'm here to tell you what really happened. During my last year there I became aware that someone was surreptitiously producing large quantities of antimatter and storing it. I knew that the only reason for building up a large stockpile of antimatter was to make weapons. When the supply ship showed up, I knew that something was terribly wrong. I made a laser pistol and hijacked the shuttle so that I could warn Helike of the danger."

"Why didn't you just send a communication?"

"The director of the lab had taken total control of all communication under the guise of security. I could not send any messages."

"I see, please go on."

"This is a recording of the events after our escape." Dr. Rubis started to play the video that ADI had constructed. "Here you can see the supply ship leaving the base. At this point, fifteen hours later, a large explosion occurred inside the base. We know this because there was a large electromagnetic pulse at that time shown here by this waveform. The explosion had to have been the antimatter in the lab being released. The explosion was so large that it would have killed everyone at the base. But unknown to the perpetrators of this heinous crime there was another group that was also producing and storing antimatter. Here you can see where it is released. The EMP signature shows that the energy released and the subsequent explosion was much larger than the first. It was so huge that it actually set off a fusion reaction, consuming all the low weight elements at the base. The EMP signature is much larger and broader indicating the enormity of the explosion and its longer duration. This was so intense that it set off a second fusion reaction that actually started to consume the moon. This reaction continued until the moon fractured."

Dr. Rubis paused the video so that the first plumes exiting the fractures could be seen. "At this time, you can still see the supply ship trying to make its escape." She resumed the video. "As the moon fractured into pieces, one of them was thrown out in the direction of the supply ship. It was so large and traveling so fast that the ship could not get out of its way. Here you can see the debris smashing into the ship, and here you can see the ship exploding and the fifth EMP event indicating that the antimatter the ship was carrying was released and it exploded."

"Dr. Rubis, some people say that the aliens did this. What do you say to that?"

"These events were set in motion a year ago. The explosion occurred when the supply ship left the base. As you can see, there is no sign of the alien starship."

"And how did you create this recording?"

"These events were recorded by the Delphineans using telescopes that were light hours away from the moon. By assembling the signal from several telescopes they were able to create this video."

"And how did they know to put these telescopes into place?"

"The explosion that destroyed the moon also disrupted the wormhole they were using to travel through space. A wormhole is a space-time tunnel between two distant locations. When they emerged in our system, they sent probes out with the telescopes to determine what had happened to cause their wormhole to collapse."

The interview continued, with the reporter grilling Dr. Rubis about wormholes, the Delphinean technology, and how she was sure that the video was true. Dr. Rubis provided convincing answers to all of the questions.

"Tomorrow, we will provide more proof about this plot to seize control of Helike."

"I'm going up to the Merlin so would you two like to come up also? It'll be safer," Catie told Ensign Nikitas and his father. "Prince Demetrius, you're welcome to bring your family."

"No, I will go to the capital to work with President Tripino, but I would like to send my wife and daughter. With all these protests and riots, I worry about their safety."

"I agree, Father. Do you wish for me to come with you?"

"No, you should go up with the princess. Take Captain Galanos also. We need Helikens up there to coordinate things. Princess, when do you plan the first move?"

"Dawn tomorrow, that is dawn where the carriers are. I think . . ."

"Cer Catie, that will be 1300 hours in the capital."

". . . at thirteen hundred tomorrow."

"Very well, I'll prepare the president. Kozma, help your mother and sister move."

◆ ◆ ◆

"Princess Acantha, you and your daughter can have my cabin. There are two bedrooms and a day cabin."

"We shouldn't take your cabin. I'm sure we will be comfortable in one of the others."

"No, mother. The others only have bunks for bed. You should take Princess Catherine up on her offer. You and Melitta will want the privacy that the princess's cabin will afford you. The regular crew cabins are very small and close together."

"Princess Catherine will share my cabin," Captain McAvoy said. "It's the same layout as hers so she'll be comfortable."

Morgan and one of the stewards were already shifting Catie's things to the captain's guest room. "We're putting some of your stuff into storage for now. But don't worry, I've kept plenty of gowns out in case you need to look pretty."

Ensign Nikitas gave Catie a weak smile as he followed his mother into the cabin.

Captain McAvoy took Catie by the shoulder and led her into the captain's suite. "Don't worry, I never notice who my roommate has over for guests."

"Does everyone know?"

"No, just your close friends."

Chapter 21   The Gloves Come Off

"Why did we transfer to the Merlin?" Lieutenant Kay Owens asked Lieutenant Mariam Beaulieu as they were flying their Foxes at Mach 4, twenty meters above the ocean surface.

"I think we decided that it would get us home earlier."

"But we know she's crazy."

"You're saying the princess is crazy?"

"Well, history shows that she keeps coming up with these hairbrained schemes."

"That's true, we should discuss that with her if we survive this one. Now, pay attention, we're ten kilometers out."

Their two Foxes were approaching the carrier group from the north, while another two were approaching it from the south. Their railguns had been modified to increase the velocity of the slugs they fired which would give them four times the kinetic energy as before. But it meant they would only be able to get off two shots in the three seconds that it would take them to pass the carrier group. The Fox that was flying fifteen thousand meters above the carriers was providing the telemetry they needed to target the guns.

"Here we go!"

The two Foxes popped off the deck, turned off their sonic suppressors, and aligned on their first targets.

"They've seen us! They're firing missiles!"

"Too late," Kay said as her Fox passed the group and started climbing.

"Ouch, that was loud," Mariam said as she passed through the shock wave from the other two Foxes that had approached from the south.

"Makes you feel sorry for the guys down there."

"Why? They're the enemy!"

"No they're not, they're just following orders. That Prince Xenakis is the enemy."

"We got eight hits. Good shooting," Catie said as the data came in from the observation Fox.

"Thank you, Cer Catie. It was a challenging problem," ADI said. ADI had had to align the vector of the Foxes with the targets. Since the railguns only could be adjusted up or down for aiming, the Fox had to be aligned with the target. And flying at Mach 4 meant there was no time to adjust the angle of the Fox between shots. So she'd aligned their vectors so they would cross both targets at the proper angle.

"ADI, how much damage?" Admiral Michaels asked.

"Two frigates and two destroyers have lost their propulsion; two of the tenders have also lost propulsion. One destroyer has a hole in its stern that can probably be repaired, another frigate has lost much of its bow. It is probable that it will sink before repairs can be implemented."

"Okay, now we wait and see what they do. Is the president contacting Prince Xenakis?"

"That's what we understand."

"Prince Xenakis, I again demand that you recall your fleet. It is senseless to risk Heliken lives in this mad quest for power. As I warned you, we've enlisted the help of the Delphineans to turn back your fleet."

"It's *King* Xenakis, and your Delphinean friends did little damage to our fleet. We will not be deterred by your traitorous action of allying with the aliens."

"*Prince* Xenakis, you have enough blood on your hands, why waste more lives?!"

"It is you who has blood on his hands. Our brave soldiers and sailors have sacrificed their lives to protect Helike. You are the traitor. Tell Prince Demetrius to surrender Zakinthos and we can end this quickly."

"You will lose this fight. We are barely tapping into the power the Delphineans have. Please come to your senses and stop this madness!"

Prince Xenakis slammed the phone down. He turned to his cabinet. "Now tell me, what the hell happened?"

"Sire, their jets were so fast that we could not catch them. They outran our missiles and our jets."

"What damage did they do?"

"We lost the Georgiadis, without one of the carriers slowing down to help, she sank. Six ships will need to be towed back to port. The Moraitis will be able to repair the hole and will catch up with the rest of the fleet."

"What should we do?" the prince asked his admiral.

"They will be able to continue to pick off our smaller vessels. We can tighten up the formation, but I fear that will just make it easier on them. They did not try to attack the carriers. Our engineers tell me that their armor will withstand these slugs that they throw."

"Why couldn't our lasers shoot them down?"

"Sire, the slugs were traveling at over Mach 10. They have a miniscule profile, and the lasers could not hold a lock on one even if they managed to target one."

"Tell the carriers to continue, send the rest of the fleet back home."

"Yes, sire."

Catie was waiting outside the airlock to flight bay three. The Foxes had just landed and the flight bay door closed. She was impatient for the bay to recompress so she could meet and congratulate the pilots.

Kay and Mariam had exited their Foxes, turning them over to the flight crew. Of course, they were still wearing their spacesuits, but that didn't stop them from giving each other a congratulatory hug. They high-fived with the other two pilots as they made their way toward the airlock.

Finally, the green light went on signaling that the bay was fully compressed. Catie cycled through the airlock immediately. By the time she was through, the pilots had removed their helmets.

"What's this I hear about a crazy princess?" Catie asked, feigning anger.

"Hey, you have to admit that was a crazy maneuver," Kay said. "Didn't you get one of your kills against Kasper by divebombing him while he was on the deck like that?"

"Yes, but you had a bit more margin between you and the water than he did." Catie grabbed the two women and hugged them. They'd been comrades in arms back during the Paraxean war and she missed the comradery. She saluted the other two pilots as she led all four of them to the wardroom where Kasper and Captain McAvoy awaited with a selection of drinks.

"Oh, I'm glad you gave us more margin above the water, it shows you care," Kay quipped.

"Congratulations on a successful mission," Captain McAvoy said, giving the pilots a salute.

Kasper echoed the salute before asking, "Did their fighter screen give you any problems?"

"Those guys were going the wrong way," Miriam said. She twisted her head from side to side mimicking what the other pilots must have done. "We were by them before they had a chance to do anything. They were probably going, 'What was that?' when we went vertical."

Everyone in the wardroom laughed, including Eliades. They'd made sure he was in attendance. The Q&A had been scripted by Catie.

"What about their missiles?"

"Missiles?" Miriam gave a jerk of her head as if shocked. "Oh, you mean those little pointy things they threw at us. We barely noticed them; they don't go very fast, maybe Mach 4. Anyway, we were probably breaking the atmosphere by the time they got up to speed."

"Definitely. Although that 6-G turn was pretty hard on me," Kay said. "I think all the fat in my body migrated to my ass." She twisted around looking down at her rear end.

"Kay, I hate to tell you this, but that fat has always been in your ass."

Kay punched Miriam in the shoulder. "I hope that next time we get to use the big guns. Hey, where's my drink?"

"Right here, ma'am," the steward announced.

Catie, Kasper, and Captain McAvoy headed to her cabin to allow the pilots to continue their celebration uninhibited.

"How long before our friend sends an updated report?" Catie asked.

"I don't think it'll be long." Captain McAvoy gave Catie a hug. "It's hard to watch them go out on a mission without you."

"Yes, I really miss being part of the group."

"I know, but you should be proud of them."

"You know, despite the bitching, those two were the first to volunteer for the mission," Kasper said.

"I know. They're good pilots."

"Yes they are. I think they'll make the promotion list for full lieutenant."

"They deserve it."

"Speaking of promotion lists, Lieutenant Commander Mischeff, you are out of uniform." Captain McAvoy barked, "Attention," while reaching into her desk. She pulled out a box and handed it to Catie. "If you'll do the honors."

Catie fought back tears as she opened the box. It contained the shoulder boards for a lieutenant commander. She replaced Kasper's shoulder boards with the new ones, then stepped back and saluted him, "Congratulations!"

"Thank you, Princess. It's an honor to have you pin my boards on."

"It was my privilege. Now, why don't we have a drink while we wait for our mole to send a message."

It was an hour before the message went out.

"The pilots returned from the mission. They were jubilant. They laughed at the thought that we would shoot missiles at them. They also talked about the need to use their bigger guns. I have not been able to determine what they meant, other than we know they have plasma cannons.

"They also indicated that they executed a 6-G turn. I will investigate further."

The next morning, ADI Commed Ensign Nikitas. "It's time for you to go back to your cabin."

"Where is Catie?"

"She left an hour ago to do her workout."

Ensign Nikitas got dressed quickly then exited Catie's cabin into Captain McAvoy's day cabin.

"Good morning," Captain McAvoy said.

"Shi . . . Sorry ma'am."

"You know, if you kept a fresh uniform here, you would be able to come in here and be early for the morning briefing instead of leaving late from last night's meeting." Captain McAvoy was trying hard not to laugh at Ensign Nikitas.

"I'll discuss that with the princess."

"You can call her Catie when we're alone. Obviously, you're on a first-name basis with her."

"Yes, ma'am," Ensign Nikitas stammered as he rushed out the door.

Breaking News: "The next installment in our series about the plot that destroyed Stási. We're on the Merlin, the Delphinean starship. After the interview, we'll be giving everyone a tour of the ship. Now, with me is Prince Kozma Nikitas, who was on the Geraki and was present when they uncovered more evidence of what was behind the plot. Prince, thank you for joining us."

"It is my pleasure. All Helikens must unite to defeat this stab at our freedom."

"I understand that you have evidence about the ship that was carrying antimatter away from Stási."

"Yes I do. I participated in a raid to infiltrate the base that built the ship and gather intel. Here you can see that this asteroid was hollowed out to create a shipyard. It is here that the ship was built."

"How did you gather this intel?"

"One of the Delphineans snuck into the base when the supply ship was docking. They were able to gain access to the base's computer systems and gather this information."

"How do we know this is true and not some concoction dreamed up by the Delphineans?"

"Because right now, Colonel Hatzis from our space station in the asteroid belt has taken over the shipyard and is able to tell us what he has found." Ensign Nikitas flicked a switch in his HUD and the display now showed a Heliken colonel standing in the cargo bay of the asteroid.

"Colonel Hatzis, can you tell us what you have found?"

"It is my honor, Prince Nikitas. We have taken over the asteroid. In it, we have found the shipyard your evidence pointed to. We have captured eight men who were crewing the base. They have acknowledged their part in building the base and the cargo ship."

The reporter interrupted, "Colonel, do you have evidence as to who was behind this?"

"We have been able to trace the shipment of material to the base back to Polemistia. It is not clear whether the government was behind the shipments or whether it was private individuals. But it was over thirty billion dollars of equipment and materials that were shipped here."

"Is it possible that the Delphineans planted this evidence?"

"It seems very improbable. We have waybills that have Polemistia stamped on them. The equipment was all manufactured in Polemistia. We will continue our investigation and interrogation, but all signs point to Polemistia."

"Tune in with us tomorrow when we will show the next chapter in the efforts to thwart this plot."

◆ ◆ ◆

The Foxes were skimming over the water as the Delphineans made their second assault on the carriers. An hour earlier, six Foxes had bombarded the carriers with railgun slugs. The plan was to weaken the flight deck so that a short blast with a plasma cannon would be able to finish it off.

"Where are their picket fighters?" Mariam asked.

"You'll be crossing under their outer line in twenty seconds," the spotter in the observation Fox informed her. "The carrier is one minute out."

"Pop off the deck in thirty!" Lieutenant Owens ordered.

Lieutenant Owens took her Fox to sixty meters, armed her missiles, then alarms started ringing in her cockpit.

"ABORT! They launched coasters. Evasive maneuvers!" Lieutenant Owens shouted. The carriers had launched missiles that were coasting at low velocity in all directions from the carrier. By coasting along, the missile only had to adjust its vector to be able to intercept one of the Foxes, it didn't have to try and catch it, just get in its way.

Lieutenant Owens fired off her rear plasma cannon, keeping it on constant firing as she banked her Fox hard to the right and then took it into an 8-G turn up toward the sky. Two missiles exploded behind her.

"Jonah has been hit! I see his escape pod ejecting!" Lieutenant Beaulieu reported. She was gasping as she was also enduring a high-G turn to evade the Polemistian missiles.

"Chute deployed! Missiles are vectoring toward the escape pod!"

"He's hit the water. He's sinking!"

"I'm after him!" Ensign Sòng yelled. He was flying a rescue Fox trailing the others. He was going slow enough that he could submerge his Fox before anything could hit him. That is if they could detect his Fox when it was flying five meters above the water.

When Lieutenant Owens made it back to the Merlin, she immediately exited her Fox and used the airlock to get into the ship. She strode quickly to her cabin where she removed her shipsuit, rinsed it out, and shoved it into the recycle chute. Then she entered the shower and let the hot water clean her body. As the water jets released the tension, she leaned against the wall and started sobbing. "I could have lost everyone!"

Mariam finally reached their cabin. She knocked on the bathroom door. "Kay, are you alright? Kay! They pulled Jonah out, he's okay."

"I'll be out in a few minutes, when's the debrief?"

"Twenty minutes. And hurry, I need a shower too."

It took Kay two minutes to finish her shower, dry, and put on a new shipsuit. "Sorry."

"No problem. Did you deep-six your other shipsuit?"

"Yes."

"Good, then I won't feel so bad about dumping mine. I'll never believe the smell is out. Gawd, I was so scared."

"Sorry, I should have anticipated the missiles."

"Save it for the debrief."

◆ ◆ ◆

"Okay, what happened?" Kasper asked as his pilots assembled in their ready room.

"They must have guessed we'd be coming back after the railgun attack," Lieutenant Owens said. "They launched missiles that coasted along just fast enough to stay aloft. When they got a lock on us, they only had to cross our path. I should have anticipated that."

"That was my job. We were under the impression that they didn't have that kind of capability."

"Cer Kasper, they must have reprogrammed their missiles. The data I have on their technology does not show that capability."

"It doesn't matter, we knew they can do it, we should have planned for it. You people did your job. It's on the command team that we didn't come up with a better plan. You're dismissed, enjoy your little party." That was the cue to go ahead and have a few drinks and spread a little information that would make its way back to the enemy.

Kay and Mariam walked over to where Jonah and Carew, the other two pilots on the mission, were chatting with Ensign Sòng.

"Jonah, are you okay?" Kay asked.

"I'm fine. Sòng fished me out just fine."

"Why were you sinking?"

"Hey, those missiles were coming at me as I was going down. I figured I had to get underwater or they'd be on me."

"Smart thinking."

"Thanks, I'm just glad that some whale-like creature didn't come along and swallow me up."

Kay laughed so hard she had trouble catching her breath. "Jonah, how long have you been waiting to use that line?"

"My whole life. I've only managed it once before."

"Good timing. Now I need a drink."

"So do I. When are we going to start using the big guns?" Mariam asked.

"Yes, I heard we're bringing some Oryxes in. One of those babies can sink a carrier from ten thousand meters without breaking a sweat."

"Yeah, remember back in the Ukrainian campaign? We took out entire military installations with one shot. That would get their attention if we dropped one on one of their shipyards."

"Okay, so that didn't go so well," Catie said as the command team gathered in Captain McAvoy's day cabin.

"How much damage did the railguns do?" Kasper asked.

"They tore the decks up pretty good, but they're already fixing them. And it looks like they're laying armor down on them to reduce the damage should we try again," Captain McAvoy said.

"Those carriers are tough. We need a few Oryxes with railguns."

"I've already requested them. But they won't be here for another week."

"In a week, they'll be able to take Zakinthos," Ensign Nikitas said. "It will be very difficult to remove them."

"How are the people reacting to the news coverage?" Catie asked.

"The pro-Polemistia demonstrations are down, and we're seeing more people demonstrating for a united Helike," Captain Galanos said. "But there is still a lot of suspicion that we're not telling the truth."

"It'll be interesting to see how they react to the next story."

"Yes, but what do we do about the carriers? We should have brought a few asteroids along with us," Captain McAvoy said.

"Asteroids?"

"Yes, we can launch them at a target from high orbit. The kinetic energy is enormous. One small asteroid could destroy one of those carriers."

"We could sacrifice a Fox," Kasper said.

"It would only damage the carrier. And I'm not excited about killing all the sailors and pilots on one of them. They're just pawns," Catie said. "But . . . the Lagrange points, I bet there's some space junk in L5 that we could use. Maybe we just need to show them how exposed they are."

"I don't understand," Ensign Nikitas said.

"Do you know about Lagrange points?"

"Cer Catie, I've translated it to the correct word in their language. One of their mathematicians developed the proof for Lagrange points many years ago."

"Yes, I know what they are."

"Well, L5 is a balance point, it collects junk, fragments of stray asteroids, parts of comets, that get swept up in Helike's orbit. Sometimes there's a big asteroid there, trojans we call them."

"So?"

"So, it's close. We can send a Fox out there with an asteroid mover, a frame with gravity drives, and bring one back."

"Just one?" Kasper asked. He was obviously starting to issue orders to send a Fox out.

"Three, two small ones and one big one. We'll adjust the energy by changing the altitude we drop it from."

"Done."

◆ ◆ ◆

Breaking News: "We have Helike's finance minister here with us. He'll explain how the Polemistia separation party has stolen from the people to finance this war and the expedition to Stási. Minister Kalivas, please explain how you came by this information and what it means?"

"An insider in the Polemistia finance ministry shared the information with me. He was horrified when he realized what had happened and wanted the help of the planetary ministry to stop it."

"Exactly what happened?"

"Someone has diverted funds from the federal employees' retirement funds to pay for their political adventures."

"How could they do that without being exposed right away?"

"They were clever. They sold bonds to the fund. But the bonds were secured by the two extra carriers that they built in secret. Carriers are not a money-generating investment. There is no way to recover the money. They also used a similar scheme to build the shipyard in the asteroid belt. Some of that money may be recoverable since the shipyard may have value. But even that is uncertain now that the Delphineans are here and will share their technology with us. You've seen their ship. It outclasses anything we have and it is just a small frigate."

"How much money was stolen?"

"Over eighty billion dollars, about ten percent of the fund." Their Comms translated the amount from dracus to dollars so they could appreciate how much money it was.

"And you're suggesting that there is no way to recover this money?"

"It is unlikely unless we can go after the people behind the theft. The bonds are probably worthless."

"And how do you know it was the separatist party?"

"The bonds are tied to companies whose only assets are the carriers and shipyard. It was obfuscated, but once you follow the trail, it is clear how the money was spent."

"What does the president plan to do?"

"The president believes that Prince Xenakis is behind this. Since he is using the carriers to try and annex Zakinthos, he clearly knew about the fraud. And all evidence points to him as the perpetrator of the attack on Stási."

"There you have it. The lust for power has led to the theft of the money that was set aside for people's retirement. Where will it end? Can President Tripino stop Prince Xenakis? Will he be able to restore democracy to Polemistia? Stay tuned."

"Sire, President Tripino is on the line."

"Put him on. .... I don't know why I'm talking to you. The lies you've been spreading about me will do you no good. Once I have Zakinthos, the people will forget all about your lies."

"I'm calling to give you a last warning. We and the Delphineans are trying to resolve this conflict with a minimal loss of life. But if you persist, we will be forced to destroy those carriers and all the sailors aboard them."

"Ha, your last attempt failed. What can you do now?!"

"We are preparing a demonstration. Let me show you." The president brought up a video of the asteroids that were now orbiting Helike. "As you can see, we have three asteroids orbiting Helike. We'll reserve the large one for later, the first will target the middle of the Zika desert. It will give you a taste of exactly how much power we wield. I've just sent you the coordinates of the impact point. The second one will be dropped in the middle of your carrier group. I'm sure they'll survive the waves it throws up. This conversation will be released in two hours and the asteroids will be launched an hour later unless you turn your carriers around."

"You're going to throw rocks at us, how absurd! Release your video, the people will finally realize how desperate you are."

"It is you who are desperate. The Delphineans have sent for additional forces which will be here within the week. They will be able to target any facility on Helike and destroy it. It is time for you to end this desperate grasp for power."

Prince Xenakis slammed the phone down and again turned to his cabinet. "Rocks, what can they do?"

"Sir, from that height they can do a lot of damage. The kinetic energy released will be enormous. Even one as small as the ones they're saying they will throw would be able to destroy a small town. They would certainly destroy a carrier."

"Sure, but how can they target them that accurately? Indiscriminate killing will turn the people against them."

"I agree," one of the other advisors said. "They may be able to toss them at us, but to be accurate, it is not possible. That is why they're targeting the center of our largest desert."

The first one shook his head. "They gave us precise coordinates of the impact zone. We will soon see how accurate they are."

"Yes we will, and with that, we will end this charade. The Delphineans don't care about Helike. They're willing to risk the lives of innocent people by throwing rocks when they cannot know where they will strike," the prince shouted. "Make sure we make that point to the press when they release their video."

Breaking News: "President Tripino gives Prince Xenakis ultimatum, relent or we will bring fury from the heavens!"

The reporter played the video that had just been released, then turned back to the camera. "As you can see, President Tripino is threatening to drop asteroids on Helike to disrupt the plans of Prince Xenakis. He claims that the Delphineans are bringing more forces that will arrive within a week, a seemingly impossible timeline.

"Prince Xenakis has dismissed their threats, and his people tell us that the Delphineans don't care about Heliken lives if they are willing to toss asteroids at us with no control of where they will land. Can the

Delphineans deliver an asteroid to a target on Helike? We will know within the hour. Stay tuned!"

The gravity drives clamped to the asteroid started to push it toward Helike. They didn't have much power, but with the asteroids starting from fifty-thousand kilometers it didn't take much to assist the 0.28-G force that Helike was exerting on the asteroid. ADI left the guidance of the asteroid to Merlin; with limited variables in play, it was a task well suited to his analytical abilities. As the asteroid accelerated and entered the atmosphere, its body shielded the gravity drives and their controller from the heat. They simply needed to make the minor adjustments for the shifts caused by the small variations in Helike's gravitational pull as they moved across the planet's surface. Without a full map of Helike, those variables could not be accounted for in advance.

At fifteen thousand kilometers the drivers released the asteroid, the effects of wind and shifting gravity would be minor during the last few minutes of its descent. It slammed into the desert at over thirty thousand meters per second.

Breaking News: "First asteroid slams into the Zika desert, only two hundred meters away from the target coordinates. The impact created an enormous shock wave that swept the region; it also triggered a 3.2 magnitude earthquake. Apparently, the Delphineans can target their asteroids."

The second asteroid landed in the middle of the carriers, sending out a shower of water and waves that threatened to swamp them.

"Sire, the asteroids landed on target."

Prince Xenakis threw a paperweight against the wall. "What is that noise?"

"Sire, there are protesters around the palace. They are demanding that you stop the carriers."

"Call the army and have them dispersed. Shoot them if they don't move!"

A small contingent of soldiers led by a colonel burst into the cabinet room.

"What are you doing here, the protesters are out there!"

"Prince Xenakis, by order of parliament, you are under arrest for treason!"

"How dare you!"

"How dare you, sir!"

The prince looked around the cabinet room for support. All of his advisors were refusing to make eye contact with him. "You traitors!"

"The carriers have turned around!" Ensign Nikitas cried out as he leapt from his chair.

"Remember your decorum," Captain Galanos scolded him.

"Yes, ma'am."

"But, hooray!" Captain Galanos added.

"What does your father say?" Catie asked.

"Father, are you there?"

"Yes, I'm here. The military has arrested Prince Xenakis. The people rose up and demanded that parliament act."

"And the military backed parliament?"

"Yes, there were some sporadic incidents of armed conflict with a few small units. But once the people made their position clear, those units stood down. The prime minister promised them amnesty if they put down their arms by the end of the day."

"Then it's over?" Catie asked.

"At least the worst part. Now we need to heal."

"I think we should play our last card."

Breaking News: "The Delphineans are our cousins. I have with me Dr. Moreau from the Delphinean starship and Dr. Christou from the Heliken Institute of Health. Welcome to our program."

"Thank you for having us."

"You're saying that Helikens come from the same planet as the Delphineans. Can you explain how that is possible?"

"Let me first explain why it is true. Dr. Moreau and I have analyzed the DNA of thirty Delphineans and of an equal number of Helikens. There is no doubt that we come from a common ancestor."

"But how can that be?"

Dr. Moreau leaned into the camera. "Your myth of Helike's birth speaks of a great ship. We believe that that ship was a starship."

"But why?"

"We don't know. We speculate that Earth was being observed by an advanced alien race. When the city of Helike was about to be destroyed by an earthquake and a tidal wave, they decided to save the people. For some reason, they brought you here and gave you the means to start a new world."

"What evidence points to that?"

"First, your story of Helike's destruction matches a similar event on Earth. The destruction of the Greek city of Helike. Second: your language shows strong similarities to Earth's ancient Greek. Third: your oral history that precedes the founding of Helike matches the history from Earth's ancient Greece. And fourth, speaking with your archeologists, they tell me that there is no evidence of a stone-age civilization. All the other worlds we've encountered have records of their civilizations evolving from a stone-age beginning. They also show evidence of their species evolving from early primates. There is no similar evidence of evolution here on Helike. Your people just burst forth twelve hundred years ago."

"That does give credence to your claims. Our scientists have never been able to explain where we came from. They have evidence of the evolution for all the other animals here, but none for Helikens."

"Hence the theory that aliens brought you here."

"And you have no idea who these aliens are?"

"No, we don't."

"Are they still here?"

"You haven't found any evidence and neither have we. But if you want, we'll help you look," Dr. Moreau said.

"There you have it, more mystery about the origins of Helike. Stay tuned as we continue to delve into this subject."

"Well at least the news media is happy about things," Catie said.

"Yes," Captain Galanos agreed. "They always find a way to pull in viewers. And Prince Nikitas looks good in front of the cameras. That always helps." Captain Galanos smiled at Ensign Nikitas.

"My mother always says I favor Alexander the Great. Maybe I should wear a breastplate to the next news conference."

Catie and Captain Galanos giggled as they both agreed it would be a good idea.

Chapter 22   Board Meeting August 7th

As soon as he saw the last person come into the video conference Marc brought the meeting to order. "Welcome everyone. Let's get started, the meeting is now called to order. Catie, I understand you've got good news for us."

"We're over the bit of drama. The Heliken government is back in charge. And I'm ready to come home. I hope you have a ship ready to head this way because we're leaving tomorrow."

"We sent the Charon out this morning. You're free to head this way as soon as you like. Are you bringing guests?"

"We've invited them to send some people with us. Some anthropologists and historians want to come. And Dr. Moreau is bringing one of their doctors. The scientists seem happy to wait for our guys to show up."

"What about the prince?" Samantha asked.

"I don't know. He's talking to his father," Catie said as noncommittally as she could.

"Okay, let us know. Now, Admiral Michaels, some good news?"

"We have actually finalized the treaty for full nuclear disarmament. It includes the decommissioning of all nuclear reactors and the sequestering of all plutonium."

"What about Iran?" Blake asked.

"You must not watch much news. The people of Iran have elected a more moderate government and forced the government to agree to the disarmament. Seems they're tired of the embargo and all the drama. Keep your fingers crossed."

"I'm sure we all will. And congratulations on the achievement."

"Remember, you have agreed to move two hundred thousand Chinese colonists over the next year."

"I remember. Blake, you have news?"

"The Roebuck has finished its refit and is now on the way to the first target planet to start the survey. It should be there in about three weeks."

"Great. We need to start up another colony."

"Have you decided who's going to be governor?"

"I am. Sam and I have agreed to move to the new planet once the base is fully established. Natalia and Paul are going to come with us."

"Cool, then Allie and Jules will get to grow up together."

"Now before we move on to the boring stuff, . . ."

"Hey, it's what pays the bills," Fred said.

"We know and we appreciate it. ADI, you had something you wanted to share."

"Yes, Captain. I wanted to report that last month the worldwide population of Earth actually fell for the first time since the Black Death in the fourteenth century. I think we should congratulate Dr. Metra on the success of her birth control program."

"Hear, hear!" The group applauded vigorously as Dr. Metra blushed and her ears flared out.

"You fixed your nose!" Catie exclaimed as she realized that Dr. Metra had changed her nose back so that it matched the other Paraxeans.

"I thought it was time. Very few will remember when I actually started here." Dr. Metra had been the first Paraxean that Marc had brought out of stasis when he'd discovered the Sakira. She'd changed her nose, which had ridges like a Bajoran from *Star Trek*, and had worn a scarf to cover her ears which could flare out like a panther's.

"I like it," Blake said. "Makes her look more exotic."

Dr. Metra continued to blush as Marc motioned for ADI to continue.

"And, we have seen another half-degree drop in global temperature. Carbon emissions are falling dramatically; it seems there is hope for you humans after all."

"Very funny, ADI."

"We do have a problem though," ADI added.

"What?" Marc asked.

"With the addition of the new colonies and your desire to accelerate the settling of Artemis and add a second Earth colony, you will deplete your stores of platinum metals within a decade."

"What?" Catie asked. "What about how rich Artemis is?"

"Unless you intend to restrict the distribution of gravity drives and other advanced technology, you will not have enough platinum metals. All three Paraxean colonies are in systems with low reserves of the metals. The new Aperanjen colony has marginal reserves and Onisiwo also lacks sufficient quantities to bring it to the same level that you plan for Earth."

"So what should we do?" Samantha asked.

"Find another system to mine," Catie said.

Marc rapped on the table, "Do you think we could find a system that would last more than ten years? It's a pretty big investment to set up mining in a system."

"We could look for big systems. A bigger star would imply that there would be a lot more solar debris around it. We've been ignoring the big ones mainly, but the solar explorers used some for waypoints, so we have some data."

"Cer Catie, we have data on two hundred B class stars. I will start analyzing it for indications of a large asteroid belt or planets."

"Thanks, ADI."

"That means we'll need to send an expedition to set up a mining starbase. Don't we have someone who's done that before?" Marc asked, giving Catie a meaningful look.

"Daddy!"

Afterword

Thanks for reading **Delphi Diversion!**

I hope you've enjoyed the twelfth book in the Delphi in Space series. The story continues in Delphi Forge.   If you would like to join my newsletter group go to ⧉https://tinyurl.com/tiny-delphi. The newsletter provides interesting Science facts for SciFi fans, book recommendation based on books I truly loved reading, deals on books I think you'll like, and notification of when the next book in my series is available.

As a self-published author, the one thing you can do that will help the most is to leave a review on Goodreads and Amazon.

Acknowledgments

It is impossible to say how much I am indebted to my beta readers and copy editors. Without them, you would not be able to read my books due to all the grammar and spelling errors. I have always subscribed to Andrew Jackson's opinion that "It is a damn poor mind that can think of only one way to spell a word."

So special thanks to:

My copy editor, Ann Clark, who also happens to be my wife.

My beta reader and editor, Theresa Holmes.

My beta reader and cheerleader, Roger Blanton, who happens to be my brother.

Also important to a book author is the cover art for their book. I'm am especially thankful to Momir Borocki for the exceptional covers he has produced for my books. It is amazing what he can do with the strange PowerPoint drawings I give him; and how he makes sense of my suggestions, I'll never know.

If you need a cover, he can be reached at momir.borocki@gmail.com.

Also by Bob Blanton

Delphi in Space

Sakira
Delphi City
Delphi Station
Delphi Nation
Delphi Alliance
Delphi Federation
Delphi Exploration
Delphi Colony
Delphi Challenge
Delphi League
Delphi Embassy
Delphi Diversion
Delphi Forge – coming soon

Stone Series

Matthew and the Stone
Stone Ranger
Stone Undercover
Stone Investigations